# The Dog Who Knew Too Much

Krista Davis

BERKLEY PRIME CRIME
New York

BERKLEY PRIME CRIME
Published by Berkley
An imprint of Penguin Random House LLC
penguinrandomhouse.com

Copyright © 2019 by Cristina Ryplansky
Penguin Random House supports copyright. Copyright fuels creativity, encourages
diverse voices, promotes free speech, and creates a vibrant culture. Thank you for buying
an authorized edition of this book and for complying with copyright laws by not
reproducing, scanning, or distributing any part of it in any form without permission.
You are supporting writers and allowing Penguin Random House to continue to
publish books for every reader.

BERKLEY and the BERKLEY & B colophon are registered trademarks and BERKLEY
PRIME CRIME is a trademark of Penguin Random House LLC.

ISBN: 9780451491688

First Edition: November 2019

Printed in the United States of America
1  3  5  7  9  10  8  6  4  2

Cover art by Mary Ann Lasher
Book design by Kelly Lipovich

*To Buttercup,*
*my sweet Jack Russell terrier who inspired this series.*
*Like Trixie, she was abandoned by someone and left*
*on the road to fend for herself. Finding her there was*
*one of the best things that ever happened to me.*

# Acknowledgments

This book was a long time coming. I thank my readers for their patience and hope it lives up to their expectations.

From time to time I am asked to include real people or animals in my books. I was delighted to use real names for two characters in this book. Naturally, the characters are not based on the actual person or dog. After all, this is fiction. But it was a lot of fun to include them.

Rose Martin very generously allowed me to use the name of her boxer, Stella. Sweet Stella turned out to be a pivotal character who rose above her tragic circumstances. The real Stella lives the good life and is pampered with watermelon, banana slices, and lots of love.

I was also asked to include Jim McGowen, who may be surprised by his character. Again, this is fiction and doesn't in any way reflect the real Jim McGowen.

Special thanks to Jim McGowen and Betsy Strickland for suggesting the method of death. My research into fentanyl was truly sobering, and I hope that it will be off the streets soon.

Huge thanks to my lovely editor, Michelle Vega, who was so patient with me. I appreciate her kindness more than I can say.

And, as always, I would be totally lost without my agent, Jessica Faust, who makes me smile and feel better, no matter how dire things may seem.

*A dog is the only thing on earth that loves you more than he loves himself.*

—Josh Billings

## MEMBERS OF THE SUGAR MAPLE INN FAMILY

**Liesel Miller (Holly's Oma)**—co-owner of the Sugar Maple Inn
    Gingersnap, a golden retriever and canine ambassador of the inn

**Holly Miller**—Liesel's granddaughter and co-owner of the inn
    Trixie, a Jack Russell terrier
    Twinkletoes, a calico cat and feline ambassador of the inn

**Zelda York**—front-desk employee of the inn

**Shelley Dixon**—waitress at the inn

**Mr. Huckle**—elderly "butler" at the inn

**Casey Collins**—night manager at the inn

## WAGTAIL RESIDENTS

**Runemaster, "LaRue"**

**Sugar McLaughlin**

**Augie and Glenda Hoover**
    Stan, their son
    Dolly, their Yorkshire terrier

**Diane Blushner**
    Stella, her boxer

**Clara Dorsey**
    Tavish, her Scottie

**PIPPIN & ENTOURAGE**

Pippin—a border collie and Labrador mix
Jim McGowen—Pippin's handler
Marlee Seidel—Pippin's media assistant
Camille Ladouceur—actor
Howard Hirschtritt—actor
Finch Morrison—actor
Rae Rae Babetski—chaperone

# One

Most cats would have fled from all the barking and yipping. But Twinkletoes, my long-haired calico, took it in stride. She sat on top of the desk in the main lobby of the Sugar Maple Inn and yawned as if the commotion was perfectly normal. A caramel spot and a chocolate spot on top of her head looked like she had shoved sunglasses above her brow. Her green eyes almost glowed as she peered at me.

"You're very brave," I whispered to her.

She mewed and rubbed her head against my hand, twisting as if she wanted to make the most of being stroked.

My grandmother, Liesel Miller, whom I called Oma, German for *grandma*, joined me in the main lobby, where the grand staircase led up to the rooms. It was the hub of the inn, where guests gathered to eat in the dining area or to lounge in the Dogwood Room, which wasn't actually a room. It was all one large open space, divided by the grand staircase. Opposite the stairs was the front door, which led out to a covered porch and, beyond that, the town of Wagtail.

In the accent that I found charming but she wished to lose, Oma said, "It is Pippinmania! I have never seen such a thing."

"I guess they're not exaggerating when they call Pippin 'America's Favorite Dog.'" I had thought that was some kind of clever marketing ploy, but if these people were any indication, it was true.

In the dining area of the inn, adults and children wore fake-fur dog ears in a creamy white color. The ears stood up at the base of the headband that held them on, but the tops flopped over. They were quintessential puppy ears. The people barked. And yowled. And the dogs who were with them joined in, undoubtedly confused about their humans trying to speak canine. Fridays were always busy, but this was highly unusual.

My own Jack Russell terrier, Trixie, sat at my feet, watching and listening as if she didn't know quite what to make of it all. She would be meeting Pippin shortly when he arrived with his costars in an upcoming TV show for what had been billed as a much-deserved vacation for Pippin in Wagtail. With fans like these, I suspected he wouldn't be getting much rest.

"They say it is like this all over Wagtail. The merchants are thrilled. We aren't the only ones who have a full house. Everyone is booked." Oma smiled at the craziness. "You would think Cary Grant was coming!"

If I recalled correctly, Mr. Grant had passed away. "I think you'd get a bigger crowd than this if that happened."

Fortunately, she understood my meaning and chuckled. Her smile faded too quickly, though. In a low voice she said, "Another dog is missing."

"No!"

As Oma was the mayor of Wagtail, that kind of problem

fell directly into her lap. It had been odd when the Hoovers' beloved Yorkshire terrier disappeared the day before, but we hoped she had simply gotten lost and would turn up. News of a second missing dog changed everything. Now it was an ominous pattern.

"This time it's Clara Dorsey's Scottie. Two dogs in two days. We have to stop this. For the sake of the dogs, but also for the well-being of Wagtail. If this kind of news gets out, people will be afraid to bring their dogs here."

"Did anyone see anything this time?"

Oma shook her head. "He was there one moment and gone the next. Some people fear that it is a coyote. They tell me that these creatures are very wily."

I shuddered. "Has anyone seen a coyote?"

"No," she said emphatically. "They say coyotes are everywhere in the United States, but none have been spotted on Wagtail Mountain or Snowball Mountain. Some speculate that Wagtail is not a popular place for coyotes due to the number of large dogs here. No, I fear it may be something else entirely . . ."

I tried to gauge her expression. It wasn't difficult. She was clearly very upset.

"The dogs weren't wearing GPS collars?" I asked.

"The Scottie was. Officer Dave is trying to track him down right now. I am crossing my fingers that they will find him. Clara has a reputation for dipping into the cooking sherry when she makes her dinner."

"Oma!"

"This is not gossip. It is true. I am not making it up. I hope she accidentally left the gate open and that her dog, Tavish, scampered away. The alternative would be horrific."

I swallowed hard. Trixie had taken off a few times, but luckily, she had come home or I had found her quickly. What a nightmare!

At that moment, Mr. Huckle, an elderly gentleman with a kindly face as wrinkled as an old map, rushed toward us waving something. Previously a butler for the wealthiest family in Wagtail, he still insisted on wearing his butler's uniform at the inn. Oma had hired him when he was down on his luck. Her kindness turned out to be fortunate for us. He gave the inn a touch of class and had quickly become the darling of our guests. Mr. Huckle was always available to lend a hand or take care of some little detail for guests, their dogs, and their cats. To be honest, I thought he seemed happier since he had come to work with us. He loved his previous employer, but he enjoyed meeting people and thrived on helping them.

"It's here!" Mr. Huckle presented us with a copy of *Dog Life*, the national magazine for dog lovers. A photo of Trixie sitting on the front steps of the Sugar Maple Inn was on the cover.

Oma took the magazine into her hands. "Little Trixie, you look beautiful! This is wonderful publicity."

At the mention of her name, Trixie gazed up at Oma. Her sweet, lively eyes didn't miss much. Trixie's fur had been yellowish when I found her, but with good nutrition it had changed to shiny white, except for her black ears and the black spot on her rump that traveled halfway up her tail. No one had docked her tail, and it was adorable, curling upward and always wagging happily.

I had found Trixie, or maybe she found me, at a gas station at the bottom of Wagtail Mountain where someone had abandoned her. She had waited for him to return to pick her up, surviving off the scraps she found in trash cans. On that fateful rainy night, she decided she had waited long enough and jumped into the car I had borrowed from my boyfriend. Dirty and wet, she promptly spilled coffee and snarfed corn chips, making a mess on the carpet with na-cho cheese powder. At the time, I thought I wouldn't be able to keep her, but as things worked out, along with Twinkletoes, Trixie had become one of my little darlings.

In the beginning, Trixie was prone to taking off, which troubled me. But I soon learned that what I thought was wandering had a purpose. Most of the time Trixie stuck by me. Her main flaw was a nose that sniffed out trouble, more specifically, corpses. And that was what had brought a reporter and a photographer from *Dog Life* to interview Trixie.

Oma opened the magazine to the article. I peered over her arm. Twinkletoes received mention too, but Trixie was the star of the piece.

An uncanny ability to locate deceased people came naturally to her. As far as I knew, she had never been trained as a cadaver or search dog. I had certainly never received any training along those lines or in law enforcement, but Trixie had led me to enough corpses that we were getting a reputation for solving murders.

"Let's put one in each guest room. Ja?" suggested Oma. "And we should frame it and hang it somewhere." She looked around but stopped and bent to pat Trixie. "You are our star, little one!"

At that moment, the front door opened and my aunt Birdie marched in. Her dark eyes flashed, and she carried something that looked suspiciously like a rolled-up copy of *Dog Life*. Aunt Birdie always dressed like she was on her way someplace special. A stylish cream-colored dress with an asymmetrical neckline hung perfectly on her slender figure. Her dark hair was smartly coiffed. Her trademark white patch at the top of her forehead waved back off her face. "Have you seen this?" she demanded.

"We are very proud of our Trixie," said Oma.

The two of them didn't get along. Aunt Birdie was my mother's sister, and Oma was my father's mother. When I moved to Wagtail, Aunt Birdie had been envious of my relationship with Oma, and she still intervened regularly.

Aunt Birdie's nostrils flared. "Your mother will be mortified. Decent young women do not have a reputation for locating corpses. What were you thinking allowing a national magazine to carry such a morbid story about you?"

"Aunt Birdie, it's Trixie who finds murdered people, not me. And it's really quite remarkable that she can do that."

Aunt Birdie drew in a sharp breath. "For your information, your actions reflect on our entire family. This is such an embarrassment!" She lifted her chin in the air. "It is a stain on our family. Your ancestors are churning in their graves."

"Birdie," said Oma, "you are making a fuss for no reason. I am very proud of our Holly. And Trixie and Twinkletoes, too!"

Aunt Birdie was aghast. "You are a terrible influence on Holly. I knew my sister shouldn't have married your son."

Good grief. We were going to rehash my birth again, were we? I was in my thirties, and while both sides of the family had been dismayed by my arrival, since my parents were still in their teens, I thought enough time had passed for all of them to get used to the fact that everything had turned out fine. True, my parents had divorced and now lived on opposite sides of the country with new spouses and more children, but they were happy. Only Aunt Birdie continued to create friction wherever she could.

I checked my watch and said as sweetly as possible, "Pippin should be arriving soon. Maybe we should cordon off the reception lobby? If word gets out and these Pippin-mania types rush to see him, it could be a madhouse."

Mr. Huckle, who had stood a discreet distance away during Birdie's tirade, nodded. "I'll help you bring up the stanchions and ropes. While you get the star settled in his room, I'll stand guard."

"Thanks, Mr. Huckle."

I waved at Aunt Birdie and fled toward the basement. I

would certainly hear about this from my mother. Luckily, she had also suffered from Aunt Birdie's cranky nature. I wished Aunt Birdie would find a hobby that didn't involve me.

Mr. Huckle and I spent the next half hour arranging crowd-control stanchions at the hallway that led from the main part of the inn to the reception lobby.

Fortunately, in spite of the ropes, the Pippinmania crowd hadn't caught on that their favorite celebrity was about to arrive. Trixie and I left Mr. Huckle to crowd management and hurried along the corridor to the reception lobby on the west side of the inn.

At the sight of me, my normally calm Oma jumped from the desk chair in our office and rushed to join us. Her eyes shone with excitement. "Did you know that Howard Hirschtritt is a famous actor? I have seen him on television!"

Oma was always impeccably dressed in what she liked to call country chic. Today that consisted of a violet plaid skirt with a white blouse embroidered with flowers that matched the colors in her skirt. Oma never wore makeup other than lipstick, so I noticed immediately that she had gussied up a bit with blush and mascara. If I wasn't mistaken, even Gingersnap, her golden retriever who was the canine ambassador of the inn, sported a new collar embroidered with the words *Best. Dog. Ever.*

Gingersnap was a sweetheart and definitely deserved that kind of praise.

Zelda, the daytime desk clerk, chirped up. "I didn't realize that Howard Hirschtritt was with Pippin's entourage. He's been nominated for three Emmys! We have Hollywood royalty coming with Pippin." Zelda tweaked her cheeks for color and fluffed her long blonde hair. "They say he has given several famous actors their start in the business."

"Are you hoping he'll discover you?" I asked. It was always interesting to meet someone famous, but I had no aspirations of finding fame in Hollywood, and I hadn't known that Oma or Zelda had Hollywood dreams.

"Well," said Zelda, "if they're going to make a TV show with a dog in it, maybe it would be helpful to have a cast member who can communicate with the dog."

She had a point. Zelda fancied herself an animal psychic. I was still a little bit doubtful about her abilities, but Zelda thought she could communicate with them. She even had a side business as a pet psychic. On occasion, she had been dead-on. I wasn't so sure, but just because *I* couldn't read a dog's mind didn't mean she couldn't.

At that moment, Shadow, our handyman, passed through the registration lobby with his bloodhound, Elvis. "All the prizes for Pippin's Treasure Hunt are hidden on the mountain, ready to go. The guys from Chowhound are supposed to set up their tents this afternoon. I get along with Augie just fine, but one of us probably ought to go up there and check on him. I'd hate to have everyone get to the top and not have any grub."

I gave him a thumbs-up. Augie was a nice guy. Sometimes he was so generous that he overextended himself and couldn't accomplish everything he had promised. "As soon as we get Pippin and friends checked in and settled, I'll take a hike up there. It's so pretty with everything coming back to life after the winter."

Trixie and Gingersnap pricked their ears and gazed expectantly toward the sliding glass doors.

Two Wagtail taxis drove up. Golf carts were the primary means of transportation in Wagtail. All visitors left their cars in a large parking lot outside of town and were transported into town by golf carts, better known as Wagtail taxis.

"They're here," Zelda breathed.

Shadow hurried outside to help them with their luggage, and Oma straightened the belt on her skirt.

After all the preparation and anticipation, the sliding glass doors opened and a blonde fashionista wearing a leather jacket and oversize sunglasses backed into the lobby snapping photos as Pippin, America's favorite dog, walked into the Sugar Maple Inn.

An adorable border collie and yellow Labrador retriever mix with bright eyes, Pippin engaged Gingersnap in proper doggy protocol for meeting a stranger. Friendly and good-natured in spite of his long flight from the West Coast, he promptly introduced himself to Trixie, too.

It was immediately clear why he was America's favorite dog. He had the fluffy fur of his border collie ancestors, but he was definitely Labrador yellow with a whitish blaze on his face. His ears perked up at the base, but the tips flopped over, which gave him the appearance of being an eternal puppy.

Pippin's human entourage followed him inside while the photographer continued to take pictures.

"I'd like to get a shot of Pippin checking into the inn," she said.

A tall man stepped toward the registration desk. He patted the top, saying, "Pippin, paws up!"

Pippin promptly left his new dog friends and stretched to place his front paws on the top of the desk. Zelda played along by handing him the key to his room, which Pippin promptly took into his mouth. It would be an adorable picture.

"Hi," I said. "I'm Holly Miller, the co-owner of the Sugar Maple Inn. Do you think we could have a copy of that?"

The photographer looked a little bit put out. She lowered her sunglasses and eyed me as if she wasn't impressed by my jeans and pink buffalo-check shirt. "Sure."

"Good grief, but you people are out in the boonies. I didn't even know places like this still existed." The man who spoke was partially bald with smooth facial skin and a prominent nose.

I recognized him right away as Howard Hirschtritt from TV shows he had starred in. But I didn't think I had seen him in anything recently. I wouldn't have known him by name if we hadn't just been talking about him, but his face was very familiar.

He stretched out his arm and made a production of looking at his watch, a modern silver style with a brown alligator strap. "That's it, kiddos," he said. "Hope I don't see you around." He spoke like a grump, with a grumble in his tone.

"Howard, wait!" cried a pretty young woman with large brown eyes and lush lashes. "Where are you going?"

The man snorted. "*I* am not a dog sitter. I may play the role of the father-in-law, but I am not a dog sitter."

She pumped her hands on her hips.

I could tell she wasn't a pushover.

"Excuse me, but isn't this your job?" she demanded. "I was led to believe that you would be in charge of this project with Pippin."

His upper lip curled as though she amused him. "It's a good thing you're pretty, sweetheart. The guy with the dog will take care of everything." He strode toward the door.

The woman followed him. "If you're not staying here, the least you can do is tell us where we can reach you."

"*Darling*," said the man in a droll tone, "*that* would defeat the purpose of leaving, wouldn't it?" Chuckling to himself, he sauntered out of the inn.

# Two

The young woman watched the automatic door close behind him and whipped around. "Can you believe him?" she asked her companions. "You'd think he would have left an itinerary and a number where he can be called. Howard Hirschtritt was one of the main reasons I was excited about this job, and now he has brought us to heaven knows where and abandoned us." She gazed at the others. "Do any of *you* know what we're supposed to do?"

They appeared to be fairly clueless.

A red-haired guy said, "At least we won't have to hear about that watch again." He imitated Howard when he said, *"It's a rare Cape Cod–style Hermès."*

The two women and two men who had arrived with Howard snickered.

The pretty woman looked at the man who had gotten Pippin to pose for his photograph. "I guess you're in charge."

He was blond with an athletic build. There was no mistaking the annoyance with which he said, simply, "Nope."

"Didn't Howard tell you what we're supposed to do?" she persisted. "He just said as much."

He held up his hands as if in protest. "I'm just Pippin's assistant. No one *ever* tells me anything. I'm here to make sure Pippin has a vacation before you guys start shooting."

"Don't look at me," said the photographer. "I handle Pippin's social media."

"Bonding," said the red-haired guy. "We're supposed to become buddies. Remember the show *Friends*? The actors were sent to Vegas to bond before they started shooting. It's not a bad idea, actually." To Zelda and me, he said, "Camille and I are supposed to be a couple in a TV show about our rascally dog, played by Pippin. Howard has the role of the grouchy father-in-law. The producer thought it would be a good idea if we all became friends and if we got to know and love Pippin. That kind of genuine affection comes across on-screen. And it's important when there are a lot of snide, teasing comments in a show. You don't want them to seem angry when they're supposed to be funny."

That explained a lot. It wasn't perfect timing for me to butt in, but they all looked tired and I didn't want them to start moaning about Howard's abrupt exit again. "Welcome to the Sugar Maple Inn." I reached out to pet Pippin and shake his paw. "I'm Holly Miller. If you need anything at all, please ask us. Everyone in Wagtail is excited to have Pippin vacationing here."

Zelda smiled at them. "Camille Ladouceur?"

The woman with the brown eyes stepped toward her. She had a mane of dark hair that rivaled Zelda's long locks. "That's me."

Zelda checked them in one at a time. While she checked in the two men, I showed the women to their rooms.

Camille and Marlee Seidel, the thin photographer, followed me.

"I can't believe that Howard took off," griped Marlee.

"What is he thinking? And why couldn't they have sent us to Miami Beach or someplace fun?"

"Do you think this is some kind of trick?" asked Camille. "Maybe it's part of their plan. You know, leaving us to our own devices so we'll have to be a team to survive?"

"Survive?" screeched Marlee. "I don't *do* survival."

"Camille, you're in Stay." The door to the room bore a little plaquette with the word *Stay*. "All the rooms in the main section of the inn are named after things dogs like to do." I swung the door open.

Camille walked in slowly, taking in the mahogany four-poster bed piled with pillows and surrounded by silky curtains. A bay window overlooked the plaza in front of the inn, and the walking zone beyond called the green.

She paused in front of the fireplace in the corner. "This is lovely. I'd like to stay in here the whole time curled up with a good book." She fingered the basket of goodies from merchants in Wagtail. "Um, Holly, I don't know quite how to ask this, but the room is paid for, right?"

"You don't have to worry about that. Your stay has been taken care of by the production company. We serve breakfast and lunch and offer limited room service. You'll find the menu on the desk. But we don't serve dinner."

"That's a relief. At least someone planned ahead. I got a little worried when Howard abandoned us. Thanks!"

I closed the door and unlocked Chew. The afternoon sun shone through the window that overlooked Dogwood Lake and the mountains. A stone fireplace on the adjoining wall was a rustic touch, and it melded nicely with the country chintz fabric of blooming peonies on a light blue background.

Marlee tossed her purse on the bed along with her expensive-looking camera. "When I signed up as Pippin's social media manager, I never expected this. I thought we might go to Paris or Tokyo. He's very popular in Japan. But no, poor overworked Pippin had to go on a *dog* vacay in the boonies."

"Maybe you'll enjoy it, too. He's going on a hike tomorrow morning," I said cheerfully.

"Ugh. They'll want pictures." She flopped backward onto her bed, hitting her head on the camera. "Ow." She rubbed her head and lay there.

I assumed that was a cue for me to exit.

I returned to the lobby to collect Jim McGowen, Pippin's handler, and Finch Morrison, both of whom were, thankfully, much more cheerful than Marlee.

It appeared to me that Jim was already flirting with Zelda. "Pippin's going on a hike and a picnic tomorrow," he said, "so he can run around in the woods off leash and play with other dogs. But I won't have anyone to keep me company. Maybe you could join us?"

Finch glanced around. "I believe I take offense to that. Camille and I will be there. We're supposed to play with Pippin. Right, Pippin?"

Pippin looked up at Finch and wagged his tail at the sound of his name. Finch knelt and massaged Pippin's ears. "We're going to play together."

Zelda was blushing. "That sounds like a lot of fun, but I'm scheduled to work. Maybe I'll see you later on in the day? We have some great bars and restaurants."

Jim towered over Finch, whom I vaguely recognized from a TV show in which he had played a hilariously sarcastic little boy. His flaming-red hair gave him away. He looked much older now that his hairline was receding, though I suspected he was only in his midtwenties. His hair waved and was long enough to tuck behind his ears. His beard was neatly trimmed, and in the middle of all that red hair, impish blue eyes still evoked memories of the spunky kid he had portrayed.

Finch was a bit portly and carried himself with all the

energy of the average couch potato. In contrast, while Jim wasn't thin, he exuded the get-up-and-go of a more athletic type. He was grinning at Zelda.

"Ready to go upstairs?" I asked.

"I'm not sure Pippin wants to leave his new friends," Finch observed.

The three dogs were romping together, all tails wagging.

Suddenly, Jacob Minifree, a local six-year-old with fat cheeks and absolutely no inhibitions, ran into the lobby and flung himself at Pippin. He wrapped his arms around Pippin's neck.

"Whoa, there!" Jim rushed to Pippin's aid. "Everybody loves Pippin, but we have to be respectful of all dogs."

To his credit, Pippin wagged his tail and bravely endured the child's hugs.

Jacob's mom was well-known around town because she subscribed to the *let them run free* theory of child-rearing. I wasn't the only person who suspected she liked that idea because she had eight children. Oma had heard endless complaints from residents about members of her brood showing up in dangerous locations without adult supervision.

At Jim's coaxing, Jacob let go of Pippin and patted his fur with the palm of his hand held flat. "Is this the real Pippin?" he asked.

"Yes, he is."

"My mommy said it would be a fake Pippin, but he looks like Pippin to me."

"What's your name?" asked Jim as he reached into a canvas bag the color of desert sand. It appeared to have all kinds of compartments and handy pockets.

"Jacob."

Jim pulled a tiny plush replica of Pippin from his bag. "This is a gift for you from Pippin for being his number one fan."

Jacob grasped the toy dog. "Thanks, Pippin! Can he come outside and play with me?"

"I'm afraid not. He traveled a long way to get here and Pippin is tired."

"Oh."

"Maybe your mom can bring you to Pippin's Treasure Hunt tomorrow."

"Okay. I'll see you then, Pippin." Jacob waddled out the door.

Jim frowned. "He's pretty young. Shouldn't someone take him home?"

Zelda snorted. "You'd think so. But his mother would just send him outside again. So how do you get a job as a dog's assistant? That sounds like fun!"

"It was a fluke. I found Pippin in a shelter and adopted him," said Jim. "He was a goofball and took a great picture, so I started training him, and before I knew it, he made more money than I did at my day job as a computer programmer. Now I'm the personal assistant to America's favorite dog."

"Thanks to Howard, you're also in charge," teased Finch.

"Sorry, Finch, you'll have to tuck yourself into bed. But I will gladly take you for a run," Jim quipped.

The doors flew open, and a woman with a helmet of unmoving platinum hair burst into the reception lobby. She wore a vivid fuchsia dress and so much jewelry on her ample bosom that she sparkled from all the bling. She pushed past the men to Zelda and placed a pudgy hand on the desk. "Rae Rae Babetski checking in. And I'll need to know in which room Howard Hirschtritt is staying, please."

Zelda shot me a desperate glance. I guessed she didn't want to break the bad news about Howard.

"Howard has disappeared," muttered Finch in a disinterested tone.

Rae Rae turned toward him and paused for a moment

while she stared at him. With a gasp, she pulled her head back. A delighted grin spread on her face as she declared, "Oh my word! You're little Tiger!" She pronounced Tiger with a deep Southern accent—*Tah-guh*.

Finch was obviously used to hearing people refer to him by the name of the character he had played. "Roar," he said in a bored voice, languidly holding up his hands and curling his fingers like pretend claws.

"You're just adorable! Are you going to be in Pippin's TV show?"

"Yes, I play Pippin's dad."

"Roscoe didn't tell me you would be here," she gushed.

"Roscoe?" asked Finch. "As in Roscoe Yates, the producer?"

"Of course. I'm your chaperone."

Jim burst out laughing. "Is he afraid Marlee or Camille will take advantage of little Tiger?"

Finch appeared annoyed.

"Roscoe said he's not having any hanky-panky. He said, and I quote, 'Pippin's show will be goin' to number one, and I don't want even a whiff of inappropriate behavior blowin' up into a scandal and messin' with the ratings.' So here I am to make sure everyone behaves. You can still have a good time. Personally, I am not averse to romance. I love romance as much as I love bling and cheese." She laughed and waved her hands. The faux-diamond bling on her dress reflected sparkles on the walls.

"Everyone with your group is staying in the main part of the hotel. The production company specifically asked that you all stay in rooms that are close together so Pippin can share in the fun and get to know everyone," explained Zelda.

"Wonderful! Is there an itinerary?" asked Rae Rae.

Finch snickered when he pointed at Jim and said, "Apparently, Jim is in charge."

Rae Rae smiled at him. "Terrific. What's the plan for tonight, sweetheart?"

Jim sighed. "Look, I'm *Pippin's* assistant. My job is to watch out for him. All I know is that we're supposed to go on a treasure hunt hike tomorrow and he's supposed to get a massage sometime. Frankly, I think he'd enjoy a swim in the lake and some downtime away from fans."

"Sounds like a plan to me." Rae Rae beamed. "A treasure hunt! Won't that be fun? We'll talk about the details over dinner tonight. I trust Howard made arrangements for that!"

I figured it was time for me to step in again. "I can reserve a table at Hot Hog. You all like barbecue, I presume?"

"I *adore* barbecue. Doesn't everyone?" Rae Rae raved with such excitement that I was beginning to wonder if there was anything she wasn't enthusiastic about.

Finch and Jim nodded as though they were just glad they didn't have to make a decision.

"Great. Would you like a Sugar Maple Inn collar for Pippin?" I asked. "They have GPS on them so we can help you find him if he wanders away."

"Pippin is extremely well trained," Jim uttered with disdain. "That won't be necessary."

# Three

Fearing I had insulted him, I smiled and said cheerfully, "Such a great dog! I hope some of his manners will rub off on my Trixie."

She looked up at me and waggled her hind end. I didn't need Zelda's mind-reading abilities to know that Trixie was laughing. She intended to continue being a rascal because it was so much fun.

Shadow carried Rae Rae's bags upstairs. A good thing because she had brought enough for a monthlong stay.

I unlocked their rooms and gave each of them my little spiel about room service and our dining hours. When I was done, I hurried to call Hot Hog to reserve a table for them. That accomplished, I left it to Zelda to inform them all of the time and place for their dinner.

I debated taking a golf cart up the back trail of the mountain but decided a hike would a nice break for me, not to mention for Trixie. I changed into comfortable walking sneakers, stashed extra treats in my pocket, and stopped by

Oma's office to ask if Gingersnap would like to join Trixie and me.

"Yes, of course," said Oma. "It would do her good to get out and walk on the trail."

Accompanied by Trixie, I strode to the main lobby of the inn and stepped outside, onto the porch that ran the length of the original building, which had been a grand home before it became an inn. Over the years, Oma had built additions, like the modern cat wing for feline guests with a screened porch on every room, but the original building was still the central hub of the inn. People wearing Pippin ears sat in rocking chairs, enjoying the beautiful early summer day. I did a double take when I saw a child licking a lollipop shaped and colored like Pippin's face. It was a good thing they had no idea Pippin was only one floor away from them.

Oma's golden retriever, Gingersnap, sat in her favorite spot at the top of the porch stairs, where she could greet guests as they came and left. Her reddish coat gleamed in the sunlight. Gingersnap took her job as the canine ambassador of the inn very seriously and loved all the attention.

"C'mon, Gingersnap. Let's go for a walk."

At the word *walk* she jumped up, the long fur on her tail swishing as she sprang down the steps to catch up to Trixie.

We ambled along the sidewalk and took a shortcut to the clearing at the base of the hiking trail. Tables had been set up, and a large red banner hung over them that read, *Pippin's Treasure Hunt*. Pippin's cheery, smiling face loomed larger-than-life on the right end of the banner. On the other side was a picture of pirate booty spilling over a trunk. I hoped that wouldn't give participants the wrong idea. As far as I knew, there wasn't any gold or valuable jewelry among the many prizes for dogs and their people to discover.

A couple of merchants were busy setting up tents. To my surprise, tourists were already buying stuffed dogs that looked like Pippin.

One of vendors yelled to me, "Is Pippin here yet?"

I felt my face flush as everyone turned to look at me. I hurried over to him and hissed, "Shh. You'll start a stampede."

I wasn't exaggerating. They clustered around me. "Is it true? Is Pippin in Wagtail? Where's he staying? Where can we see him?"

Good grief. What could I say to calm them down? "Pippin has arrived in Wagtail, but he's resting after his long flight." And then I dodged past them and fled up the trail.

In a matter of minutes, the town of Wagtail was left behind us. The voices at the bottom had faded, and all we heard were cheery birdcalls. It wasn't until I was well into the woods that I remembered my discussion with Oma about coyotes.

A flash of white scampered by me as Twinkletoes dashed ahead. "I didn't know you came with us. You better stick close by," I warned her. The thought of coyotes weighed on me. I reasoned that none had been seen. Surely, Gingersnap and Trixie would bark if any appeared.

Happily, the woods were peaceful and tranquil. Pine needles on the broad path gave it a cushy feeling underfoot. Trixie took the lead with her nose to the ground, sniffing on and off the path. There was something special about the solitude among the trees. I caught a whiff now and then of honeysuckle perfuming the woods. And Trixie and Gingersnap discovered some of the hidden goodies meant for dogs to find during the treasure hunt the next day. I lured them away with treats.

I knew we were approaching the clearing at the top when they raced ahead. They could probably pick up the scent of people before I could hear voices. I emerged from the trail to see tents set up with tables and a banner that read, *Lunch with Pippin!* Twinkletoes already sat on a table rubbing her head against Stan Hoover's hand.

He tickled her cheek like only a devoted cat lover could. "I believe I have a new friend," said Stan.

In his early twenties, Stan was tall like his father, but quite slender. The short sleeves on his T-shirt hung loosely on his thin arms. "Working for your dad this summer?" I asked.

"Yeah. For my dad *and* for my mom. Kind of boring. Hey, has Holmes shown up yet?"

Holmes Richardson, my childhood crush and the man who made my toes tingle, was moving back to Wagtail any day now. I had expected a delay before he could move home from Chicago, but it was already summer and he still wasn't in town. "No sign of him yet."

"I can't wait. Maybe things will pick up around here."

Stan's dad, Augie, overheard. "I'm lookin' forward to that, too," he called out to us.

Someone nabbed Stan to help set up a tent, and I wandered over to Augie. His wife usually pitched in on occasions like this. "Where's Glenda?"

The contented look on his face changed to bitterness and worry. "Ever since Dolly disappeared, Glenda can't concentrate on anything except finding her. I bought her that sweet little Yorkie for our twenty-fifth wedding anniversary. Paid three thousand dollars for that puppy. Plus all the clothes and bows and such. Dolly was like a baby to us. Neither one of us can get any sleep. Glenda spends her days searching the Internet and calling shelters. But Dolly hasn't turned up anywhere."

"I'm so sorry. I can't even imagine how difficult that must be."

"Keep a close eye on Twinkletoes and your dogs."

"Will do!" I tried to change the subject. "This looks great!"

"Wait till tomorrow when it smells like food. We're gonna cook bacon burgers on a grill. Everything tastes better when it's served alfresco." Augie licked his lips in anticipation. He gazed at Trixie and Gingersnap. "Even doggies will be eating big up here tomorrow." Augie pulled a sheet of paper out of his breast pocket. Looking at it, he said, "My understanding is that the treasure hunt kicks off at ten in the morning. By my guess, most people will make it to the top between eleven thirty and one thirty, depending on their speed. We'll have some drinks and snacks ready for people who come up the back way in golf carts. Some of the old-timers don't hike anymore, but they might like to join in and enjoy the view."

I smiled at him for being so thoughtful. He was right about the scenery. You could see for miles. It was like being on top of the world. "Sounds about right to me. Plus, some people probably won't be searching for treasures and will walk very fast. Others will dawdle and take a more leisurely pace."

Augie snorted. "That's what I would do. I'm glad someone had the foresight to put in that back path for vehicles. It would be tough getting the food and grills up here. I'd have to hire Sherpas!"

Augie looked around before whispering, "Sugar McLaughlin is having that thing done today where they freeze your fat. Have you seen her lately? Got hair extensions, too. Looks like a Barbie doll."

I groaned and wondered how to respond. I knew perfectly well what Augie was trying to tell me. I wasn't the only one with eyes for Holmes. Sugar had made no secret of her attraction to him. I opted for the most gracious thing I could think to say. "Sugar is Stan's age. She's beautiful just the way she is. She doesn't need all that stuff."

Still keeping his voice low, Augie fixed me with a stern look. "Now you listen here, Holly Miller. Sugar used to date Stan, so I know her pretty well. That young woman is bound and determined to get her man. I thought we were going to lose Holmes to that city slicker fiancée of his. Good thing that didn't work out! I am not going to lose our buddy to a screwball like Sugar McLaughlin."

I probably should have been flattered that he thought I wasn't a screwball, but he was clearly telling me I needed to step up my game to compete with Sugar. "This isn't a competition, Augie. And you should have more faith in your old friend Holmes anyway."

Augie shook his head slowly. "Holly, darlin', there will come a day when I'll say I warned you. Sugar and her momma, Idella, have had their sights set on that man since last Christmas. You best think about that. Ain't no fury like a woman scorned, you know."

I laughed aloud. "You make it sound like they're out to get me."

Augie didn't smile. Serious as he could be, he looked me straight in the eyes. "Don't underestimate Sugar and Idella."

"Oh, Augie. Sugar and her mom are Holmes's problem, not mine."

"One other thing, Holly. I need you to talk to your grandmother. Much as I hate to say it, I believe our little Yorkie, Dolly, and Clara's dog, Tavish, were snatched by coyotes. Liesel won't listen to me. She thinks if nobody's seen a coyote, they're not around here. But she's dead wrong. Coyotes can grab a dog like that!" He snapped his fingers to demonstrate. "They don't care if dogs are pure-bred or expensive. It's all the same to them. We have to do something to keep those critters out of Wagtail."

"Why don't you come by the inn and talk with Oma? I'm sure she'll be receptive to your opinion. Maybe you can make some suggestions about how to handle them."

Augie, a man of some size who could probably win most amateur weight-lifting competitions, took a step back and looked at me in horror. "To tell you the truth, she scares me. I believe I'd rather look a coyote in the eyes."

I laughed aloud. "She's very nice."

"You know, some people are frightening because they're strong and menacing, but some people, like your Oma, are like the alpha dog in a pack. All they have to do is look at you, and you know not to disappoint them."

I walked away thinking that Oma had made it to alpha dog status in Wagtail. That was actually something to be proud of. I wasn't keen on people being afraid of her, but Augie regarded her as a formidable leader, and that was probably a good thing. She had clout and respect.

We walked back on the main trail, enjoying the mild afternoon weather. Leaves on trees were still young, but they had filled the woods, blocking a distant view. It would be easy for a coyote to lurk among the evergreens yet remain well hidden. I kept a close eye on my companions. The white fur on Twinkletoes and Trixie was easy to see in the shadows of the trees, but Gingersnap's reddish fur melded with the colors, and I called to her more than once when I lost sight of her for a moment.

Then Trixie stopped short. She raised her nose into the air, and I could see it quivering.

# Four

A man stepped onto the path, his gaze fixed on
Trixie.

I didn't like to make snap decisions about people—after
all, we come in many shapes and sizes—but there was something about this man that gave me the creeps. I guessed him
to be in his fifties. His mouth curved downward at the edges
as was often the case on perpetually grumpy people. A pale
blue golf shirt with short sleeves revealed muscular arms, as
though he chopped wood or worked in construction.

He squatted and called out, "Come here, Dummy. Don't
you remember me?"

Thin auburn hair suited his ruddy complexion. But his eyes
made me leery. They were cold as stone and the gray color of
slate. I didn't like the way he was looking at Trixie.

Apparently, Trixie wasn't keen on him, either. She tucked
her tail between her legs and flattened herself against the
ground. She pinned her ears back. I couldn't remember her
acting that way before.

He held out his hand. "Come on. Come here, Dummy."

Had he really called her Dummy? Maybe I had misunderstood.

Trixie didn't take her eyes off him. Grudgingly, she inched toward him on her belly. The poor baby was afraid. What was going on?

Gingersnap, who loved everyone, must have picked up on Trixie's discomfort. She actually growled.

That was enough for me. I whipped Trixie up in my arms and held her tight.

The man rose to his feet and took a step toward us. "She remembers me. Barkiest dog I ever had. Had to lock her in the shed all the time to keep her from runnin' off."

A tremor ran through me. "You must be mistaken. Trixie has been my dog for years." It was a slight exaggeration, but I felt like she'd been with me forever.

"Tricksy? That's what you call her? She's not smart enough to do tricks. All she knows is how to make trouble and bark her fool head off." He held out large, rough hands. "I'll take her now."

I tightened my grip and pressed her against my chest. Since his dog ran away from him, I felt pretty sure the dog was smarter than he was, but I wasn't going to risk telling him so. "I'm sorry, sir. Maybe your dog looked like Trixie. But this is *my* dog, and anyone in Wagtail can confirm that."

The man snickered. "That there is my dog. I ought to know."

Could he be the man who had dumped her? Shivers ran through me. Could he make some legal claim that she belonged to him? Surely, he hadn't named her Dummy? "Look, mister. I'm sorry, but you're wrong. This is *not* your dog." I spoke as bravely as I could, which was no small feat because I was scared out of my wits. The thought of setting Trixie down and yelling at her to run flashed through my mind.

"Yeah, she is. I got Dummy as a puppy. The guy who

bred her can confirm that." In a low voice he grumbled, "She's *my* dog. Hand her over."

I took a step backward. "You have her confused with another dog."

"Nope, that's Dummy all right. Never was smart enough to come when I called her."

That didn't prove anything. In fact, maybe it was shrewd not to come when *he* called. "I don't think so." I could hardly breathe. What if he wasn't making that up? Could I be forced to give Trixie back to this ogre? I would move away and hide her before I let that happen. Taking another subtle step back, I mustered my best no-nonsense voice and wished I had some of Oma's moxie. "Then take me to court. This is *my* dog."

"I don't need some idiot judge to decide anything for me. I'll take her now. Just put her down and I'll take her."

My heart beat in my chest like a drum. "I understand that your Jack Russell might have looked like her, but you're not taking Trixie anywhere." I was afraid to turn away from him, so I slowly took step after step backward down the path away from him.

Suddenly, his eyes grew wide. He nodded at me coolly and said, "See you around."

He strode away and disappeared into the woods. I watched until he was gone, immensely relieved that he had left. I set Trixie on the ground, wondering what I had said that finally convinced him. Whatever it was, I would have to keep Trixie close by until I knew that creep had left town. My hands still trembled. I took some deep breaths and swung around calling, "Come on, guys!"

And then I let out a scream so loud I thought they might have heard it on the next mountain over.

Standing not ten feet away from me was the Runemaster. I hadn't seen him in years. In fact, I had forgotten all about him. He stood quietly, his weathered face not reacting to my scream. He clutched a gnarled walking stick in his hand, just as he had the only other time I had seen him. The top of his dark green shirt was loosely closed with rawhide lacing. In spite of the warm day, he wore a brown vest over it, long enough to reach the tops of his knees, and rustic, as though he might have sewn it himself.

"Hello, Miss Trixie," he said. "This little girl gets you in a heap of trouble. Do you think she really belonged to that man once?"

Twinkletoes wound around his ankles as though they were old buddies. He bent to tickle her cheek. "You're looking very pretty, Miss Twinkletoes."

I was surprised that he knew her name. "I don't think so," I replied. "It scares me that he wants to take her away from me." I walked toward him and held out my hand. "Holly Miller."

He took my hand into his. It was as weathered and rough as the stick he carried. "LaRue."

It did not escape my attention that he omitted telling me his full name. "Is that your first or last name?"

He shrugged. "Whatever you like."

"I don't see you often. Do you live in Wagtail?"

A sly grin crept over his lips. "I live *on* Wagtail. You'd best keep little Trixie close by you. I don't like the looks of that character. He's likely to dognap her when you're not looking."

I gazed down at my sweet little girl. "Don't worry. I wouldn't dream of letting him take her. Speaking of dognapping, would you know anything about the two dogs missing from Wagtail?"

When I looked up, LaRue had disappeared. I turned in a complete circle, feeling a fool. How could he vanish like that? It dawned on me that while he hadn't worn camouflage, the greens and browns of his clothing probably helped him blend with the forest.

Trixie was gazing up at me. "You stick close to me, okay? No running off. And you bite that man who called you Dummy if he tries to come near you." The word *dognap* stuck in my head. Could that creepy guy have stolen the two missing dogs?

"Let's get out of here." I hurried down the path with Gingersnap, Twinkletoes, and Trixie leaping ahead of me.

I didn't stop until we were back at the banner announcing Pippin's Treasure Hunt. A few people still worked on setting up booths and tents, which gave me a degree of comfort. All three of my four-legged companions were already acting as if nothing untoward had happened.

I waved at some people as we passed them but headed straight back to the inn. We entered through the sliding glass doors in the reception lobby. When they closed behind me, I let out a huge sigh of relief. We were home and safe.

Zelda emerged from Oma's office. She stopped short. Cocking her head, not unlike a confused dog, she asked, "What happened to Trixie?"

Okay, now that was weird. I was probably disheveled, which might have tipped her off, but how could she know something had happened that involved Trixie?

Zelda stared at Trixie. She finally looked at me and said, "Trixie wants to stay here with you."

Chill bumps rose on my arms. I picked up Trixie and held her tight, stroking her round tummy. "Some guy says she belongs to him."

"She doesn't like him."

"Neither do I."

The sliding doors hummed as they swished open and Sergeant Dave Quinlan walked in. Affectionately known as Officer Dave, in spite of his promotion, he worked for the Snowball Police Department but lived in Wagtail and was our primary law enforcement officer. He nodded a greeting at us. "Is Liesel in?"

Zelda nodded. "I think she's in the main lobby."

"Any news on the missing dogs?" I asked.

Dave sighed. "We tracked the GPS collar the Scottie was wearing and found it in the lake."

I held my breath. "I hope it wasn't on the dog."

"Nope. Just the collar. That's why I'm here. I think we can eliminate coyotes as suspects. I've never met a coyote who could throw a collar into a lake. If it had been near the shore, then maybe."

"We have a dog thief in Wagtail," I uttered under my breath.

"Or a ring of them. Both the dogs that went missing were pricey purebreds. You better keep an eye on Trixie. That magazine story about her is pasted in windows all over town."

"Odd you should say that. Some guy showed up and claimed that she belongs to him."

Dave scowled at me. "I don't like the sound of that. Have you got a noseprint for her?"

"A what?"

"Noseprint. It's like a fingerprint for people. No dog nose is exactly like another. They all have little lines on them that can be used to identify a dog."

I must have looked doubtful, because he continued.

"This is nothing new. The Canadian Kennel Club has been using them since the 1930s to identify dogs. Shutter Dogs sells kits to make noseprints. Bring one to me and I'll put it on file."

"I will! I had no idea."

"Yeah, well, most of the time there's no dispute over ownership of a dog. But in a case like this, it's best to have a way to identify her." Dave crouched to pet Trixie and Gingersnap.

When he left to speak to Oma, Trixie and I hustled over to the hardware store, Shutter Dogs, for a noseprint kit. Just like most businesses in Wagtail, the store was named for an important segment of our population. In reality, shutter dogs were clips that held shutters open, but many of the stores had fun with creative names that involved cats and dogs.

Formerly a resort for people who sought the natural spring waters for their health, Wagtail suffered a decline when such places were no longer popular. The little town in the mountains of Virginia had been visited by famous people in its heyday, many of whom built magnificent homes and considered Wagtail their summer vacation spot. In an effort to revive the economy, Wagtail had gone to the dogs and cats. It was now the premier destination for those who longed to travel with pets. Dogs and cats were welcome everywhere in Wagtail. The restaurants offered special menus just for them. The stores carried everything a dog or cat could wish for, from collars and coats, to beds and cat trees. While they had hoped to turn things around, no one had anticipated the steady stream of new residents and visitors.

We walked across the green, the sun still high in the early evening. The grassy park in the center of Wagtail teemed with people and their dogs and cats. There was nothing to fear.

Trixie nosed around, probably following the scent of a squirrel.

To my surprise, people pointed at Trixie and called her by her name. Even the tourists! I thought about what Dave had said. Maybe he was right. The man probably saw the article about Trixie.

A lady stopped and cooed over her. But if Trixie knew she was featured in *Dog Life* magazine, she showed no sign of a swelled head.

As we approached the sidewalk, I saw that Dave had not exaggerated. The magazine was prominently posted in shop and restaurant windows. It seemed that everyone knew Trixie. She wriggled with joy, stopping for the occasional pat or to greet another dog, but mostly continued on her way, more interested in the scents on the ground than in the people admiring her.

Applause broke out when Trixie trotted inside Shutter Dogs. The owner, Grady Biffle, brought her a cookie in the shape of a Jack Russell terrier.

"We had these made in honor of you. We never had such a famous canine resident before," exclaimed the owner.

Trixie wagged her tail and happily munched on the little cookie that looked remarkably like her, right down to the spot on her rump. But one treat wasn't enough for our new starlet. Trixie sped straight to the dog biscuit section of the store. I kept an eye on her, but she was behaving and hadn't helped herself—yet.

Trixie lifted her nose into the air. I could see her nostrils flaring as she picked up the scent of something.

I realized that someone was watching her. Was that how it felt to be a star? Even when you were sniffing out your favorite cookies, people were observing you?

A flash of blue caught my eye. I swept Trixie up in my arms out of an abundance of caution. I didn't see the man who claimed Trixie was his. She wriggled and kissed my nose. I was overreacting. I set her down and selected a dog noseprint kit.

Diane Blushner, whom we guessed to be in her fifties but didn't look a day over forty, sidled up to me. "Noseprinting Trixie?" asked Diane. "That's a good idea. Especially after what happened to the Hoovers' dog, Dolly, and Clara's Scottie."

Diane was a natural beauty. She didn't wear a drop of makeup. Her high cheekbones and symmetrical features didn't need any assistance. The tiniest hint of crow's-feet and laugh lines had begun to take shape, and she had a small beauty mark just below the outer edge of her right eyebrow.

A boxer breeder, Diane had the distinction of owning Stella, reportedly the top boxer in the east in her younger years. Stella nuzzled my hand. She had a stunning fawn coat with a black mask on her muzzle, which had begun to gray. A spot of white on her chest looked like she'd been splashed with milk. She had a disposition as sweet as her expression. She was Diane's baby, and she knew it.

"Did you noseprint Stella?"

"You bet. I noseprint all my dogs, including the puppies. In my sales contract there's a provision that if a buyer can't keep one of my dogs, it's to be returned to me. I try my best to make sure the buyers are good people, but some of the dogs I've sold have turned up in shelters. A noseprint comes in handy to prove that they're one of mine."

"You've actually had to use a noseprint before?"

"A few years back, some sickly dogs started turning up. Some of the other breeders and I tracked them down to the most awful man. A noseprint confirmed that he was using one of my dogs for breeding. Heaven only knows how she fell into his hands, but I got her out of there and helped shut him down."

"Was he local? Do you think he could be stealing dogs around here?"

# Five

She grinned. "Not a chance. He's doing time in prison for credit card fraud. At least that scumbag is locked up!" She looked at me sadly. "But there are so many more like him. It breaks my heart."

She knelt on one knee and held out her hand to Trixie. "Congratulations on that cool article."

"Thanks. Trixie seems to be taking it in stride."

Diane accepted a nose kiss from Trixie. "That's the great thing about dogs. People get swelled heads. Dogs are proud, but they never brag."

Diane glanced at her watch. "I've got to run, but I'll see you tomorrow at the treasure hunt. They've roped me into blowing the starting whistle."

I wandered on, eyeing a dog surveillance video camera. Trixie was with me all the time, so I certainly didn't need one, but it was amazing.

And then I saw Glenda Hoover of Pierce Real Estate

making keys. I had to say something. Ordinarily, her little Yorkie, Dolly, would have been with her.

Glenda and Augie were a good match. In Wagtail, when someone was in need, they were often the first in line with a homemade casserole or a Bundt cake.

"Glenda! I'm so sorry about Dolly. Have you gotten any leads yet?"

Glenda looked worn-out. Like she hadn't been sleeping. She'd told me once she never met a doughnut that she didn't like, and her figure reflected her fondness for them. "Nothing. Not a word. It's just horrible. The rental office sent me over to make some keys. You must have the same problem at the inn. Do people walk away with the keys to their rooms?"

"All the time."

"They're supposed to swing by with the keys to the rental houses on their way out of town, but they always forget."

"Oma and I have discussed some of the fancy systems available, but they're all very pricey. And we both think there's something kind of quaint about having a real key instead of a piece of plastic that looks like a credit card."

"I totally agree. Anyway, I thought I'd buy some thumbtacks to put up pictures of Dolly around town. She's such a little barker that I can't imagine why no one has heard her!"

"If there's anything I can do to help you find her, please let me know."

"Thanks, Holly."

Trixie followed me to the cash register.

The owner of Shutter Dogs asked, "Would Trixie give us a pawtograph?"

"How do we do that?"

He pulled out the magazine page with Trixie's photograph on it and a small container of ink. "This ink is just for making pawtographs," he explained. "It's not toxic to dogs or cats."

"No kidding? I'll take one. We could start a pawtograph wall at the inn!"

Trixie cooperated patiently as he dipped her paw into the ink and then onto the page.

"That's perfect! Come back soon, little Trixie!"

We left the store and headed for home, keeping to the sidewalk, where we could always dodge into a store or restaurant if need be, though I had no real reason to fear the peculiar man when I was in Wagtail. I doubted that he would be as bold about confronting me when lots of people were around. Luckily, there was no sign of him. He was probably just a visitor to Wagtail who had seen Trixie's picture all over town, I assured myself. Of course, that didn't mean he wouldn't steal her if he got the chance.

As soon as we got back to the inn, I made noseprints for Trixie and Gingersnap. They weren't crazy about having me press against their noses, but the little chunks of cheese they received as a reward seemed to make up for it. Twinkletoes watched in fascination, but when I walked toward her, she made a mad dash for the hidden dog door in my dining room and disappeared to the private inn kitchen below.

When I lived in Arlington, Virginia, and worked as a fund-raiser in Washington, D.C., Oma had hoped I would come to help her at the inn as she grew older. Unbeknownst to me, when she added the reception lobby and a new apartment for herself, she carved another apartment out of half of the attic on the third floor of the main building for me, complete with a balcony to the front and a larger terrace to the south, overlooking Dogwood Lake and the mountains in the distance. She also built two hidden stairways. One led from the private inn kitchen to my dining room, in which there was a dog door so my cats and dogs could roam the inn as they pleased. The other led from Oma's apartment down to the inn office. They were nice shortcuts for the two of us, and sometimes came in handy when we didn't want to walk through the main lobby.

I wrote the names of the dogs on their noseprints, as well as the phone number for the Sugar Maple Inn. I added my name to Trixie's noseprint sheet and Oma's name to Gingersnap's sheet. That done, I went in search of Oma. I found her with Dave and Twinkletoes in the private kitchen that was off-limits to guests.

It was a large but homey room with a giant turquoise island in the middle. In the winter, we gathered there around the fireplace, and sometimes enjoyed cozy dinners with friends.

"I hope I'm not interrupting," I said.

Dave swallowed a bite of what appeared to be a turkey sandwich. "Not at all."

"We are discussing the problem of the missing dogs." Oma's sandwich lay untouched on her plate. She sipped from a mug.

Unless I missed my guess, she was drinking tea to calm her nerves.

"Are you okay?" I asked.

"Holly, it could ruin Wagtail if a dog theft ring is operating here. Tourism is the heart of our existence."

I sat down opposite her and reached for her hand. "Dave will get to the bottom of this. Don't worry. Wagtail will be fine." At least I hoped it would be. I loved the little town where we lived in concert with other residents who adored their cats and dogs.

"You will help Dave." Oma looked straight at me. "I am too old to chase dogs. You do it for me, please."

I gazed at Dave, who was probably offended by her implication that he couldn't find the dogs on his own.

Dave wiped his mouth with a napkin. "I can use all the help I can get, Holly. Frankly, I'd be pleased if you pitched in. You and Trixie have a knack for sleuthing."

"A dog theft ring? Doesn't that sound dangerous?" I asked.

"I suppose they can be. I'll handle the police work. You and Trixie just keep your noses to the ground and pass along any information to me. Don't do anything risky."

I wasn't about to do anything dangerous. But I could make some inquiries and see what I could find out. I handed Oma Gingersnap's noseprint and explained what it was. "You should probably sign it."

Oma studied it for a moment. She gazed at Dave. "This is true? A dog's nose can be used to identify him?"

His mouth full, Dave nodded at her.

"Why did I not know this? We should have a noseprinting event in Wagtail. The sooner the better!"

Dave picked up his mug. "Liesel, that's brilliant. We'll know most of the people who come, and if any more dogs are stolen in Wagtail, it will be easier to prove it."

"Where did you buy this?" asked Oma.

When I told her, she picked up the phone and made a call to Grady at Shutter Dogs. She was smiling when she hung up. "He has a whole case of them and can get another case by tomorrow evening. Wagtail will pick up the tab for residents who attend. Tourists can pay a token fee if they want to join in. How about Sunday at one in the afternoon on the plaza in front of the inn?"

Dave reached across the table and high-fived her. "Holly, can you put it out on social media and send a blast to Wagtail residents?"

Over the winter I had finally set up an e-mail list and emergency notification system for residents of Wagtail. It was a small community, but the time had come for us to rely less on gossip and word of mouth, which weren't always accurate.

"Absolutely." I was getting hungry watching Dave chow down on his turkey sandwich. I hustled to the magic refrigerator in search of turkey for my dinner.

My parents had sent me to Wagtail every summer to stay with Oma. They had been sun-filled days of fun and work at the inn with my cousin and Holmes, the grandson of Oma's best friend. Most of the day's leftovers from the inn's dining services were delivered to less-fortunate people who lived on Wagtail Mountain, but quite a bit also landed in the fridge, which never seemed to be empty, earning it the moniker *the magic refrigerator.*

"Has Gingersnap eaten yet?" I asked.

"Not yet," Oma replied.

I filled bowls for Trixie and Gingersnap with something called Gobble Gobble Goodness. The inn offered special homemade meals for our dog and cat guests. We also kept an array of commercial dog and cat foods because some people preferred to have their furry ones eat the foods they were used to. Gobble Gobble Goodness appeared to be chunks of turkey breast, onion-free gravy, broccoli, quinoa, and linguine, sprinkled with a few rosy cooked cranberries. I located a similar version for cats called Turkey Mousse and spooned it into a small bowl for Twinkletoes.

Dave looked over at the dogs. "Too bad Trixie's nose can't lead us to the missing dogs."

"Shh!" Oma hissed. "I wish to find the dogs but not next to a murdered person. We have had enough of those incidents. Holly, when you send out the e-mail blast, perhaps you can mention that everyone should be on the alert for the barking of dogs where there were none before."

I glanced at Dave for his approval and bit into my sandwich.

He nodded. "If it's really someone stealing dogs, there's a good chance he's not through yet and the missing dogs are still in the area somewhere. We should all be on the alert for whimpering and barking. When things calm down in town tonight, I might take a drive down the mountain to see if I hear anything on the outskirts."

While we ate, I described the incident with the gray-eyed man and how LaRue came to the rescue. Oma was horrified.

"What do you know about LaRue?" I asked.

Oma's eyes met Dave's.

"Not much," he said. "He's retired and chooses to live quietly among the blessings of nature."

"It looked like he might have sewn his own clothes. Have you been to his house?"

Dave grinned. "It's kind of neat. He builds with things he finds. The stuff the rest of us throw away. He constructed a whole wall in his entranceway out of glass that he found. It's like a mosaic that lights up from the inside."

"So he's creative and pretty smart," I said. "Does he live off the grid?"

"Ja," Oma muttered. "He is very intelligent."

Why did I feel like they were keeping something from me? In any event, they seemed to approve of him and didn't warn me to keep my distance.

I noted that Dave changed the subject quickly. "If you see the gray-eyed man tomorrow, give me a call. I'd like to know who he is and keep an eye on him."

I was more than happy to do that!

# Six

After dinner, I closed the hidden dog door in my dining room so Trixie wouldn't wander through the inn. I spent the next few hours in my quarters working on e-mail blasts and social media. Still, I glanced around for Trixie every few minutes, even though I knew she hadn't left my apartment.

At midnight, I slid a harness on Trixie and attached a leash. She gave me a curious look. It had been a long time since she had to walk on a leash. We headed downstairs to the empty lobby. Our night manager, Casey, ought to be around somewhere.

I pushed the front door open and we stepped outside. The bars and a few restaurants stayed open for night owls, so the sidewalks weren't deserted despite the late hour. We strode along for a bit. The stores were locked, but lights glowed in their elaborate window displays. Several of them featured everything Pippin, from keychains to dog beds.

Jim must be making a mint on merchandising Pippin's name and image.

We turned to the left and walked along the quiet street. The night air was blissfully warm. It was a lovely night for a stroll. Every so often we stopped and listened. Trixie continually lifted her nose to the air, picking up scents that I couldn't smell. We heard no barking or whining.

But even in the dark, there was no mistaking Rae Rae as she whipped by us in a golf cart on a cross street. Rae Rae's jewelry flashed under the light of the moon as if it glowed in the dark. Interestingly, she was headed away from the inn.

Trixie stopped to investigate a boxwood. I closed my eyes and concentrated on the sounds of the night. Crickets were busy rubbing their legs together to make their chirping sound. The engine of a boat puttered on the lake. Probably someone fishing. In the distance, to my west, I could hear a lone dog barking.

"Let's stroll over that way, Trixie."

She readily changed direction. In a few blocks, we were back in the heart of Wagtail.

As we crossed the green, I spied Jim striding somewhere fast. But Pippin was nowhere to be seen. I followed him briefly to be sure. I couldn't believe he would have left Pippin alone. But on second thought, they had had a long plane trip and poor Pippin was always the center of attention. He deserved some rest.

The Wagtail Springs Hotel was the only other inn-type facility in Wagtail. Some visitors to town stayed in a bed-and-breakfast or rented a house for their time here. Across the way, just on the outskirts of Wagtail, there was a popular subdivision with houses that looked like hobbits lived in them. But owners were not allowed to rent them. So it stood to reason that if there were someone nabbing dogs, he would have to hide them in a rental house or outside of Wagtail. And if it were the latter, he would need a means of transporting them out of Wagtail without anyone noticing. Unless he was a resident, he couldn't bring in a car or truck. But some of the rentals came with a golf cart for the tenant's use, I mused. He could probably sedate a dog and transport it to a vehicle in the parking lot outside of Wagtail without anyone noticing.

A couple of dogs barked at us as we wandered through residential neighborhoods. But I knew those dogs. They were where they belonged.

We walked back to the inn, where I collected a key for a golf cart. Trixie and I headed outside, and she hopped on the golf cart like a pro.

We drove along the same road Rae Rae had taken. I didn't see another golf cart parked anywhere, but she could have turned off on one of the smaller side streets. We drew up to the huge parking lot outside of town where visitors left their vehicles. I recognized the lot's night manager helping some people with a flat tire.

Grateful for the quiet engine of the electric golf cart, I paused and listened.

"Trixie, speak!" I said.

She looked at me and breathed a quiet *woof* in an indoor kind of voice like she couldn't believe I wanted her to be noisy.

I reached into my pocket for a treat. "Real speak!"

Her eyes locked onto the liver treat in my fingers, and she barked once, loud and clear.

I fed her the treat and listened for any whimpering or barking. We drove on, and Trixie barked four more times for a treat.

Before we left, I stopped to speak with the night manager. "Could you keep an ear open for any barking inside of vehicles?"

"Dave's a step ahead of you. He told all of us what's going on. The whole parking lot crew is on the lookout."

"Great. Thanks a lot."

I drove slowly, winding through streets on the way back to the inn. As I parked the golf cart at the inn, I heard voices and could make out two figures running and giggling in the dark. They passed under a light, and I saw then that it was Camille and Finch.

I didn't see Pippin or his group again that night, which I hoped meant things had gone well for them.


Trixie and Twinkletoes bounded out of bed in the morning, eager to get going. I wished I had their energy at that hour. I showered, pulled my long hair back into a ponytail, and dressed in a navy skort, sleeveless white shirt, and comfortable sneakers for the walk up the mountain.

As we ventured downstairs, the aroma of coffee and bacon wafted up to us from the inn's kitchen.

I glanced around the main lobby, which had begun to get busy. The phone buzzed at the front desk. I strode over and answered, "Sugar Maple Inn."

"Holly?"

I recognized Augie's voice. "Hi!" I said. "Please don't tell me there's a problem with the food for Pippin's Treasure Hunt."

"Not the food exactly. I was wondering if we could borrow Shadow today. Diane Blushner has gone missing, and two of my employees are joining a search team to look for her."

My breath caught in my throat. "What do you mean *missing*? I saw her yesterday at Shutter Dogs."

I could hear Augie inhale sharply. "Her dogs were heard barking last night. And today, no one can find her. She's not home, and no one has seen her. It appears that she didn't feed the dogs this morning."

"There's no way she would neglect her dogs. She lives for them!"

"Stella is gone, too."

If it hadn't been for the other two missing dogs, I would have assumed Diane had taken Stella somewhere with her. It was as unusual to see Diane without Stella as it was to see me without Trixie. "Does Dave think there's a connection to the other missing dogs?"

"That's what worries us. We're hoping for the best, but you know Diane. If someone tried to take Stella, she'd have said, 'Over my dead body.'"

I hoped that wasn't the case. "Shadow is free to help you out today if it's okay with him. Who is feeding Diane's dogs?"

"I'm taking care of them until we find her."

"Keep me posted?" I asked.

"Yes, of course. See you at lunch."

Oma was heading toward me. "I never want to be famous." She pointed at the outdoor patio where Pippin and Jim were enjoying the sunshine. While they ate their breakfasts, people at the other tables watched, clearly fascinated.

"I presume you've heard about Diane?" I asked.

"Dave called me an hour ago. This is unimaginable."

I explained about Augie's call and that Shadow would be helping him.

Oma nodded. "I hope that Diane will turn up soon, and that she is surprised to learn people are searching for her." Oma winked at me. "Maybe she has a boyfriend we don't know about."

I took Trixie out the front door for her morning stroll. She turned left and headed to greet friends at the area of grass designated as a doggy bathroom.

The sun shone, and there was little humidity. Perfect for a hike. People passed me on their way to breakfast at the inn, some with small backpacks, others with hiking poles. The Sugar Maple Inn was well-known for decadent breakfasts and drew diners who were staying elsewhere. We were the only restaurant in Wagtail that served afternoon tea, which was also a big draw. Our reputation for good food was one reason Oma chose not to serve dinner. Oma felt guests and visitors should get out to other restaurants and bars for their evening meals.

When we returned to the dining area, I opted for a table indoors, away from the Pippin fanatics.

Seconds after I sat down, Camille appeared. Her long brunette hair hung in informal beach waves. It was a casual look that I knew she had worked to accomplish. She was in full makeup, ready for photographs. Her hiking boots made clumping sounds as she walked toward our table. "Hi, Holly. I don't see any of my group. Would you mind if I joined you? I hate to eat alone."

"Trixie and I would love that. But Jim and Pippin are outside if you'd rather eat with them."

"Oh?" She tromped over to the window and peered out at them before clomping back. "I really don't want to be in pictures when I'm eating. Not unless I'm posing like I'm eating. You know what I mean? Holding a spoon of something and saying, 'Yummy!'" She sat down. "Chewing is not when we're at our best."

"It must be hard to be in the spotlight all the time."

"This is all new to me. The show was developed for Pippin. They pulled Finch and Howard in because they're already famous." She leaned toward me and whispered, "This is my big break. Roscoe Yates as producer, Howard Hirschtritt, Finch, and Pippin? It's like a dream come true. I'm trying to make the best of it. I was so lucky to be chosen. But it's easy to goof up. All it takes is the wrong tweet or photo and I'm dead in the water." She grimaced. "Why do people wear these boots for hiking? They're so uncomfortable." She glanced under the table. "Is that what you're wearing for the treasure hunt? Sneakers?"

"Unless you're planning to be in rough terrain, I think sneakers would be fine."

"Ugh. I'll change right after breakfast."

Shelley Dixon, the chief waitress at the inn, came over to our table and poured coffee. "Sorry to keep you waiting. It's been a madhouse this morning."

I smiled at her. "No problem."

"The special today is, what else—Pippin pancakes with chocolate chips and maple syrup. For those who aren't wearing Pippin ears, I recommend the broccoli and ham quiche or Oma's German pancakes with fresh strawberries."

"Oma's pancakes for me, please. Is there a doggy version?" I asked.

"Of course. Instead of fruit, Trixie will have ground chicken and veggies with a bite of pancake."

"Perfect."

"I'm sorry to trouble you," said Camille. "Do you have any plain yogurt? Maybe some strawberries without any sugar on them?"

Shelley smiled sweetly like she had heard this kind of order before. It reminded me of the way I ate before I came to Wagtail. Of course, in those days I spent most of my day seated at a desk. I wasn't on my feet all day long like I was now.

Shelley nodded. "Are you going on the treasure hunt? You might want to eat something more substantial."

"Just the yogurt and berries, please."

"Sure thing." Shelley hustled off.

"I hate asking for special orders," said Camille, "but I don't dare gain an ounce."

"It's no problem. There are several healthy low-calorie breakfasts on the menu. Including one with plain yogurt, berries, and nuts."

"That makes me feel much better."

Rae Rae showed up in the most bling I had ever seen for

a hike in the woods. Her sneakers were covered with turquoise sequins, which matched the sequins on her T-shirt in the shape of dog paws that ran from the bottom of her shirt to her shoulder on a diagonal. "Isn't this adorable?" Rae Rae asked. "I did some shopping yesterday before dinner. I had no idea there would be such wonderful stores here. It made me miss having a dog, too."

"There's a terrific shelter here. Maybe you should stop by and have a look," I suggested.

"I might just do that. It's time I had another fluffy sweetie in my life." Rae Rae took a seat beside me just as Shelley served our breakfasts.

"I want what Holly is having, please! That looks delish. Oh! And with a side of bacon, please."

When Shelley left, Rae Rae turned her attention to Camille. "Where's the rest of your troupe?"

"Jim's outside with Pippin, but I haven't seen anyone else. Rae Rae, do you know why Howard dumped us? It troubles me. I feel like it's some sort of test."

"Darlin'"—Rae Rae fidgeted with a giant glitzy ring on her middle finger—"that's just Howard. He may have awards and a reputation for being a marvelous actor, but Howard has been an undependable, self-centered horse's patoot since the day I met him."

"But he has such a good reputation," Camille protested.

"He's good at what he does," Rae Rae drawled. "I'll give him that. But he is a thoroughly miserable excuse for a human being. Trust me on this. Once upon a time, I was engaged to be Mrs. Horse's Patoot."

# Seven

Camille gasped. "Then you must know him very well."

"Why do you think Roscoe called me to keep an eye on things? Howard was mad as a hornet when he found out that I was here."

"Isn't it hard on you to see him?" I asked.

Rae Rae laughed aloud. "Oh, you sweet thing. It was a long time ago. But I'll admit that our breakup on our wedding day came as a blow to me. In all honesty, though, his wandering eyes did me a favor. I got out before we tied the knot. It was a painful lesson back then, but it saved me a lot of heartache in my life."

Rae Rae pointed at Camille. "Do not succumb to his charisma. He may be a flabby, middle-aged man without much hair, but he can still be very charming. And he'll suck you into his vortex before you know what's what. Here's the thing, sugar. He can do a lot for your future, but he'll do more if he can't catch you."

Camille appeared horrified. "I'm lucky you're here. He should come with a manual."

"You'll do fine. If he gives you any trouble at all, you just come to Rae Rae. Now, speaking of which, where do you suppose Finch and Marlee are?"

Camille shrugged and promptly ate some of her yogurt as if she didn't want to reply. Luckily for Camille, Shelley arrived with food for Rae Rae, which distracted her for the moment. I had a hunch that not much got by Rae Rae.

I excused myself when I finished breakfast. I needed to hustle over to the staging site to take care of any last-minute issues that might arise. After leaving some Cow-a-Bunga Stew for Twinkletoes in our apartment in case she got hungry before our return, I grabbed harnesses and leashes for Gingersnap and Trixie and returned to the lobby.

We stepped onto the porch. One guest sat in a rocking chair with a cat on her lap and a steaming mug of coffee on the table next to her. She nodded at me.

"Good morning," we chimed simultaneously.

At that moment, Jim and Pippin joined us on the porch.

Pippin immediately bowed to Trixie in the canine gesture to play. A second later, Gingersnap joined in and the three dogs galloped down the front steps and onto the plaza in front of the inn.

"This is exactly what Pippin needed," said Jim. "I love watching him play with other dogs. He never gets a chance to do that."

"It's nice to see him having fun. I guess days are long when he's shooting a television program."

"They can be. And no one wants a wild and crazy dog on a set." Jim laughed in delight as Pippin ran like he had the zoomies. There was no denying that the goofy smile Pippin wore meant he loved prancing and playing with the other dogs.

"Are you ready for your treasure hunt?" I asked.

Jim groaned. "Marlee complained about it nonstop during dinner last night." He gazed around. "She really ought to be getting photos of this for social media. Honestly, Camille is the only one with any energy. Finch hasn't even made an appearance this morning." He glanced at his watch and heaved a great sigh. "I guess I'd better go bang on Finch's and Marlee's doors and get them out of bed. Would you mind keeping an eye on Pippin? He's having such a good time with his buddies that I hate to bust up the fun. I should be back in five minutes."

"No problem." While Jim went inside to wake Finch, I chatted with a few guests on the porch.

Jim returned with a look of dismay. "Either those two are dead to the world or they're very good at hiding their heads under their pillows. Neither of them had the decency to get up and open the door. Guess we'll have to go without them. This is exactly why I didn't want to be in charge. They're adults. Right? No one should have to chase them down to do what's expected of them."

We started walking toward the gathering site at the foot of the mountain.

Camille caught up to us wearing a bright pink sleeveless top and blue jean shorts. She had swapped her hiking boots for plain white sneakers but still wore ample makeup. She probably had to be ready for photos, even on a treasure hunt. "You look great," I said.

"No sign of Marlee or Finch yet?" she asked.

Jim gave her an unabashedly admiring glance.

Uh-oh. I suspected the wrong people might bond on this trip.

"I tried. If they can't be bothered to get up and do their jobs, well, that's just too bad," said Jim. "They know what the plan is, and they're old enough to be responsible. I'm neither their dad nor their boss. We'll just do this without them."

Camille grinned. "Finch is living up to his character on the show. He's supposed to be kind of a slouch. Besides, it's Pippin who is the star attraction, not Finch. Right, Pippin?" she asked, holding out her hand to him.

He gazed up at her and swished his tail. I could have sworn he was smiling.

We walked to the starting point, where Clara Dorsey sat in a lawn chair handing out cold drinks for the hike.

"Holly!" she called.

I excused myself and walked over to her. Closing in on seventy, plump Clara could be a little scatterbrained. Her husband had died the previous year. Unfortunately, he had handled everything from finances to roof repair on their cottage. After his death, Clara had been overwhelmed until Shadow, Augie, and a few neighbors stepped up to help her. They had painted her cottage recently and repaired the gate on her fence. She handed me a bottle of water. "Any news on Diane?"

"Not yet."

Clara moaned. "I hope nothing bad happened to her. I wanted to join the search for her, but they said I would be more helpful filling in here." She glanced at her cane with annoyance. "I can't wait until my foot heals and I can get around better. Diane has been such a dear to me. Do you think she got a lead on who took my sweet Tavish?"

I had no idea. "Why would you think that?"

"She stopped by my house yesterday with a basket of fresh blueberry muffins because she heard Tavish had disappeared. She promised to do her best to find him."

"Did she have any idea what might have happened to him?"

"I don't know. She brought Stella with her and let her sniff around."

"You must miss Tavish."

"I don't know what to do without him. I haven't slept a

wink since he disappeared." Tears filled her eyes. "It was so unbearably quiet in my house last night that I drove the streets in my golf cart looking for him. I can't stand to think of what might have happened. He was in our yard! I miss the little guy so much." A tear rolled down her round cheek. "And now everyone is out looking for Diane. What's happening around here? I always felt so safe in Wagtail."

"You're still safe here. I'm sure Diane will turn up." I stopped short of reassuring her about her beloved Tavish, though. I honestly didn't know if we would be able to find the dognapper. I thanked her for the bottle of water. "And if you're ever feeling lonely, come on over to the inn and visit with Oma and me."

Clara smiled and pointed at someone. "Thank you, honey. Is Liesel joining the hunt today?"

I looked in the direction she indicated, and to my surprise I saw Oma. I wandered over to her. "I didn't know you were planning to hike."

Oma shook her head. "I would like to, but there will be no hiking for me today with everyone looking for Diane and the three missing dogs. It wouldn't be right if I were having fun. Not to mention that I would be miserable because I would be thinking of Diane constantly."

"Then what are you doing here?"

"They asked me to blow the start whistle. It was Diane's job . . ."

"Liesel!" A young man ran up to her. I backed away to give them some privacy to speak.

Vendors were doing a bang-up business selling stuffed Pippins from mouse-sized to life-sized. While Jim kept a watchful eye on the real Pippin, children and adults alike cooed and posed with him for selfies. Marlee should have been there to manage the social media aspect of things. She was missing some wonderful moments that would have made terrific photos.

Pippin was a good sport, wagging his tail and taking all the attention in stride as people patted him.

Jim sidled up to me. "This is a great crowd. But doggone it! Where's Marlee? This happens to me all the time. What's wrong with people? Why does everyone expect me to do their jobs? Marlee ought to be out here taking care of the social media stuff and dealing with all the people who want their pictures taken with Pippin." He heaved a sigh. "First Howard and now Marlee. I should have just brought Pippin here by himself. The two of us could have had a great time." He shook his head. "Seems like I always end up doing all the work."

I understood where he was coming from. It wasn't right for the others to be lounging around while Jim handled everything for them.

I gazed at the leashes and harnesses in my hands and wondered if I should put them on Trixie and Gingersnap.

They had wandered away from the crowd of people and sniffed the trail with excitement. Pippin finally had enough of posing for pictures and raced to see what interested his canine friends.

I gazed around. There was no sign of the man with gray eyes. And the dogs would have a ball mingling with other dogs and hunting for treasure. It didn't seem fair to not let them join in the fun. Could I take a chance and allow them to run loose like I would have two days ago? There were so many people participating in the hike. Surely, he wouldn't try to snatch Trixie in front of a crowd.

Pippin zipped by Gingersnap and Trixie, who chased after him. I smiled as I watched them enjoy themselves. I didn't want to deny them that. I would just have to keep a close eye on them.

From a small podium, Oma announced, "The great Treasure Hunt with Pippin begins! Don't forget that the person who finds a five-inch-tall statue of Pippin will win the coveted grand prize—a picnic at Dogwood Lake with Pippin, America's favorite dog!" She blew the whistle.

As if they understood, dogs yapped and yowled and headed up the path. Children ran after them. The adults moved a little bit slower, but everyone began hiking up the hill.

Trixie, Gingersnap, and Pippin ran ahead, taking the lead. I rushed to catch up to them. We hadn't gone far before I heard children exclaiming about the treasures they had found.

Personally, I was looking forward to the Pippin party at the top of the mountain.

The woods on each side of us were dark. The emerging leaves blocked the sun from filtering down. New growth on the ground was beginning to fill the forest so that it was more difficult to see deep into the woods.

I chuckled when I spotted a leash that glowed in the dark as a prize. It hung from a branch that looked to be about three feet off the ground. I didn't think anyone would miss seeing that.

Everyone seemed to be in good cheer. Rae Rae caught up to me. "This is such fun! But it appears that two of our crew are still missing. Roscoe will not be pleased that there are no photos of Pippin going viral."

"A lot of people took selfies. Maybe one of them will be popular."

"Wouldn't you think that they would get up and participate? After all, this is a paid vacation for them. And that Marlee! She should be working, not sleeping off a hangover! Roscoe will be quite put out."

I agreed with Rae Rae. "Was Marlee out late last night?"

Rae Rae threw me a wicked glance. "Let's just say she didn't go back to the inn with the rest of us."

I glanced at her sideways. Clearly, Rae Rae didn't realize that I had seen her out and about after midnight.

Rae Rae paused to chat with someone, but I kept walking. I searched for Trixie's white fur among the dogs romping around, but I didn't see her.

"Trixie? Gingersnap?" I started to panic. "Trixie, come!"

Seconds later, I heard Jim calling Pippin in a fearful voice.

We were a little over halfway up the trail when I heard the thing I had come to dread—Trixie's howling bark.

# Eight

It wasn't her ordinary cheerful bark. Not the one that meant she wanted a treat or the bark that indicated she heard someone outside our door. It was Trixie's way of setting up an alarm. Surely, I had heard wrong. It was a beautiful, sunny day. We had been up and down the path only the day before. Wouldn't we have noticed something then? It couldn't be . . .

I could hear her off in the woods, wailing.

Jim ran over to me, his brow creased. "Pippin followed Trixie, but I don't see them anywhere."

Rae Rae huffed and puffed to catch up to us. "Why are they barking? Where's Pippin?"

Jim paled. "Do you think they ran into a bear or something?"

"Or something," I muttered, fearful that they had found a corpse. Jim and Rae Rae wouldn't know about Trixie's nose for murder unless they had read the article about her. "I'll check on them." Following the sound of Trixie's barking, I veered off the trail onto a smaller path that was probably used more by deer than by humans.

Rae Rae and Jim were right behind me, calling Pippin's name.

"Pippin always comes when I call. I'm getting very worried. Has Trixie ever run off like this before?"

I didn't want to admit that she had, but I thought I'd better warn him. "Trixie has a knack for . . ." I stopped in the middle of my sentence. We were well off the path and had reached a point where the woods plunged into a hollow. "This looks like an animal trail. See how there's a little alley here?"

I stepped toward the edge and looked down.

And there it was. The thing I had feared. Trixie, Gingersnap, and Pippin sniffed at a figure who lay among the briars at the bottom of the ravine. I couldn't tell much from the clothing. The person lay facedown with their legs pointing toward me, as though he or she had stood over the hollow and tried to dive headfirst. My heart sank when I saw the woeful face of a boxer lying alongside the person, her head resting on the person's back. It had to be Diane Blushner who lay there, because that was Stella, faithfully staying by her side.

"Is that a body?" Jim whispered.

"I'm afraid so." Blood pounded in my ears. There were two options. I could phone for help, but that would probably mean walking most of the way back, or I could try climbing down to Diane. What if she was alive? I knew what I would have wanted if it were me lying there. I would have been grateful if someone had comforted me. "Diane?" I called. "Diane? Can you hear me?"

"Diane?" asked Jim. "How can you tell who it is?"

"Just a guess. The dog with her looks like her dog, Stella."

I handed my phone to Jim. "Try calling 911." The dogs

had managed to reach the body. Surely, I could, too. I
wished I had gloves, but that wasn't the case. I also wished
I had worn jeans, but I hadn't anticipated venturing into
overgrown areas. I took my time placing my feet into piles
of dead leaves and testing the strength of rotting trees that
lay on the ground. I could only hope that the dogs running
through the area had caused snakes to slither away. It was
steep but not as treacherous as I had thought. If it hadn't
been for the new growth of briars grabbing at me from all
directions, it might not have been that bad.

The angle was such that if I made a misstep I would
probably land on my bottom and slide, not careen, downward. At least I hoped so. Moving slowly, I sat down to be
on the safe side and scooted carefully lest I dislodge something and slip. I scooched along, dodging briars until I
reached the person's head. "Diane? It's Holly Miller. We're
going to get you out of here. Okay?"

There was no response. Not even a twitch.

But Stella seemed very glad to see me. Her tail beat
against the dead leaves. She didn't leave Diane's side, but
she stretched her broad head toward me and I stroked it.
"You're such a good girl to stay with your mama."

I reached out to touch Diane's neck. Maybe she was un-
conscious? But up close she was solid deadweight and
frighteningly still. Brushing away the leaves that cushioned
her face like a pillow, I finally confirmed that it was indeed
Diane.

I didn't know a lot about corpses, but I felt fairly sure
that she was dead and had been out there for a while.

"I can't get a signal!" Jim shouted.

I looked up at him. He was desperately punching his
finger on the screen of his cell phone.

"Try mine. There's only one carrier that works in Wagtail, and it's spotty at best."

"Still nothing. Not a single bar. Do you think we can pull her up here?"

Diane's eyes were closed, and I didn't like the way her head had been buried in the leaves. Although I thought it hopeless, I asked, "Diane, can you hear me? Diane?"

Above me, Rae Rae shrieked, "She's dead! Oh, dear heaven, she's dead!"

Trixie sniffed Diane's head and yowled mournfully as if she was trying to tell me what she knew but I didn't want to accept. I didn't move Diane in case she had spinal cord injuries, but I slid my fingers around her throat in search of a pulse.

I didn't feel one. I tried her wrist. Still nothing. It was probably too late . . .

I raised my voice so they could hear and said as calmly as I could, "I think she's dead. We're going to have to walk down to report this to the police. Jim, you better catch up to everyone since Pippin is the star attraction and he'll be missed. Rae Rae, you take my phone and walk down until you can reach the police. If you see any children coming this way, shoo them up the trail, please. We don't need any kids to be scarred for life."

"Shouldn't I remain here with you?" asked Jim.

I shook my head. "I don't think we have much choice. Everyone will be waiting for Pippin."

Jim handed my phone to Rae Rae. He called Pippin, who clearly didn't want to leave. But after some coaxing and promises of cookies, Pippin hopped his way up to Jim and Rae Rae.

I tried not to disturb the area too much because it was probably a crime scene. I couldn't imagine why Diane would be up here with Stella. It was remotely possible that they had gone for a hike and gotten lost. Maybe Diane had fallen. But as I considered the possibilities, it dawned on

me that Trixie had never barked mournfully around someone who died of natural causes. Maybe I was reading too
much into Trixie's talent for discovering corpses, but so far,
she had only barked like that when she found the body of
someone who had been murdered.

With all the leaves on the ground, almost any kind of
evidence could be hidden. And I had most likely already
kicked the leaves around too much. Given the location, I
was certain they would be moved around a lot more when
rescuers came to haul Diane out of there. Over the next
hour, I sought a pulse several more times without luck. The
peculiar thing was that I didn't observe any obvious cause
of death. She wasn't bleeding anywhere that I could see. It
didn't appear that her head had hit a rock. I did think her
limbs seemed stiff, which suggested to me that she had
been out there several hours at least.

Trixie's ears perked up, and she uttered a muffled bark.
Seconds later, I could hear voices as Dave and Rae Rae
arrived on the scene.

Dave clambered down to us. Much as I had, he sat beside Diane. After a cursory examination, he let out a long
breath and patted Stella. "I wish you could tell us how you
came to be here."

Stella gazed at him sadly as if she understood.

"Holly, I give you a lot of credit for climbing down here.
But we've got to get you out. This is a crime scene."

"You think she was murdered."

"Diane was a strong and competent person. Even if she
had come up here last night or at the crack of dawn this
morning for some reason, even if there had been an injured
dog down here and she slid down to get it and fell, she
would most likely be alive. There's always the slim possibility that she hit her head or broke her neck, but you and I
managed to get down here with nothing more than a few
scratches, so I think that's unlikely."

He was right. "Someone must have coaxed her up here."

Dave's mouth pulled tight. "There's a broken screen at her house. I'll have to talk to some neighbors to be sure it wasn't like that before, but it suggests that something untoward happened there." Dave looked around. "Did you move or touch anything?"

"Leaves. It's not possible to be down here without stepping on them. But I didn't move fallen branches or her body, if that's what you mean. I just cleared the leaves away from her face and checked for a pulse."

"It's going to take some work to get her out of here. I have someone coming up the back road in a four-wheeler."

In the distance, we could hear the faint voices and happy laughter of people who were still walking up the mountain. Their fun was oddly incongruous given the deceased woman beside me.

"So this is exactly how you found her?" asked Dave.

I nodded. "Weird, huh? Like she thought she was diving."

Dave's eyes met mine. "Or someone pushed her."

# Nine

"You don't really think that?" I asked.

"All I know is that when people fall forward, it's instinctive to hold their hands out in front of them. If she had done that, her hands would probably be under her somewhere."

"Maybe she didn't die right away."

"Uh-huh. And left her face buried in the leaves?"

I had to agree that didn't make sense. "Maybe she broke her neck. You did say that was a possibility."

"Or maybe she was already dead. And someone dragged her out here and gave her a shove." He gazed around. "It's a pretty good site to hide a body. Not too far from the back road. Chances were good that she wouldn't be discovered quickly. If ever."

"But the treasure hunt!" I protested.

"You would have walked right on by like everyone else if it hadn't been for Trixie. Whoever brought her here wasn't thinking about Trixie's nose for trouble. You need a hand getting back up?" asked Dave.

"I think I can scramble to the top." I turned over onto my hands and knees and tried to stand. How on earth did I get down this far? The terrain looked like a sheer wall of rock from this vantage point. Digging my nails into the stone and taking one careful step at a time, I started the ascent. I could feel my fingernails breaking. Ugh. I loved the outdoors, but this rock climbing wasn't my thing. How could it be so steep going back up?

As I neared the top, a muscular guy wearing a police uniform reached out to me and propelled me upward. I recognized him and a crew of guys from the Snowball Mountain Police and Rescue Squad.

One of them gave me a grim smile and plucked a little pine branch out of my hair. "Dave called for assistance. Does someone have a broken leg?"

"You obviously didn't hear Trixie barking."

The smile faded from his face. "Dave," he shouted, "do you want us to come down or do you need the camera?"

"Camera?" Rae Rae whispered.

"To document the crime scene."

She inhaled sharply and placed a hand over her mouth.

The muscular cop from Snowball turned to us. "Thanks for your help. Try to disturb as little as possible on your way out. Okay?"

"What about Stella?" I shouted to Dave.

"There won't be room for her on the four-wheeler. Think she'll go with you?" asked Dave.

So far, Stella had stayed by Diane's side. I wasn't at all sure she would leave Diane. Dogs were smarter than people about death, so she probably knew Diane wasn't coming back. Still, she'd stayed by her until help came.

I called Trixie, Gingersnap, and Stella, hoping that if Trixie and Gingersnap made their way up the hill, some pack instinct would compel Stella to go with them.

I watched her reaction when I called the dogs. Using a

higher-pitched voice to get their attention, I promised "cookies and treats."

Stella seemed worried. She gazed at Diane. Wrinkles formed between her eyes, and for the first time since we found Diane's body, she whined.

I called her again by name. This time Stella came, following Trixie and Gingersnap. I dug in my pocket. "Treats for everyone!"

Trixie and Gingersnap readily took liver cookies from me. But Stella turned her nose away. I couldn't blame her. She was in mourning.

I knelt next to Stella and stroked her soft fur. "You're a good girl, Stella. Diane loved you very much. Will you come with me?"

As we walked on the path, I feared Stella would tear away and return to Diane. I leaned over occasionally to touch Stella's shoulder with my fingertips so she wouldn't feel alone. I hoped it would reassure her that she was doing the correct thing by coming with us.

As Rae Rae and I cut through the woods back to the main trail and the other dogs ran ahead, Stella walked along with us. She trudged, though, and didn't leap and sniff like the other two.

"Thanks for helping us, Rae Rae."

"'My pleasure' doesn't sound quite right under the circumstances, does it? I'm glad I could help. Who was she?"

"Diane Blushner."

Rae Rae stifled a little gasp. "I heard you say Diane, but . . ."

"Did you know her?" I asked.

"I know a Diane Blushner," she said. "But it couldn't be the same one. There must be hundreds of women named Diane Blushner. Right?"

"I've never known anyone else named Blushner, but that doesn't mean anything."

We walked in silence for a few minutes.

"What did Diane do? Was she married? Did she have children?" asked Rae Rae.

"Diane bred boxers. She was totally devoted to them and traveled the country showing them. Very respected in her field, apparently. I don't think she had kids or a spouse. At least not that I know of."

Rae Rae didn't say anything. I glanced over at her.

I didn't expect to see her looking so suspicious. Her eyes narrowed and her lips tucked in.

"What's wrong?"

She stopped walking and bent to stroke Stella's head. "Howard knew Diane, too. I can't help wondering if he arranged this entire trip as an excuse to see her." Rae Rae straightened up. "My Diane had a very small—"

I knew what she was going to say.

"—beauty mark," said Rae Rae.

I finished the description for her. "At the outer edge of her right eyebrow."

Rae Rae sagged and covered her eyes with her fingers. "I can't believe it," she sniffled. "I heard you say 'Diane' over and over, but it never occurred to me that it could be my friend from so long ago."

Rae Rae sank to her knees.

Stella nudged her nose under Rae Rae's hands and licked her tears.

Rae Rae smiled and held Stella close. "It almost seems silly to cry about someone I haven't seen for so many years. We were roommates back in the day when we were both aspiring actresses. If I had never seen her again, it wouldn't have bothered me. I would have been okay with it. But to find her accidentally and not be able to hug her and catch up or have a laugh about old times over a drink . . . well, I feel so terribly bereft. Like I lost an opportunity."

Rae Rae kissed the top of Stella's head and got to her

feet. "She was my age. Way too young to die! It really makes a person stop and think. Why would anyone want to kill her?"

"I have no idea. As far as I know, she was well-liked in the community."

"*Someone* didn't like her."

We walked quietly for a little bit. In an effort to change the subject, I asked, "So you almost married Howard?"

# Ten

❀ ❀ ❀ ❀

"Almost? I'd had my hair and makeup done and was already in my beautiful white lace dress embroidered with the tiniest little pearls you've ever seen. It was my brother who gave me the bad news."

I looked over at her as we walked. "Howard stood you up?"

Rae Rae snickered cynically. "That might have been preferable. You know, I've always been a pretty happy person. I like most things, and I get along with most folks. There just isn't much in life that I wouldn't forgive. And I'm a firm believer in second chances. But my best friend wasn't such a great friend after all. Diane was pregnant with Howard's child." Rae Rae scratched the side of her face. "It would have been so much better to tell me before my parents spent all that money on a wedding and the guests were waiting to hear the processional music, but she chose to wait and share that mind-bending information with my brother at the last minute. You can imagine that I went storming down the hall to confront Howard. He reeked of Scotch. To this day I cannot abide the smell. It just turns my stomach."

"I can see why."

"The biggest problem for me wasn't that he cheated on me. It wasn't that he cheated on me with my best friend. And it wasn't even the baby who was on the way. My problem was that he didn't seem to think it mattered! What kind of person wouldn't take his own child and the mother into consideration? He insisted the wedding should go on as planned. I thought I knew him. But that was the end for me for a hundred different reasons. After the initial shock of it all, I was very grateful that it happened. I would never have been happy married to someone who was so selfish and uncaring. He showed his true nature that day."

"And that friend was Diane Blushner?"

"It was. As you might imagine, it put a big crimp in our friendship," she said sadly. "I heard through the grapevine that she lost the baby. Howard never did marry her. Honestly, the man couldn't even bring himself to do the right thing."

"I gather you think he continued to live his life in the same manner?"

"Good heavens, yes. He was a star. Very highly regarded, and in those days it didn't matter what kind of jerk you were in your personal life as long as your shows were a success."

"So that's why the producer sent you here?" I wondered if she had been reluctant to get involved or whether she wanted to see Howard again.

"I refused at first. But in the end, I figured I should let bygones be bygones. After all, I'm probably one of the few people who can put Howard to shame. And I know what he's capable of. Besides, the producer is my brother. I was happy to do him a favor."

"Did your brother know that Diane lived in Wagtail?" I asked.

"I doubt it," said Rae Rae. "Why would he have kept up with her? He just knew that Howard can be trouble and that I'm not afraid of telling him exactly what I think."

"Why did your brother hire Howard if he knew the truth about him?"

"Investors! Howard was part of the package. Say what you will about his personal character—on-screen he'll make that show sing. And my brother is no dummy. He can smell a good show. Pippin is the star attraction. Those kids are going to make a huge splash." She smiled at me. "This walkin' in the woods must be makin' me hungry. I could swear I smell bacon cooking."

"You're absolutely right. They're serving bacon burgers."

We walked into the clearing, where dozens of participants were chowing down on lunch. Trixie and Gingersnap had beat us there. Gingersnap waited politely with her nose lifted to the yummy scent. Trixie had no manners at all and nosed around the grill, clearly hoping a burger would land on the ground.

Stella wasn't interested. She stayed with Rae Rae and me, as though she didn't know what else to do.

To my great surprise, Marlee and Finch had shown up. They ambled toward us with Camille and Jim. Marlee kept her head down and wore a large sun hat.

"There are our slowpokes!" cried Finch.

Jim swallowed hard. His eyes wide, he shook his head.

I assumed he was trying to tell us that he hadn't shared what happened to Diane.

"Maybe we shouldn't mention anything to them just yet," I whispered to Rae Rae.

"You're probably right. It would spread through here like wildfire and spoil the day for everyone. I can't begin to imagine what the parents would tell their children."

"I'm glad you made it," I said to Marlee and Finch.

Camille tsked at them. "Can you believe they drove a golf cart up the mountain? They were already here enjoying the view and drinking soda when the first hikers arrived."

Marlee wore her signature huge sunglasses under the broad-brimmed hat. She wrinkled her nose and spoke so softly that I strained to hear her. "I can't believe you doubted us. I don't know about Finch, but I wouldn't ditch a job. We got some great pictures!"

It was Finch who gazed at us with suspicion. "What took you two so long?"

Rae Rae answered before I could. "Trixie took us on a detour."

Hmm. Rae Rae was quick with that response. I wondered if she was adept at lying. Actually, it wasn't even really a lie. Trixie had drawn us away from the trail.

Finch stared at her. A tiny smile flicked on his lips. "Why would you follow the dog instead of the trail? And where did the boxer come from?"

Rae Rae lifted her chin as though she were up to the challenge. "Trixie was after a fox. And this beautiful boxer lost her way."

"A fox?" screeched Marlee. She clapped a hand over her mouth and lowered her voice. "I'm glad we brought the golf cart. It's probably rabid."

That was all we needed. A panic based on a lie. "We took a detour," I said simply. I changed the subject fast. "I'm starved. How's the food?"

They all concurred that the burgers were great. Rae Rae and I left their little group quickly to avoid additional probing questions and walked toward the food. We grabbed plates, and Augie slid bacon burgers off the hot grill for us and plain burgers for the dogs.

He frowned when he saw Stella. "What's Stella doing here? Did they find Diane?" he whispered.

In the lowest voice I could muster, I said, "It's not good news, but we don't want to spread it around here."

He winced. "Aww. I'm sorry to hear that. I hope she's just sick?"

"I'm afraid not."

Augie paled. "What happened?"

"I don't know." That was the truth. Besides, I didn't want to go into lengthy details.

"It smells divine," gushed Rae Rae.

I loaded my plate with sides of baked beans, corn bread, and potato salad, thinking that Diane's death should have made me lose my appetite. But the sad truth was that I was ravenous.

Rae Rae and I found a great perch on a flat stone overlooking the valley between Wagtail and Snowball. Finch came to join us while Pippin and Camille posed for photos.

Marlee steered them away from the food tents.

Finch sat down cross-legged. "I'm glad I didn't miss this. It's nice to be out of the city and see this kind of beauty."

"It really is remarkable," said Rae Rae in between bites.

It made me feel a little better to see that she had piled her plate full of food, too. I wasn't the only one who was hungry.

In a low voice, Finch said, "You two are terrible liars. In the future, you really ought to work out a story in advance."

"Why, Tiger!" Rae Rae exclaimed. "You speak like someone who has a lot of experience lying."

"Of course I do. People assume kids don't catch on, but I grew up watching my mom lie to get jobs. She wanted so desperately to be a star."

Rae Rae handed a bite of hamburger to Gingersnap and coaxed Stella to try a morsel. "It must have been hard on her when you became such a success."

Finch studied Rae Rae for a moment. "Yeah." He took a deep breath. "It was. She didn't have a sitter, so she took me along when she was auditioning for the role of Tiger's mom. They took one look at me and forgot all about her. She was happy for me, of course, but being a stage mom wasn't how she had envisioned her life."

"Is your dad in the business?" I asked.

"That's how they met. But it's a tough racket. One day my dad decided he had waited on enough tables while hoping for his big break. My mom wanted to stay in LA, so they split. Dad took off for Arizona, opened an ice-cream shop, and now has six of them." He gazed at the mountain view. "So what's going on?"

Rae Rae and I exchanged a look.

"Okay," she whispered. "Trixie found a local woman who was dead."

Trixie heard her name and perked her ears. I could tell she was hoping for another bite of beef. I pinched off a piece of my burger and handed it to her.

"Dead?" Finch said much louder than he should have. Realizing his mistake, he said, "Dead-on!"

"We're trying to keep it quiet. This is her dog, Stella."

Finch blinked at Rae Rae as though he couldn't believe what she was saying. "You're making this up." He gazed from her to me and back. "Whoa."

"How come Marlee is whispering?" I asked.

Finch shrugged. "She's been doing that since we arrived. It's as though she doesn't want anyone to hear her. She passed on the food too and asked me to bring her a soda. It smells so good that she wound up stealing from my plate!"

In spite of Augie and Finch knowing about Diane's demise, we were able to keep it quiet on the mountain. But by the time we reached the staging area at the bottom, everyone's phones were working and the news of Diane's death traveled fast among locals.

When Pippin and his group dispersed in the main lobby

of the inn, I headed for Oma's office to fill her in on the details.

Oma sat quietly in an armchair in our office, gazing out the window at the lake. Gingersnap ran to her and laid her head in Oma's lap.

"I guess you heard." I dusted off my skort and dropped onto the sofa.

Trixie trotted to Oma's chair and placed her paws on Oma's knees as though she knew Oma needed comforting.

Stella stopped at the door and looked around.

Oma stroked Trixie and Gingersnap. "Diane was a wonderful person. I can't imagine why anyone would have done this to her. It is heartbreaking."

Stella ventured farther into the room, treading cautiously. Her nostrils twitched as she took in the new scents.

"Is that Diane's Stella?"

I nodded. "Stella stayed with Diane until we coaxed her away. I think she's kind of lost and confused right now."

Oma held her hand out to Stella. "We will keep her here until everything is settled."

"Fine by me." I fetched a GPS collar from the registration desk and fastened it on Stella. I didn't want to lose her if she wandered off or went home. "Does Dave have any leads? Any ideas?"

Oma stared at Stella. "She knows. You saw what happened, didn't you, Stella?"

# Eleven

Stella lay down by Oma's ankles, her eyelids heavy. She had been through a lot over the last twenty-four hours. She was probably worn-out.

"Do you think she could have bitten the person who killed Diane?" I asked.

"It's possible. Or perhaps she ripped their clothes."

"Dave said a screen was torn. All the dogs must have been barking and making a big fuss."

"Perhaps Diane was out with Stella when the person broke into her home and hid?" Oma postulated.

The thought turned my stomach. "Either way, the neighbors must have heard barking."

"They did," said Dave from the doorway. He walked in and sat down beside me, wearily rubbing his face with both hands. "I've had at least three calls from people who heard barking at Diane's house last night around two in the morning. I'll be very surprised if the coroner doesn't find that as the approximate time of death."

"So someone killed her at her house and then drove her up the mountain in the middle of the night to dispose of her body?" I was aghast.

"I think that pretty much sums it up. Except for the torn screen, the house looks like she left to go to the supermarket. No blood. Nothing turned over or out of place. No evidence of a struggle or confrontation."

I felt a little bit guilty for what I was about to say. Still, Dave had to know. "One of our guests, Rae Rae Babetski, knew Diane. It's been a long time, but if anyone had a reason to hate Diane and Howard, it's Rae Rae. She was best friends with Diane, who was having an affair with Howard, who happened to be Rae Rae's fiancé. She didn't find out until the day of the wedding. And as if that wasn't bad enough, Diane was pregnant with Howard's child."

"Our guest?" Oma frowned at me. "Surely you don't think she killed Diane?"

"I don't know that she had anything to do with Diane's death. She said she hadn't seen her in years. But I did see Rae Rae driving around in one of our golf carts after midnight."

"Liesel, would you mind if I used your office to ask Rae Rae some questions?"

Wagtail didn't have an official satellite police station. Dave often borrowed the office at the inn when he needed to question people in private.

Oma stretched and stood up. "Ja, of course. I'll take Stella with me."

Dave held up his hand. "Let's leave Stella in here if it's okay with you. It might be interesting to see her reaction to Rae Rae."

"Stella walked up the mountain and back with Rae Rae and me. I'm pretty sure Rae Rae even fed her some hamburger."

"Mmm. Thanks for telling me that. Stella probably

thinks Rae Rae is wonderful. Still, you can leave her here
if you don't mind."

Oma and Gingersnap set off for the main lobby.

I hadn't done my rounds in the inn yet that day. "I'll stop
by Rae Rae's room and send her down here."

Weariness was beginning to set in, but I got to my feet
and took the back stairs up to the second floor of the inn.
Trixie trotted along beside me.

Rae Rae was staying in Jump. I knocked on the door and
heard someone stirring in the room. "Rae Rae, it's Holly."

She opened the door holding a tissue. Mascara and eye-
liner had smudged on her cheeks. It appeared that she
had frantically wiped her face. She forced a smile and sniffled. "I'm sorry. I had a little meltdown when we came
back. All the way down the mountain I kept thinking of
Diane and the times we spent together. We were so young.
Like Camille and Marlee are now. Everything seemed possible. We had such big dreams." She struggled to smile
while tears ran down her cheeks. "I'm a mess. It all came
pouring out."

"Officer Dave from the police department is here. He'd
like to speak with you."

She closed her eyes for a moment and took a deep breath.
"I'll pull myself together and be there in a moment."

"He's in the office." I pointed toward the stairs. "Just go
to the registration desk and Zelda will show you."

"Thank you, Holly." She closed the door.

I walked away thinking how hard it must have been for
her to stay composed while we were on the mountain. Out of
habit, I stooped to pick up a scrap of paper that someone had
lost on the floor. I continued walking through all the hall-
ways, checking to be sure nothing was out of order. Though
I longed for a nap, I would have to make do with a shower.

I let myself into my apartment and tossed the scrap of
paper into the trash. It lay there, almost as if it were taunt-

ing me, and when I looked closer, I noticed there was a photo of Stella on it.

I grabbed a plastic food storage bag from my kitchen cabinet, turned it inside out, and stuck my hand in it. I had probably already ruined any fingerprints on that scrap, but I might as well be careful. I picked up the paper and flipped the bag over it. It had been torn but was readily identifiable. Someone at the inn had ripped and dropped Diane's business card.

Forgoing my shower, I hurried back downstairs with my scrap of paper to hand it over to Dave before he left. As I approached the reception lobby, I heard a loud voice.

I scrambled down the stairs and found myself face-to-face with Howard Hirschtritt. Up close, he looked much older than I remembered from his TV shows. I wanted to imagine him as the wisecracking detective he had played, but in person, there was no disguising his true colors. His eyes flashed with anger.

Zelda, who was no cowering lily, had taken a step back from the registration desk as though she was fearful.

I sucked up courage. "May I help you?"

"At last. I hope *you* have half a brain. I should like to check into my room, please."

I desperately wanted to defend Zelda, but if there was one thing Oma had pounded into my head when I was a kid, it was to always be polite to guests. Always! "I'm so sorry, but you gave up your reservation yesterday and we're filled to capacity."

"I did not give up my reservation. I merely did not exercise it for one night."

I gave him my best sweet smile while thinking what an annoying dolt he was. Did he really get away with things like this because he was a star? "Now, Mr. Hirschtritt, I think we both know that if that were the case, we would have to keep all our rooms open indefinitely in case someone changed his mind. Your confirmation stated very clearly that if you did not check in by six p.m., you would forfeit your room and it would be given to someone else."

"That's just nonsense. I know that's hospitality business speak for overbooking."

"I'm afraid not. In any case, we gave your room to someone else after you left here, because you made it very clear that you were not staying."

His eyes softened, and he stepped toward me. "Listen," he murmured, "there was a murder in town last night. I need to stay someplace where there are other people." He gazed around and pointed at the sliding doors. "Someplace that has a security system like you do."

He'd be mighty disappointed to meet our nighttime security system. Casey Collins resembled Harry Potter and spent most of his time noshing in the kitchen or napping. Besides, I was fairly sure that Howard wasn't sincere and was playing a role that he knew very well.

"I heard about the murder. But it doesn't change the fact that we don't have any rooms available. You can check back with us daily to see if the situation changes."

He nervously twisted his hands. "You don't understand. I can't go back there. I might be next."

Zelda gasped.

"I hope you're being melodramatic," I said, trying to keep my voice level and calm. "Why would anyone murder you?"

He stared at me silently, which prompted me to wonder if he needed a script for his next line.

At that moment, the door to the office opened and Rae Rae emerged with Dave.

"Perfect timing," I said. "You can tell Officer Dave all about it."

Howard launched himself at Rae Rae. "How many beds are in your room? Is there a sofa? Can I shack up with you?"

Rae Rae drew away from him. "Hello, Howie. It's nice to see you again, too," she uttered sarcastically.

He shot her an annoyed look. "I'm serious."

Rae Rae's face wrinkled up. "Is this some sort of joke? Absolutely not! What kind of example would that set?"

"Kindness. Generosity." Howard's fists clenched, but his face seemed hopeful. "Love."

Rae Rae snorted and laughed. "Get your own room."

"They gave it away."

"Then stay wherever you spent last night."

A sly look came over him. It occurred to me that when he looked that way on TV, it made me laugh. In person, it wasn't so funny.

"We're supposed to be bonding." He opened his hands and held them palms up. "C'mon, Rae Rae. For old times' sake. We used to have great times together."

"And who ruined that?" asked Rae Rae.

"Don't tell me you're still holding a grudge all these years later?"

To Dave I said, "Howard thinks he's going to be murdered next. And if I'm not mistaken, he knew Diane Blushner very well."

Howard turned toward me in wretched horror.

Dave beckoned to him. "Why don't we have a little chat in private?"

"Well, now you've done it. Thanks a lot," he grumbled at me.

Rae Rae laughed like she was truly amused. "If you're going to play the victim then you have to expect the consequences."

"You know me so well." And with that, Howard took a bow. "I'm sorry if I scared anyone." He hooked his arm through Rae Rae's. "You look terrific. May I buy you a drink?"

"Not so fast." Dave crooked a finger at Howard. "I'd like to have a word with you first."

It seemed as though Dave had knocked the steam out of Howard. His shoulders sagged as he trudged into the office.

When the door closed, Zelda whispered, "I'd like to be a fly on the wall in there."

Rae Rae smirked. "Not me. I've heard enough of Howard's lies for a lifetime. If you'll excuse me, I believe I'll take a little nap."

She ambled away, her expression revealing her real feelings of heartache.

Zelda leaned over the counter toward me. "Do you think they could possibly be involved in Diane's death?"

"Seems unlikely. And Rae Rae doesn't look too worried. But I did see her barreling along the street after midnight in one of our golf carts."

Zelda's eyes grew large. She rustled around under the counter and pulled out the golf cart log. She pointed at a signature. "Casey signed one out to her last night. I guess we'd better tell Dave, huh?"

"I already did." I was eager to hear what Dave would say, so I busied myself tidying the registration lobby.

It wasn't long before Howard reappeared, looking none the worse for his interview with Dave. "Where's Rae Rae?"

"She went to her room to take a nap," said Zelda.

"Okay. Which room is she in?"

I pointed at the house phone. "You may call her if you like."

Howard stared at me as though I was a nut. "What do you people think you are? The Ritz? I could just stand right here and yell her name and she'd probably hear me."

That might be true. But I stood my ground.

"Aw, forget it. Forget all of you!" Howard marched out the sliding glass doors.

"He's a real disappointment, isn't he?" said Dave. "I don't think I'll ever be able to enjoy his shows again."

"Do you think he was playacting when he said he would be murdered next?" I asked.

"How does a guy come to Wagtail for the first time in his life and less than twenty-four hours later he's afraid for his life? I don't think so," said Dave. "But I do think he's worried about something."

"Maybe he angered someone enough to drive him to murder," I said.

Zelda handed Dave the golf cart log.

"Thank you."

I couldn't read his expression. "Is Rae Rae a suspect?" I whispered.

"I'm not sure. Rae Rae readily admits that she was out and about last night."

# Twelve

"Did she see Diane?" I asked.

"She claims she didn't even realize that Diane lived here. She went out checking up on the others. Said she didn't want one of them acting in an unbecoming way or lying in the street intoxicated. It was her job to prevent that."

"But they're all adults," Zelda protested.

Dave's eyes narrowed. "Yeah. Seems like something is going on with this group, though. Y'all keep me posted on what they're up to."

"I hope Howard doesn't come back," said Zelda. "Where's he staying that he dislikes so much?"

"He rented the house with the red roof on Elm Street. It's a pretty nice place." Dave chuckled. "Maybe he just likes it better when he can call for room service."

"No wonder he's scared. That place is set way back on the lot with trees all around the rear for privacy." Now that Howard was gone and the drama had ceased, I remembered the partial business card I had discovered upstairs and handed it to Dave. "I found this on the floor where Pippin's group is staying."

Dave's eyebrows rose as he examined it. "Now *that* is interesting. Sheds a new light on things. One of them must have had some interest in Diane. Maybe even had contact with her." Dave grinned at us. "You know the trouble with these actors? Their chosen profession makes it so much harder to tell when they're lying!" He walked to the door. "Tell Liesel I said thanks for letting me use the office."

I finally took the time for my shower. But I had barely stepped out when my phone rang. I threw on the plush Sugar Maple Inn bathrobe that Oma had embroidered with my name. My hair wringing wet, I answered the phone.

"Holly, liebling, a number of residents are gathering in the dining area to discuss the missing dogs and Diane's murder. Could you please help Mr. Huckle put out some things to nosh on?"

"Absolutely. I'll be right there." On days like this I was glad to have long hair that could air-dry and be pulled into a ponytail. I threw on a summery white skort and a violet top. Trixie watched me dress, pacing and stretching, as though she was restless.

We hurried down the back stairs and through the private kitchen. In the main lobby, residents of Wagtail had begun to gather. I spotted Augie petting Stella. "Please, won't you come and have a seat?" I gestured to the dining area.

Poor old Mr. Huckle was trying his best to roll a buffet table into place. He gave me a grateful look and a pat on the shoulder when I offered to take over.

I shoved it against the wall and threw a vibrant rose-colored cloth over it. While Mr. Huckle arranged platters in the kitchen, I started coffee and tea brewing and brought out napkins, cutlery, plates, and mugs. In a matter of minutes, the buffet was covered with hors d'oeuvres. Mr. Huckle might not be a professional chef, but he knew how

to throw together lovely platters of mini ham quiches, crudités, and smoked trout toasts.

I searched the freezer and found chocolate cupcakes.
They would thaw in half an hour before anyone was ready
for them. I looked for a three-tiered server and loaded it up
with the cupcakes.

I left them in the kitchen to thaw and joined the throng
in the dining area as Oma was clinking her mug with a fork
to get their attention. "Ladies and gentlemen, please have a
seat. First, I would like us to share a moment of silence in
memory of our wonderful Diane, who was taken from us
far before her time."

Everyone grew quiet and bowed their heads. I noticed
that Augie's wife, Glenda, reached out for his hand.

After the moment of silence, it was Dave who got the
meeting going. "A lot of you have been asking me questions
about Diane. At this point, I don't have much to tell you. I
can say with confidence that I don't think anyone else is in
danger. At least preliminarily, Diane appears to have been
targeted."

"But she's a dog breeder," someone called out. "A lot of
us are, too. And the two dogs that went missing are purebreds that can fetch a good price. How do we know we
won't be killed so they can steal our dogs?"

"That's right," said a man with a white beard. "I think
Diane died protecting her dogs. It could have been any
of us."

"Do you think there's a connection between Diane's
death and the dogs that were stolen?" asked a woman.

Dave responded quickly. "We don't know yet, but it's
clearly something we have to consider. However, none of
Diane's dogs are missing, so it seems unlikely, at least at
this time, that she was killed by someone intent on stealing
them."

I could understand why Dave had said that, but I wasn't

sure it was true. Stella had been by Diane's side. If Diane was murdered in her house, how did Stella get out unless the killer meant to take her and she managed to escape?

Augie stood up and eyed the people in the room. "It had to be someone local. No one else would have known how to get up the mountain the back way."

People in the crowd nodded and murmured.

Dave spoke calmly but in a firm voice. "Now, let's not get carried away with unsubstantiated theories. Augie, you might not notice them because you see them every day, but there are signs all over town pointing to the access road for handicapped visitors. Golf carts and electric wheelchairs go up and down there all the time."

Clara Dorsey stood up. She leaned on her cane with her right hand and waved a photo of her Scottie in her left hand. "This is my precious Tavish. I'm just lost without him. Obviously, because of my foot surgery, I couldn't walk him, so I let him out in my fenced yard at ten o'clock at night like I always do before I go to bed. That was the last I ever saw of my sweet boy."

Glenda Hoover rose quickly and flashed a photograph of Dolly. "Clara just described exactly what happened to us. I'm telling you, folks, it's not safe to let your dogs out at night by themselves. There's a thief prowling our streets and stealing our babies."

"Why?" shouted the owner of Café Chat. "Why would anyone take them?"

"To sell them," said Augie.

The owner of Café Chat stood up. "Let me get this straight. You're saying someone is stealing purebred dogs to sell them? Dogs aren't like knockoff watches that can be sold on the street. Who would buy a purebred out of the back of a car? Why wouldn't people just buy them from a breeder?"

Dave nodded. "Apparently, there's a market for it. With

all the dogs sitting in shelters, you'd think people would go there, but it seems they buy these stolen dogs. Some bring in hefty prices."

Someone called out, "The buyers don't realize that they're stolen."

Dave continued, "They also take them for puppy mills. So you breeders with high-profile dogs need to be especially careful."

I looked over at the lobby to be certain Trixie and Gingersnap were still in the building. They were happily visiting with Stella and some of the dogs other people had brought with them.

Just past the dogs, Camille stood by a window alone. It appeared almost as though she was watching someone but didn't want to be seen. Did she intend to eavesdrop on the meeting?

I fetched the cupcakes from the kitchen and placed them on the buffet. Then I surreptitiously sidled away from the crowd and tried to act casual when I ambled over to Camille.

"Hi! Everything okay?"

Camille's cheeks flushed. "I'm fine. I'm just watching the Yappy Hour parade."

Through the window I could see Pippin leading the parade of dogs and cats. A goat dressed as a pink unicorn with a horn jutting off its head was getting a lot of attention, too. I couldn't help laughing. "People are so creative with the costumes. I see Finch and Marlee out on the porch. Wouldn't that be more comfortable?"

"I'm good here. It's, um, too hot for me outside."

I looked at her flushed face, but I didn't think those rosy cheeks had been caused by heat. It was already late afternoon, and the temperature outdoors was very pleasant. Maybe she had a falling-out with Finch or Marlee. In any event, whatever it was appeared to embarrass her. "You're certain that everything is all right?"

Camille hesitated. She pulled the curtain aside ever so slightly, and I spied the gray-eyed man in the middle of the crowd that watched the Yappy Hour parade. My pulse quickened. Was he watching the inn? Had he expected Trixie to be in the parade? She often was. Or was I overreacting? The Yappy Hour parade was always well attended.

I was so unnerved by his presence that I gave a start when Camille spoke.

"Everything is fine," she insisted. But then she added a soft, "I think."

I studied her, not sure whether she was afraid or upset. I didn't want to pry. Some people liked to confide their troubles and others didn't. It was her choice. "If you need a friend, I'm always available." I turned to walk away.

"Holly?"

I looked back at her.

"Thanks."

I nodded and returned to the meeting, wondering what she was thanking me for. Was she relieved I hadn't pressed her for the truth, or was she glad that I was looking out for her?

The meeting appeared to be wrapping up. I made a beeline for Dave.

Oma was on her feet holding up a sheet of paper. "Those who would like to volunteer for night shifts between the hours of nine and midnight until the dognapper is caught, please sign up here. You can walk during your shift or use golf carts. If you should see anything suspicious, do *not* take matters into your own hands. You must phone Dave immediately. I'm going to repeat that for the logic impaired. Do not take matters into your own hands under any circumstances. Your job is to be an extra set of eyes and ears, *not* to take action."

I heard Augie mutter, "I'll take action if *I* see someone steal a dog. He'll be sorry he ran into me."

People began to sign up, help themselves to food, and mingle.

I bent over and whispered into Dave's ear, "The man who thinks Trixie belongs to him is outside watching the parade."

Dave jumped to his feet. I followed him to the front porch.

"Where is he?" asked Dave.

I scanned the crowd. He had moved. Hopefully, he hadn't grabbed a dog and made off with it! "Rats, it looks like he's gone."

"Too bad. I'd like to talk to him. I think I'll stay out here for a little bit and keep an eye on things."

I was so frustrated. I walked back into the inn and noticed that Camille had left her position at the window.

There was nothing to do but start cleaning up. I gathered discarded plates and napkins.

The fellow with the white beard was speaking with Augie, and I couldn't help overhearing their conversation.

"Augie, you're dead-on. I think someone local murdered Diane, too. What I can't figure out is who had a beef with her."

"I'm afraid I agree with Dave," said Clara. "She bred top boxers. How do we know someone from the show circuit didn't do her in?"

"She was such a genteel woman and a kind neighbor." Augie wiped a teary eye. "She wasn't the type to make a fuss or alienate people through her behavior. I don't understand why anyone would kill her."

"Holly," called Oma, cutting into my brash eavesdropping. "I think the two of us should take evening shifts patrolling. Ja?"

"Sure. I'd be happy to do that." I signed the paper just as Grady, the owner of Shutter Dogs, rolled in a dolly with boxes stacked on it.

"Liesel, per your request, noseprint kits!" said Grady proudly.

"Wonderful! Come with me to the office and I will write you a check. Holly, do you have everything under control?" Oma asked.

"You bet." I was left to deal with the boxes, which I stashed in the storage room off the hallway. The door was open, but I was hidden from view when I heard two people speaking in the hallway.

They sounded like Marlee and Camille.

# Thirteen

"What do you think of Howard's invitation?" asked Camille.

"Are you kidding? This is our big chance. I was devastated when he dropped us on arrival. To be invited to his house is a huge deal."

"I'm not so sure. Doesn't it bother you that he didn't include Finch or Jim? Not to mention Rae Rae. For a while I really suspected that his departure was some kind of test. Something they had planned to force us together. But now I'm not so sure. If we're supposed to be bonding, wouldn't he invite everyone?"

"You're overthinking this, Camille. Who cares if the others aren't included? Rae Rae has nothing to do with the show. And Jim's just a dog handler anyway. He doesn't matter."

There was a prolonged silence. I felt guilty for listening to their conversation. Not that they had said anything particularly private. Maybe I was the one overthinking my guilt. They could see the open door, couldn't they?

My conscience bothering me, I was about to rattle some boxes to alert them to my presence, when Camille blurted, "No. I'm not going without everyone else. Do you remember when we arrived and he said it was a good thing I was pretty? That was an insult. He thinks I'm an idiot. Well, I'm not stupid enough to trot over to his private house and drool over him. If he wanted to talk with us or get to know us, he could have invited us to lunch in a public restaurant. Marlee, there's something wrong about his invitation. I'm not going, and if you ask me, you shouldn't go, either."

And then it dawned on me. Marlee had said that Jim didn't matter because he was just a dog handler. From Camille's perspective, which she was kind enough not to voice, Marlee fell into the same category. She was just a social media manager for Pippin and played no role in the show. Camille was probably right. Howard invited the pretty girls on purpose. It had nothing to do with the show.

"No! Oh, Camille, don't do that to me. Don't you get it? This show is your big break. You did it. You got there. But this is my only chance to catch Howard's attention."

"I'm sorry, Marlee," said Camille. "I understand why you feel that way. But I'm not going. Marlee, I'm telling you, there's something weird going on."

"Ugh. I can't believe you! Okay, fine. Be that way. I'm going with or without you."

I could hear heels clicking down the hallway. I peered from behind the door. Camille was walking toward the lobby, and Marlee was heading in the other direction.

I closed the door behind me and looked out the hall window. Camille was right. Something strange was going on, but I didn't have a clue what was up.

I gazed down at Trixie.

She wagged her tail and studied me with those soulful brown eyes.

"That's a smart pup you have."

I picked her up fast and turned around. It was only Jim and Pippin. "Thanks." I set Trixie on the floor. "You mean because she sniffs out dead people?"

"That, too. I've been watching her. She'd be great in commercials. She has such an expressive face."

I stared at him in shock. Was he just complimenting her, or was he in the market for another dog? Surely, someone who doted on Pippin the way Jim did couldn't be a dog thief.

"Did I say something wrong?" he asked.

The man with the gray eyes had me on edge. I smiled at Jim. "No, of course not. I think she's smart, too. I have loved all my dogs, but sometimes it's like Trixie seems to know what I'm thinking."

"Ah. The sign of a very trainable dog. She wants to please you."

I tickled the top of her head. "She can be a rascal, but there's usually a reason for it when she misbehaves."

"Pippin and I are having a great time. Honestly, I hoped Pippin would have fun, but I didn't think I would, too." His eyes opened wide. "Oh! I didn't mean that the way it sounded. I'm sorry about the lady who died. Do they have any leads on who murdered her?"

"I don't know. Poor Dave is kind of swamped right now."

"I'm not from around here, but if there's anything I can do . . ."

"That's very kind of you. Don't give it another thought. You're supposed to be enjoying your stay in Wagtail, like the other guests. It was just bad luck that Pippin went along with Trixie when she smelled a body."

"I heard about your noseprinting event tomorrow. How about if Pippin comes and gets his nose printed first?"

"That would be great! He can be an example, and it would draw a lot of people."

"Super. We're on then." Jim waved and walked away with Pippin by his side.

I returned to the dining area to finish cleaning up after the meeting. Dave was the only one left. He was standing in front of the window overlooking the terrace and the lake, with his back to me. He held a phone to his ear.

As quietly as I could, I stacked the empty platters from the buffet and took them to the commercial kitchen. Trixie sprawled on the floor as if she knew this would take a while. When I returned with a tray to collect cups and saucers, Dave walked over and helped me load the glasses. "What do you know about Diane?"

I glanced up at him in surprise. "Just the usual stuff. Well-known boxer breeder. Well-liked in town. She was always very cordial to me."

"Did you ever hear any rumors about her?"

I squinted at him, wondering what he was getting at. "Nothing springs to mind."

"In her twenties she was an aspiring actress."

"That's not exactly a rumor. It's not surprising either—she was very beautiful."

He nodded. "Do you know if she was seeing anyone?"

So that's what he was looking for. "You think she had a secret lover who killed her?"

Dave's mouth twitched to the side. "It's possible."

"This is such a small town. I'm sure everyone would have known if that were the case."

"But you haven't heard anything?"

"Dave, just come out and tell me. You clearly know something." I poured a glass of ice water for each of us and took a swig from mine.

"Any chance that she could have been having an affair with Augie?"

I spewed water. "I'm so sorry!" Laughing and more than a little bit embarrassed, I grabbed a wad of napkins and wiped off my shirt. "You can't be serious. Diane with Augie? That has to be the most unlikely combination of people on the planet. No way!"

"That's what I thought, but strange things happen. It would have been easy for them since they lived next door to each other."

"Augie and his crew had been hauling tents and food up the mountain on that back road. But if I had killed someone, I don't think I would have tried to hide the body in a place where I would be going the next day."

"Glad to know that," joked Dave. "You'll leave plenty of clues and there won't be any other reason for you to have been there."

My grin vanished. "Good point."

"Everyone who commits a crime leaves something behind, Holly. We just have to find it."

"That's not going to be easy with all those dead leaves up there. How did Stella react to Rae Rae?"

"Loved her."

"So Rae Rae didn't kill Diane," I mused.

"I don't know that I'd go that far. Stella's behavior doesn't exonerate Rae Rae. But it was interesting to me that she didn't care for Howard."

"Did she snarl at him?"

"Nothing quite so dramatic. Mostly she just ignored him." Dave set his glass on the tray with a thunk. "Let me know if you hear anything that could be helpful."

"What about Howard? What's he afraid of?"

Dave shook his head. "He claims he was making a scene on purpose to get Rae Rae's sympathy and attention. Seems he still has a thing for her."

I had not expected that! "Really? According to Rae Rae, it's been years since she saw Howard. Did you believe him?" I asked.

"This job has made me a little bit jaded. I'm suspicious

about most things folks tell me. Up until something confirms it, anyway. Did you know that most people blink more rapidly when they're lying?" He strode across the lobby and out the door.

Now exactly who had been lying to him? Howard? Rae Rae? Augie? I finished cleaning up and ran the dishwashers, thinking about Howard and Rae Rae. Unless I was mistaken, Howard had put on that little scene in the reception lobby to cover up his real emotions. Maybe he was an ace actor, but I was under the impression that he truly was afraid of something. Or someone. But who?

As I walked out of the kitchen, I caught a glimpse of Marlee sitting on the terrace by herself. I wasn't sure I should interrupt, but Trixie pawed at the door. I went with her intuitions and let her out.

Trixie ran to Marlee, who picked her up and cuddled her. Trixie's little tail wagged.

I ambled over to join them. "Would you like some company?"

"Sure."

She was very sweet to Trixie. "Do you have a dog?" I asked.

"My parents do. I really miss her, but I rent an apartment and my building doesn't allow dogs."

"You live in Los Angeles?" I asked.

"Pasadena."

Marlee sniffled a little bit but kept stroking Trixie, who reached up and licked Marlee's cheek.

"Is everything okay?" I asked. "You seem a little sad."

"It's a long story. It's just that I've been trying so hard to land an acting job. I've done everything I've been told, but I just can't seem to break in. My parents have suggested the time has come to realize that it won't happen for me. I guess I'm a little envious of Camille."

"I can understand that. I gather this wasn't exactly an

overnight thing for Camille, either. If you keep trying, maybe you'll be cast in a show, too."

"Sometimes I think I don't take advantage of everything that comes my way. You know? I'm here with all these people involved in what's going to be a sensation, but I'm not really part of it. But if I play my cards right, maybe I could be."

Ohhh. She was talking about Howard and his invitation to the girls. I feared Camille was correct. I hoped I wouldn't give away the fact that I had heard their conversation. I dared to say, "I think you'd be wise to steer clear of Howard."

Marlee turned her head to gaze at me through her oversize sunglasses just as Trixie moved her nose to sniff Marlee's ear, shifting what was apparently a wig. I tried not to show my surprise when a dark brown hairline appeared.

Marlee tried to covertly adjust it, but it was too late. I had seen her real hair. If she realized it, she gave no indication. She watched a dog splashing in the lake. "It's so peaceful here," she said. "No noisy traffic or congestion."

"Marlee! There you are," Rae Rae called from the door.

"Oh my gosh!" cried Marlee. "What time is it? I'm supposed to have dinner with the group." Marlee looked at her Apple Watch. "I'm late!"

Marlee set Trixie on the terrace floor and jumped up. She briefly rested her hand on my arm. "Thank you for being nice and listening to me babble. I feel better just having talked to someone." She ran into the inn.

I got up and followed in the same direction.

Rae Rae was dressed in an eye-catching purple dress with a rhinestone-encrusted V-neck. "It's like herding puppies to get these kids together. Finch is the worst. I don't know what's up with him. He's always last. At least I know where to find Jim. All I have to do is look for a crowd of Pippin ears. He's usually in the center of it." She gasped. "What did you think of Howard's little show?"

"Are you sure it was a show? He's not really afraid of something?"

"He always has to be the center of attention. That was complete and utter nonsense about being murdered next. Wouldn't you think he would be sorry about Diane's death? He knew her very well, but he didn't so much as mention her name! How on earth could he leap to the possibility that he would be the next victim? Can I tell you how glad I am that I didn't marry him? Imagine what an awful life that would have been. No, thank you!"

I debated whether to tell her he claimed to still carry a torch for her. Might as well. Maybe she would be flattered. "Apparently, he still loves you."

# Fourteen

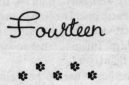

Rae Rae's smile vanished. And then she laughed so hard that tears ran down her face. "That would be such a nice thing to hear—if he had *ever* loved me. The man doesn't know how to love. He has never given a single thought to anyone but himself. Hmm, I guess he does know how to love someone after all—himself!" She walked away still laughing.

I suspected I would find Oma in the private kitchen. I swung the door open. Sure enough, Oma was eating dinner. She had fed Gingersnap and Stella. Twinkletoes sat on the fireplace hearth washing her face.

"Don't you feed Twinkletoes?" asked Oma.

"Of course I do!"

"She acts as if she is starving."

"*Acts* would probably be the operative word. I left food for her in my apartment this morning. I guess she didn't want to wait for me to decide it was dinnertime. Thanks for feeding her. What's for dinner?"

"Pasta primavera. It's delicious!"

I helped myself to some, poured a glass of iced tea, fed Twinkletoes, and joined Oma at the table.

She chatted about inn matters and my father's second wife while we ate. Only when I had finished eating did she ask, "What is this fentanyl?"

I blinked at her. "Fentanyl? It's a very powerful drug. A small amount can kill you. Apparently, it was designed for patients who were in terrible pain. Why are you asking about it?"

"That is what killed Diane."

"How do you know that?" I asked.

Oma pursed her lips. "The new doctor in town, Engelknecht, is very good. When Diane was transported to the office of the medical examiner in Roanoke, he followed the transport. He was highly suspicious because he knew Diane was in good health and there was no apparent cause of death. He asked them to expedite a test for fentanyl. How can such a dangerous drug be here in Wagtail?"

"There are people in pain everywhere, I guess. If Diane was healthy, I suppose it wasn't prescribed to her. I can't imagine that she took it intentionally. I hear a tiny bit can kill a person."

Oma placed her hands on the sides of her face. "Someone must have poisoned her with it. Does one swallow it?"

I didn't know. I'd heard of fentanyl but hadn't paid it much attention. I pulled out my phone and looked it up. "It says here that it comes in a patch, a lozenge, or powder. When people want to get high they swallow, inhale, or inject it." No wonder Oma hadn't wanted to talk about it while we ate.

"Does it have any flavor?" asked Oma.

"It says it doesn't have a distinctive taste, which is one of the problems with identifying it."

"Holly, there is one other problem." Oma sighed. "You need to know because it could impact us."

It couldn't be that serious. But Oma looked very worried. I sipped my tea and waited for her to tell me.

"They look at the stomach contents when making the autopsy."

I nodded. I had heard that before.

"The most recent thing she ate was a brownie."

I shrugged. "So?"

"I presume it could have come from one of the bakeries in town. But we were serving brownies with powdered sugar on top yesterday."

## Fifteen

That could be a problem. "Did Diane eat here yesterday? I don't remember seeing her at the inn."

"We will have to check with Shelley and Mr. Huckle. They would remember. Holly, it would have been so easy to mix powdered fentanyl with powdered sugar and sprinkle it on a brownie."

"Oma, don't look so worried. And stop jumping to conclusions. In the first place, we didn't poison any brownies. In the second place, maybe the fentanyl was injected or applied to her skin and it had nothing to do with the brownie she ate."

Oma shook her head in disagreement. "If it was found in her stomach, then she ate it."

"There must be half a dozen places or more in Wagtail where she might have bought brownies."

Oma took a deep breath. "Poor Diane. Why would anyone want to kill her? Of all the people I can think of off the top of my head, she's the one who minded her own business and was always a perfect lady."

"Maybe there are things we didn't know about her. She told me about shutting down a puppy mill. That was the right thing to do, of course, but the owner of that puppy mill might be angry with her."

"Does Dave know about this?"

"I don't know, but I'll be sure to tell him. Now quit worrying so much. Do you want to watch the inn tonight or take our shift patrolling for dognappers?"

"Hmm?" She seemed to be thinking about something else. "Yes, that would be fine. You patrol. You excuse me?"

"Of course. I'll clean up in here."

She rose, and on her way out, she planted a kiss on the top of my head. Gingersnap and Stella followed her out the door. Poor Oma. I could tell how worried she was. She loved Wagtail. It had been her home for decades. "Trixie, we'd better figure this out."

Trixie placed her paws on the edge of the seat of my chair. "You're supposed to be thinking about who murdered Diane, not about pasta primavera."

She didn't give up, and she didn't seem ashamed about it. I gave her a tiny bite of pasta.

I thought about Diane while I washed the dishes. It did seem more logical that someone local had murdered Diane. Still, there were at least two visitors in town who had known her once. It probably wasn't a coincidence that she died the night of their arrival. And who was to say that they hadn't been in touch more recently than they claimed? Just because Rae Rae said she hadn't known Diane lived in Wagtail didn't mean that was true. Could Rae Rae have ordered brownies upon arrival? Or had she baked them herself and brought them with her? Was she really looking for Camille and the gang at midnight when she went out on the golf cart? Or did she have a different destination? Like Diane's house?

That line of thought brought me to another idea. Maybe

the screen in Diane's window had been torn for weeks or months. Could she have been an addict who took fentanyl on purpose? She never struck me as the type, but I guessed anyone could become addicted to pain meds.

Leaving Trixie in the kitchen, I went to the professional inn kitchen in search of brownies. I found two pans in the refrigerator, waiting to be cut into squares and served. At this point, no powdered sugar had been dusted over the tops. I stared at them. It was only Oma's conjecture that the fentanyl had been mixed with the powdered sugar. It could have been baked into a brownie. But topping it with powdered sugar would be quick and so easy that anyone could do it.

I rummaged in the pantry for powdered sugar and found several large bags of it. Someone could have tainted it with fentanyl between the manufacturer and the inn, I supposed. But if that had happened, if the brownie Diane had eaten came from the inn and it had been poisoned with powdered sugar, then wouldn't more people have keeled over dead? I felt certain she wasn't the only one to whom we had served a brownie.

I picked up the phone and called Dr. Engelknecht, who agreed to stop by.

I loaded the brownies and powdered sugar onto a tray and carried them into the private kitchen, where Trixie was sitting near the sink, looking up at a cabinet.

Setting the tray down, I watched her. It startled me when the door to the cabinet thudded as if someone had pushed it from inside and it banged shut again.

Trixie barked and pranced in a circle.

Surely, we didn't have mice or rats. I walked closer, and a furry white head popped out of the cabinet and looked at us. "Twinkletoes! What are you doing in there?" She knocked a box of dog cookies down to the counter, jumped out of the cabinet, and fled. "Dog cookies?" I opened the cabinet door wider. Aha! Dog and cat treats.

Twinkletoes returned, hopped on the counter, and walked under my chin, rubbing against me.

"You sneak! You know you shouldn't be up there. Was this a ploy to gain favor with Trixie by knocking her favorite treats down to the floor?" I asked her.

She purred, evidently quite pleased with herself.

I scooped up Twinkletoes and placed her on the floor. Even though it had been terrible behavior, I gave her a fishy cat treat, and Trixie received a cookie. I knew I was breaking every rule about animal training. I had just rewarded both of them for something they shouldn't do, but they were so adorable, and Twinkletoes wasn't just being sneaky. She was smart enough to know where those yummies were.

I was laughing when I heard Dr. Engelknecht's voice in the lobby calling my name. I swung the door open. "Thanks for coming. That was quick."

He walked into the kitchen. "I was in the neighborhood." He gazed around. "I've never been in here before."

"Only very special people are allowed in the private kitchen," I joked. "When my dad and his sister were children, Oma felt they needed a room where the family could gather and eat privately. It can be taxing to always be in the public eye. Plus it's hard to have private family conversations if you constantly eat with everyone else."

"I suppose it can be. I think I'd hang out in here all the time."

"Could I get you a cup of tea or coffee?"

"If it's not too much trouble, I'd love an herbal tea. It's been a long day and I'm bushed."

"Peppermint, lemon, or rose hip?"

"Peppermint!"

"Coming right up."

He talked to Trixie and Twinkletoes while I made his tea and a strong cup of English breakfast tea for myself.

When we sat down at the table, I said, "I wanted to ask you about Diane."

He held both his palms in the air. "Even though she's dead, I can't tell you much because of the privacy laws. Besides, the full report isn't out yet. It could be several days before that happens. Given where she was found, it looked to me like she had been murdered, but there weren't any obvious signs like knife wounds. I've been concerned about fentanyl, because it's spreading across the country so fast. I had a hunch when I saw her, so I asked the medical examiner to rush a test for it. I needed to know if it's in Wagtail, because we'll be seeing other cases."

"I understand completely. I only have one quasi-personal question about her, which I hope you can answer. Was Diane a drug addict?"

He snorted. "Okay, I will answer that one. Most certainly not."

"So she wouldn't have intentionally used fentanyl?"

"That's more than one question, but I have no reason to think that would be the case."

He gazed at the brownie pans.

"You know where I'm going with this," I said. "Could someone have tampered with a brownie so that Diane consumed fentanyl without knowing it?"

He smiled. "Now that's the kind of question I like. And one that occurred to me, as well as to the medical examiner. In a word, *yes*. Apparently, fentanyl can be almost flavorless, or very slightly bitter depending on the batch, but mixed with something sweet, it would probably be disguised. And it's important to note that a surprisingly small amount can kill someone."

"So it would be possible, for instance, to mix it with powdered sugar and dust it on top of one of these brownies?"

"Absolutely. It would be diabolical, but one could do it.

What's worse, a wicked person could blow it into someone's face so they would inhale it or even get it in their eyes."

"I guess this would be a better question for Dave, but do we have a fentanyl problem here in Wagtail?"

"They tell me it's readily available in Snowball. I'd like to think that we don't have a lot of drug dealers in Wagtail, but that doesn't mean visitors don't bring it with them."

Dr. Engelknecht finished his tea. "I guess you know that it's part of my job to investigate the circumstances of Diane's death. I've heard you're pretty good at solving murders, so I hope you'll keep me in the loop about what you find out."

"I'd be glad to do that."

"Thanks. I'd better be getting home." He rose to leave but stopped at the door. "Holly? May I take the brownies and powdered sugar to test them?"

Brownies were one of my favorite sweets. But I certainly didn't want to take any chances. We couldn't serve them to guests, and I wouldn't dare eat them. I would have given them to Dave anyway. I gladly handed them over to Dr. Engelknecht.

Guests kept me busy for the next couple of hours. As usual, things settled down after dinner. Some guests were relaxing in their rooms, and others were out enjoying the balmy air of the summer night.

Gingersnap and Stella tore through the hallway, probably looking for Trixie and letting me know that Oma had finished whatever she was doing. The dogs accompanied me to the registration lobby.

"I'm ready to go on patrol," I said.

Oma gazed at Stella. "Perhaps Stella should spend the night with Gingersnap and me?"

"Whatever you think is best."

"Come on, Stella. We will wait for Casey in the main lobby. Ja?"

Trixie and I headed for the inn golf carts to go on dog-napper patrol. She jumped up on the front seat with me, and I would have sworn she was smiling.

"You were meant to be a little sleuth, weren't you?"

She nosed my pocket for a treat.

"Okay. Maybe you were meant to be a treat taster."

She crunched happily on a tiny, thin, bone-shaped carob cookie. I started the electric golf cart, and we were off. I was always amazed by the lack of sound from the electric engine. You really could sneak up on someone.

It was a lovely Saturday night. Trendy pear-shaped lights glowed in backyards. Cats stole across the street to visit friends and chase mice. An occasional couple walked home from a late dinner.

For no particularly good reason, I steered toward Elm Street. The quiet engine made it easy to hear dogs barking. I guessed a lot of dogs were snoozing by now, because I heard very little yapping.

The house Howard had rented was set back off the street. Nevertheless, I could see lights blazing from the windows. I didn't hear voices or music or anything indicating a lively party. We drove on. It was a boring night in Wagtail. All things considered, though, that was a good thing.

I drove around the neighborhood and back by Howard's rental. A lonely figure stood at the curb. I squinted to see her more clearly. It looked like Marlee. But as we neared and she saw the lights of the golf cart, she took off running toward Howard's house.

I stopped the golf cart and stepped out. "Marlee?" I called. There was no answer.

Maybe she didn't want to be seen at Howard's house. Camille and I had told her it wasn't a good idea. But sometimes people just had to find out for themselves. I hoped it would work out okay for her.

I shrugged and stepped back into the golf cart. This time

I drove on streets closer to the stores and restaurants that lined the green. I heard a man yell, "Hey! Hey, you!"

I looked around to see if he was in trouble.

Unfortunately, it was Howard who tripped toward the golf cart, shaking his forefinger at me.

"I want a word with you," he slurred.

Ugh. I wasn't even close to him and I could smell the booze on his breath. "Do you need a ride home?"

"You! You turned me in to the cop. A pretend country bumpkin cop, that's true. I was a smarter detective on TV than he is in real life, but still, you bet-bet-betrayed me."

"Can I call someone to help you get home?" I asked.

He snorted and waved his arm at me in a jerking, intoxicated motion. "Honey, we are not on my turf right now, but beware, because I will not forget your treachery. You might want to watch your back."

# Sixteen

I should have been shocked by his threat, but all I could think of at that moment was how odd it felt to have a man who portrayed kind and wise characters on TV say such a thing.

"I'll get you fired," he added. "I have a lot of clout. Wait until your boss hears how you've treated me."

I met the ugly gaze of his intoxicated eyes. He clearly didn't know that I was a co-owner of the inn and my own boss. "I look forward to that."

Trixie barked at him ferociously. Undoubtedly, in my defense.

The nice thing to do would have been to take him home. But after being harassed by him, I decided he could find his own way home. After all, the rental house was only a few blocks away.

I turned the golf cart down the closest street to get away from him. I looked back, though, and felt reassured when I saw him staggering toward his rental in the correct direction.

Rae Rae was right. She was lucky that she hadn't married him. They would probably have divorced in short order, but he would have made her life miserable.

As I drove along, I thought about how amazing it was that he could come across as a good guy on the screen when he was so different in real life. And now poor Marlee was at his rental house waiting for him. Well, she was only a few years younger than me. Surely, she would leave when she saw how drunk he was. I wondered if there were other people in the house. Or had he left all the lights ablaze when he went out?

Trixie and I spent another hour cruising the sleepy streets of Wagtail before calling it a night and heading home.

Unless we were expecting someone to check in, the registration lobby door was locked at nine every evening. After I parked the golf cart, Trixie and I strolled to the front of the inn and entered the building to the sound of hysterical laughter.

Twinkletoes waited for us on the grand staircase. I picked her up and tickled her chin. It didn't take long for Trixie to find the fun.

Casey, our night manager who looked remarkably like the young Harry Potter, right down to the round wire glasses and a shock of dark hair that fell onto his forehead, was playing poker with Finch, Jim, Camille, and Pippin.

"Pippin knows how to play poker?" I asked.

"Not really," said Camille. "We deal him an open hand. He's pretty happy about it. Instead of chips he plays with dog treats."

"That sounds like fun." Trixie sniffed at Pippin's pile of dog treats from a safe distance. "Pippin seems to be winning."

They collapsed into giggles.

Finch finally recovered enough to choke out, "It's painfully embarrassing that we're not smart enough to beat a dog."

I watched them with a smile. Finally, they were bonding, becoming friends. "I'll see you in the morning."

Trixie and Twinkletoes ran ahead of me up the grand staircase to our apartment.


I slept later than usual the next morning. Small wonder after two nights of excursions. Although it was Sunday, I saw that Mr. Huckle had snuck in and left a tray for us. My tea was still hot in an insulated carafe. Twinkletoes and Trixie enjoyed their treats, but probably not as much as I loved my chocolate croissant. It was the perfect way to start a day. Neither Oma nor I had anticipated that kind of service by Mr. Huckle, but he enjoyed doing it, and it made us feel like royalty. We missed being pampered on his days off.

A gentle breeze touched my gauzy white curtains. Outside the sky was a heavenly blue. Not a single cloud dared mar the summer sky. I stretched and looked out the French doors. But the sight of the man who claimed Trixie belonged to him cast an immediate shadow over my day. He sat on a bench in the green that was so close to the plaza, he could watch the comings and goings from the inn.

I showered in a hurry and dressed in a black skort with a pink floral pattern. I slid on the matching pink top as fast as I could. Black sneakers completed my noseprinting ensemble. I took the time to pull my hair back in a ponytail.

When I peeked out the French doors again, he was still there, looking so comfortable that if I hadn't had a run-in with him, I wouldn't have even noticed him. Adding tiny gold hoops in a hurry, I grabbed a leash that I hadn't used in ages. I wasn't taking any chances on Trixie getting away from me. Besides, there was something about a leash that

seemed to connote ownership. It didn't actually mean anything. After all, if that guy snapped a leash on Trixie, it
wouldn't mean she belonged to him. Still, I fastened a harness on her and hooked a leather leash to it. I swung the
large loop of the other end over my shoulder and head like
I would the strap of a cross-body bag.

I phoned Dave as we walked down the stairs. He wouldn't
be able to do much, but, if nothing else, I hoped he could find
out who the man was.

Dave answered right away. When I told him the guy who
wanted Trixie was watching the inn, he agreed to come
over as soon as he could.

We scooted through the main lobby and over to the reception lobby, where I could take Trixie out to the potty
without being so obvious. The dog bathroom was probably
somewhat visible from the plaza, but the man might not
notice us if he was focused on the front of the inn.

I was relieved to see Rae Rae walking toward the inn.

"Oh! You look so pretty," she said. "I love pink. But
honey, you need some bling!" Rae Rae actually flashed when
she moved. The sun caught the tiny crystal beads adorning
the neckline of her yellow dress. Large, chunky crystals on
her bracelets caught the light as she reached out to me, and
matching crystals hung from her earlobes.

"I'll keep that in mind."

"You'd better. Rumor has it that Sugar is pulling out
everything in her arsenal."

"You sound like a resident of Wagtail. How can you possibly know about that?"

"I have often wondered that myself. As far as I can figure, I look safe, like everybody's crazy aunt. And they tell
me things. I don't even have to ask. They just pour their
hearts out to me. So I have heard quite a bit about your
friend Holmes. Everybody is rooting for you, except maybe
for that darling Dr. Engelknecht."

This was just too embarrassing. "You went to see Dr. Engelknecht?"

"I didn't actually go to see him. I met him the first night we were here." She winked at me. "Dr. Engelknecht is awfully cute."

I was already embarrassed, and now I could feel the heat of a flush rising in my cheeks and to the tops of my ears.

Folding a dog waste bag over my hand, I walked over to collect Trixie's poo. When I stood up, I spied Camille jogging in a loose-fitting heathered-blue T-shirt that read *Wake Up and Run* and a pair of black pants that were skintight. Her hair was pulled back into a ponytail.

My gaze drifted to the bench where the man had been watching the inn. He was still there.

Camille slowed to a walk as she neared the bench. She glanced casually in his direction and did a double take. She looked like she had seen a ghost. Her eyes wide, she turned her head away from him quickly and ran past him like the devil himself was behind her.

When she saw Rae Rae and me, she ran toward us. Breathing heavily, she panted, "Good morning!"

We greeted her, but I noticed that she made a point of standing where the man on the bench couldn't see her. "Do you know the fellow on the bench?" I asked.

"Who?" she asked innocently.

I grinned. She was a pretty good actress. I pointed in his direction. "That guy."

"I don't think so. Whew! I'd better hurry and shower. I'm starved. Save some breakfast for me."

The second the doors closed behind Camille, Rae Rae turned to me. "Who is he, and why is she lying?"

# Seventeen

❀ ❀ ❀ ❀

At that moment, Dave strolled up.

"He's still there." I tried to look nonchalant so the man wouldn't take off. "See him? In the navy blue shirt?" I explained to Rae Rae that the man on the bench had claimed Trixie belonged to him.

"You must be terrified!"

"I am. I don't like him sitting there. I'm worried that he's waiting for an opportunity to grab Trixie."

"Relax, Holly." Dave patted my shoulder. "I've got him in my sights now. I'll figure out what he's up to."

"Thanks, Dave."

Rae Rae and I walked inside the inn and paused at the ladies' room to wash our hands.

Rae Rae eyed me. "That's awfully peculiar. What in the world would Camille have to do with that man, and why would she deny knowing him?"

We walked toward the dining area. "I'm glad you picked up on that, too. I plan to find out. I'm just not sure how."

"Oooh, I love being a sleuth. I've always thought I would have been an excellent private detective. No one would ever think a thing of me nosing around asking questions. You know, it's that crazy-aunt image that I seem to project."

I sidled over to the window in the lobby and looked out. Rae Rae peered out beside me.

Dave was chatting with the man. We watched as he pulled out a wallet. I guessed he was showing Dave identification.

"I'm ordering breakfast," said Rae Rae. "I'm absolutely famished." She walked over to the dining area.

I followed her somewhat reluctantly with Trixie still on a leash. She didn't appear to mind it much until she saw Gingersnap and Stella and wanted to run to her friends. Dave was right outside. It wasn't as though the man could dash in and steal her in front of everyone. I unlatched the leash, and Trixie sprang happily toward her buddies.

Rae Rae and I joined Oma and ordered eggs Benedict. I even splurged on a side of bacon.

Shelley had just delivered tea and coffee when Dave arrived and took a seat at our table. She hastily brought Dave a cup of coffee, too.

"The mystery man says his name is Wade Holt. He's here on vacation and read about Trixie in *Dog Life*. According to him, he recognized her as his missing dog right away. He never imagined she would still be alive." Dave gulped coffee like he was parched.

"Because he abandoned her!" I huffed.

"I told him he would have to take you to court and bring some evidence to prove ownership."

"And?" I asked, afraid to hear what he had said.

"He got a little surly about that. At any rate, he knows I'm watching him."

"Well, that doesn't help at all. He could just sweep in and steal her when I'm not looking."

Dave tilted his head and smiled. "Really, Holly? When exactly is Trixie not right by your side?"

"When she smells corpses."

"She's already done that this week. Once was plenty. Just keep her close by. Wade will probably give up and go home."

"I hope you're right," I grumbled.

Dave shot me another look. "He hasn't done anything illegal yet, unless you want to press charges about your encounter on the mountain."

Oma frowned. "Did he threaten you?"

"Mostly, he scared me. I don't know what would have happened if LaRue hadn't shown up." I shook my head. "I hope you're right, Dave."

He raised his coffee mug to me. "Okay, then. I have to get back to work. I've got a murder on my hands."

I winced. "Sorry. I just don't want a confrontation. Or to lose Trixie."

"Call me if he gives you any trouble." Dave stood up.

"What?" asked Oma. "No brunch for you?"

"Some other time, Liesel. I have a lot of work to do."

"Is it about Diane?" asked Rae Rae.

"I'm trying to get to the bottom of this. But for once, none of the local gossip is leading me anywhere."

He waved and strode out of the inn like he was in a hurry.

After brunch, I helped Shadow set up tables on the plaza in front of the inn for noseprinting. I was much relieved to see that Wade had left. Nevertheless, I kept Trixie on my hands-free leash.

I unfurled a banner that Oma had ordered from the local printshop. It read, *A noseprint is a dog's fingerprint!* That certainly got the point across. I hung it on the front of a long table while Shadow retrieved the noseprinting kits from the storage room.

Oma carried a basket outside. "These are rewards for dogs who get their noses printed."

I peeked inside. They were white-iced dog cookies in the shape of every dog's archenemy—the squirrel. "They'll love these!"

We hadn't started yet, so I stepped aside to phone Clara Dorsey and the Hoovers. It might be wise for them to attend, in case someone showed up with their dogs.

When Pippin arrived, his entire entourage was with him. Marlee wore her blonde wig and oversize sunglasses. There were a lot of reasons that women wore wigs, so I didn't want to jump to conclusions, but the sunglasses caused me to believe she didn't want to be recognized. There was something strange about it.

Pippin demonstrated how a good dog patiently waited while his nose was printed. And then he happily chomped on his squirrel cookie while his fans applauded.

We opened for noseprinting. I passed around forms to be filled out and accepted payments from non-residents of Wagtail, while Shadow did the actual printing. Several people brought their cats for noseprinting as well. Generally speaking, the dogs were better behaved about it. The cats seemed to consider it undignified and take it as a personal affront.

Meanwhile, Pippin posed for pictures and played with fans. Jim was teaching Finch and Camille the correct commands for Pippin to roll over, hide his eyes with his paws, and look guilty. The crowd in line loved it.

At four o'clock, we ran out of steam and noseprinting ink. Shadow and I folded up the tables and carried them back to the inn. It was tough going with Trixie on her leash. I figured it was safe to take the leash off since we were inside the inn.

We loaded the tables into the elevator, which Trixie refused to enter. Maybe being closed up in a shed was the reason she was afraid of small, confined spaces. Shadow took the tables to the basement, and I used the stairs so Trixie could come along. When they were neatly stashed away, the three of us walked up the stairs.

Right in front of us, Pippin led Jim, Camille, and Finch down the hallway. They wore bathing suits and carried towels.

"Time for Pippin's swim?" I asked.

Jim rubbed his hands gleefully. "I don't know if Pippin has ever been swimming before. This should be interesting."

I was glad to see them bonding. Even Finch appeared to be having a good time.

We followed them as far as the registration lobby. Shadow seemed very happy to be going home.

"It's been a busy weekend for you. Why don't you take tomorrow and Tuesday off?"

"No kidding?"

I laughed. "Go on and get some rest."

Shadow high-fived me and rushed out the door.

"That was nice of you," said Oma from our office. "I'm glad you did that."

Trixie and I walked into the office, where I flopped onto the sofa. "I'm glad we made all those noseprints. It might turn out to be a blessing in the future."

"It might also discourage people from stealing our dogs. I hope word gets out that Wagtail is not an ideal place for dog theft."

"Still no news on the missing dogs?"

"I'm afraid not. And with Diane's untimely death, all eyes have moved to that instead." Oma glanced down at a scrap of paper. "Her sister Donna is arriving today. If I'm not mistaken, the police cleared out her refrigerator and pantry to test the food for the fentanyl that killed her."

"Want me to put together a basket of goodies for her?"

Oma smiled. "I think that would be lovely. You can leave Trixie here with Gingersnap and Stella. I'll keep an eye on them."

"Great. I'll just dash upstairs to change."

I closed the door to Oma's office and ran up to my apartment. After a super quick shower, I slid on a violet summer dress and sandals, grabbed my purse, and was off to Wagtail's primary grocery store.

I found it surprisingly difficult to shop for someone I didn't know. I liked two-percent milk, but a lot of people didn't drink milk at all. She probably drank coffee for breakfast. But did Diane have a coffee maker or a Keurig? Yikes! In the end, I did the best I could. Fresh raspberries and blackberries, cereal, a loaf of bread, butter, sliced ham and the deli's fabulous potato salad, milk, sugar, salt, a bottle of wine, and eggs fresh from a local farm. I hoped I had hit enough items to tide her over until Donna could buy what she liked. On the way to Diane's house, I stopped at Sweet Dog Barkery. The owner's grandfather, Mr. Ledbetter, dusted off his hands and rushed to the pastry showcase to help me. He was adorable with fluffy white hair and perpetually red cheeks.

"Howdy, Miss Holly. What can I get for you?"

"Everything looks so tempting. How about an assortment of a dozen cookies"—I was tempted by the brownies but thought better of it—"a cannoli, and a blueberry turnover, please."

Mr. Ledbetter carefully prepared a box for me and tied it with their trademark chocolate pawprint ribbon. "You be sure and tell your aunt Birdie that I threw in something extra just for you." He smiled and winked at me.

Okay. I had no idea what that was about. "Thank you for your help. I'll give Aunt Birdie your best."

At the door, I turned to look back at him. He waved at me.

When I pulled up in front of Diane's house, a Sugar Maple Inn golf cart was already parked there. I recognized the inn's logo on the front. Laden with groceries, I walked to Diane's door and rang the bell, which set off a torrent of barking.

When Donna opened the door, I saw the family resemblance to Diane immediately. She had the same nose and high cheekbones. She was chubbier than Diane and wore her hair in a very short cut. I introduced myself and handed her two grocery bags.

"This is so thoughtful! Won't you come in?"

I followed her to the kitchen, where Rae Rae sat at a small table surrounded by boxers. "Well, hello!"

"Hi, Holly. Should I leave?"

"Please don't," said Donna. "I'm so glad for your company. I've almost stopped crying." Her eyes were rimmed in red. Tears welled in them again. Donna sniffled and wiped them away with her fingers. "Holly, the police told me you stayed with Diane until help came. Thank you so much. That was so kind of you. I shudder to think of her all alone there during the night."

"But she wasn't alone. Stella was with Diane when I found her. I imagine Stella was with her all night long."

Tears came to her eyes again. "Stella was devoted to my sister. How does a dog recover from that kind of loss? How does a person cope with it?" She clutched the sides of her face. "Diane's death is overwhelming. I can't believe that she's gone. I keep expecting her to come running into the house all breathless and happy. It's unimaginable that she's gone."

Rae Rae rose. "Do you have any coffee in those bags?"

"I do."

Rae Rae and Donna high-fived like they were old friends.

"We were just saying we could use a cup of coffee," said Donna. "Oh! And wine, too. You thought of everything."

Rae Rae was already spooning coffee grounds into a filter.

"I was almost afraid to stay here," said Donna. "They say just a little bit of that fentanyl can kill you. But the thing is, I knew my sister very well. She never was a drug user. Someone had to be pretty crafty to get her to take that stuff."

"Did she say anything to you about problems she might have been having with someone?" I asked.

"I knew about the fellow with the puppy mill that she put

out of business. When Dave Quinlan of the police department called to tell me about her death, that was the first thing I thought of. But the cops followed up on that guy right away. He happened to be in police custody out in Kansas, so that eliminated him." Donna looked through cabinets for mugs, found some, and placed them on the table.

"Was she seeing anyone?" asked Rae Rae, pouring coffee into three mugs.

Donna placed milk, sugar, spoons, and napkins on the table.

"Not romantically. The two of us had such bad luck with men. Our sisters found great husbands! Diane and I joked that we would have to grow old together because we didn't have anyone else." Donna's face screwed up, and she choked back tears. "I'm sorry. I can't seem to stop crying."

She wiped her face with a tissue and looked Rae Rae in the eyes. "Diane always said she lost her best friend over a man who wasn't worth fighting for. I know it's not much consolation, but after her experience with Howard, she was very critical of those who had affairs with married people. She had her fair share of married admirers, for sure. But she put them in their place. She asked me once, 'Why do men think I'm so stupid that I would believe their wives don't understand them?'"

Rae Rae laughed. "Oh my. I've been on the receiving end of that line from men, too." She let out a little sigh. "Having you here is almost like talking with Diane. She was so right. We should have both kicked Howard out of our lives and kept our friendship. Funny how things look so different years later."

Donna took a deep breath. "They're not giving me her body yet. I figure I'll take her home and bury her in the cemetery where the rest of our family is. I need to scrounge around for her will. Knowing Diane, I'm sure she made provisions of some sort for her dogs." She gazed at the gang that sprawled comfortably on the floor. "I hope I can be of help in figuring out who murdered her, but mostly I came to take care of the dogs. They were her babies."

"I guess Rae Rae mentioned that Stella has been staying with us."

"I love Stella! She's such a sweetie," blurted Rae Rae. "Let me know what you find out about Diane's dogs. I went over to the shelter yesterday. They had such lovely pooches, but if one of Diane's dogs needs a home, I'd really like to adopt him or her."

"That's wonderful!" I looked at Donna. "Don't you think Diane would feel good about Rae Rae taking one of her babies?"

Donna nodded. "I just have to make sure she didn't want them going to someone else. Ugh. It will be so hard to look through her things."

"Maybe I can give you a hand," offered Rae Rae. "I'll be in town all week."

"Should I bring Stella home?" I asked.

Donna sagged a little. "Is she being a problem?"

"No. She's wonderful."

"Would you mind terribly keeping her a little longer? I'm sort of overwhelmed with dogs right now. I wish Dawn and Debbie were here to help me."

"Your parents gave you all names that begin with *D*?" I asked.

"There were four of us, Diane, Debbie, Dawn, and me, Donna. Our mom thought it was cute to have all our names begin with the same letter. She even named the cat Darin. We had fun growing up. Oh, we argued and teased mercilessly, but we all loved one another so much. And now one of us is gone. We're like a puzzle with a piece missing from the center."

Rae Rae reached out and placed her hand over Donna's.

"Why don't we go out to dinner tonight? Holly, would you like to join us?"

"Maybe tomorrow night?" asked Donna. "I have a lot to do around here and so much to figure out. I'm tired from the drive, too."

I took that as a major hint to depart. "If you need anything while you're here, just give me a call." I scribbled my number on a pad by Diane's phone.

"And I had better catch up to my gang," said Rae Rae. "But we are definitely on for dinner tomorrow night."

The two of us walked out to our golf carts. "Do you think I'll get one of the boxers?" asked Rae Rae.

"I honestly don't know what kind of arrangements breeders make for their dogs in the event of their deaths. I've heard that sometimes the breeding community rallies around them and helps place the dogs, but I don't really know."

"Cross your fingers for me!" Rae Rae stepped into her golf cart.

I walked on toward mine and thought about Diane on the way home. She had seemed to live a quiet life. She was always friendly and participated in town events. And I never heard anyone complain about her or even gossip about her for that matter. Mr. Huckle was always on top of town gossip. He denied it, of course, but there wasn't much he didn't know about the goings-on in Wagtail. I would have to remember to ask him.

It wasn't very late yet, but I was a little worn-out. I parked the golf cart and headed for the main lobby. Oma was probably there with the dogs keeping an eye on everything.

A group of people gathered there, including the Pippin entourage. It alarmed me when they turned to look at me and fell silent. I glanced around. "Where's Trixie?"

# Eighteen

I couldn't breathe. "Trixie? Trixie!"

"We've been trying to reach you." Jim sounded panicked.

I glanced at my phone. The sound had been turned off by accident.

"Liebling, I'm so sorry," said Oma. "I never expected her to run out."

"I'm sure she's around here somewhere," said Camille in a soothing voice.

My heart thundered. It was as if I couldn't hear anything. Voices and faces swirled around me. What happened to Trixie? Could she have gone up to our apartment? Why, oh why, had I left her?

Food, she loved food. I hurried to the private kitchen. There was no sign of her. The dining area was empty. I checked the terrace overlooking the now-darkening lake. Still no sign of Trixie.

My heart heavy, I stood in the middle of the lobby and screamed, "Trixie!"

They watched me with pity, which I hated.

Jim grabbed my arm. "Will you stop moving for a second? I'm trying to tell you that Pippin went with her."

"What?"

"Trixie shot out the front door. She nearly tripped me in her hurry, and Pippin whipped around and followed her."

I ran to the front porch. "Trixie? Trixie!"

"Holly! Listen to me. I chased them until they wriggled under a fence. I tried going around it, but I had lost sight of them." Jim sounded as worried as I felt.

She hadn't been stolen. I tried to tell myself that was a good thing. It *was* a good thing! "The GPS collar," I blurted.

I ran inside and down the hallway with Jim right behind me. I pulled out an iPad, connected to our GPS system, and entered the number of Trixie's collar. "She's on Elm Street."

I grabbed a golf cart key and ran out the door. Jim kept pace.

Pushing the cart to travel as fast as it could, I drove north past the church and cut to the right. One more turn and we would be on the east side of Wagtail. Trixie and I had driven in this neighborhood last night. It had been so quiet and calm.

Jim watched the GPS screen. "The collar stopped moving."

"Good! We can catch up to them."

I glanced at the screen. We were almost there. We needed to turn right on Elm and figure out exactly where they were. Only then did it dawn on me. Someone was dead. Trixie wouldn't have run out of the inn like that otherwise.

"Pippin!" called Jim. "Pippin, come!"

I thought I heard a bark. "That must be Trixie."

I slowed down as we approached the spot where the collar was supposed to be. We stopped in front of the house that Howard had rented.

Jim shouted, "Pippin!"

I yelled, "Trixie!"

Jim gazed at the iPad. "Could they be inside the house?"

Darkness was falling rapidly, and I wished I had brought a flashlight. I remembered that my phone had one and flicked it on. It wasn't great, but it was better than nothing.

The house was completely dark. I knocked on the door anyway. "Howard?" I called. Less politely, I banged on the door and tried to turn the doorknob. It was locked.

"They must be inside." Jim grimaced. "Do you think he's dead?"

A shiver ran through me, and I looked at Jim. "If he's dead, how did they get inside?"

"Maybe a back door is open."

I phoned Dave while we dashed around the side of the house. Fortunately, the call went through. "Something's wrong at Howard's rental on Elm Street," I blurted. "Hurry!"

Jim tried opening the back door. "It's locked."

"Maybe they're not inside after all. Could we be reading the map wrong?" I peered at it. "If we're in the right place, we should hear Trixie barking." I wished I had brought an extra GPS collar with me to verify that we were in the correct spot.

Jim was looking around the base of the house.

"What are you doing?" I called.

"Maybe they got in through a basement window."

I tried looking through the windows in the back of the house. When I shone my light inside, I saw a sofa and a TV, but no dogs and no Howard. Frustrated, I tried the kitchen door myself. It was a fairly simple doorknob without a dead bolt.

"Jim! Did you bring your wallet?"

"Yes." He pulled it out of a back pocket. "How's that going to help?"

"I'd like to borrow a credit card, please. One that you don't use much."

He handed it to me. "I'm not following you."

I carefully slid the credit card into the crack between the door and the frame. Positioning it at an angle above the point where I thought the latch would hit the strike plate, I eased it downward while pulling it toward me. The door opened.

Jim raised his eyebrows. "You do realize that this is breaking and entering, or trespassing at the very least?"

"Do you want me to close the door and wait for Dave to call the rental company and have them bring a key?"

"No!" He almost shouted the word.

"Okay, then." I swung the door open wide and flashed the beam on my phone around the walls in search of a light switch. "Trixie!"

Jim was so close behind me that I could feel his breath on my hair. "Pippin!"

The house was silent. Dead quiet.

I found the switch and flipped it. The rear of the house came to life. We slowly walked into a combination kitchen and family room. An empty pizza box lay open on the counter.

"I think they would be making a fuss if they were in the house," said Jim.

I handed his credit card back to him. "Thanks. I hope I didn't mangle it."

"No problem. I can always order another one."

Jim took the lead and ventured into another room. He flicked on a light. "Gah!"

I rushed in.

Jim turned and stopped me. "You don't want to see this."

That was the wrong thing to say if he really wanted to prevent me from seeing it. I pushed my way past him.

Howard lay on the sofa at an awkward angle. His body looked like it had keeled over, but his legs dangled toward the floor. I was pretty sure he wasn't breathing.

# Nineteen

I screamed. I couldn't help it. The scream was an involuntary reaction. Howard's face was pale, and his lips were blue. I crept closer. There was a bluish tint around his perfectly manicured fingernails.

Thanks to Trixie's nose, I had seen more than my fair share of corpses, but I hadn't seen anyone with blue lips. His eyes were closed. If his body hadn't been somewhat contorted, I might have thought he was sleeping.

"He looks like he'd been sitting up and suddenly fell over," Jim whispered.

An empty old-fashioned glass was tipped over on the floor. A scrap of paper lay on his thigh.

I watched his chest for any sign of breathing.

"Should we should try chest compressions?" Jim touched Howard's legs. "Ugh. He's already stiff. We're way too late to help him."

A shudder ran through me. "Do you think someone killed him?"

"I don't see any blood or wounds."

"Holly?" It was Dave's voice.

"In here." I was enormously relieved that Dave had arrived. I had seen some awful deaths, but there was something different about this one.

Dave walked in and stopped short at the sight of Howard. For a long moment, he said nothing. "Have you touched anything?"

"I tried to move his legs. And we touched the doorknob," said Jim.

"And the light switches," I added.

And then I saw something that struck fear into my heart. "Trixie and Pippin are here somewhere. That's a dog's paw print on the hardwood floor."

Dave ushered us outside and called his police department for backup. "Someone could still be in the house," he grumbled. "You two took a huge risk going in there." He stopped fussing at us. "Do you have reason to think anyone else is inside?"

"No," said Jim. "All we wanted was to find Trixie and Pippin."

Dave drew his gun. "Stay out here. That means you too, Holly."

It was fine with me. My major concern was Trixie. But if she was inside the house, why hadn't she come running to us? I refreshed the page on the iPad and entered the number of Trixie's collar again.

Jim watched over my shoulder. "I don't understand. If Trixie isn't here, why does her collar show up? Do you think she's at the house next door or something?"

The two of us started calling Trixie and Pippin. We walked out to the front yard and called them. No one barked, no one whined, no one bounded toward us.

I tried to be calm. It wouldn't help if I acted as irrational and upset as I felt.

I faced Jim. "We know they were here."

"That could have been the paw print of another dog." He sighed. "But since Howard didn't bring a dog, it was probably Trixie's or Pippin's print."

Fear clutched at me. There were only two logical reasons for the GPS to indicate the collar was here. Both were horrific. Either the collar had been taken off Trixie, or it was still on her, but she was no longer moving.

Dave emerged from the house through the front door. "It's all clear."

"Any sign of Trixie or Pippin?" I asked.

"No dogs, no cats, no people except for Howard. And I can't find a pulse on him."

"I know you don't want us in there messing up the crime scene, but do you see a GPS collar lying around?"

"Yeah, there's one right next to the dog door."

"Dog door?" That explained a lot. I breathed a little easier. She must have gotten caught and backed out of it.

A police car and an ambulance arrived.

I phoned the inn and Oma answered. "Have Trixie or Pippin returned?" I asked.

"Liebchen, I'm so sorry this happened."

"Oma, it's not your fault. I guess they haven't come back to the inn?"

"Not yet."

"Thanks, Oma. We'll keep looking." I hung up. "Wade Holt. The gray-eyed man," I said. "He killed Howard, trapped Trixie and Pippin, and took them with him."

"You don't know that," Dave scolded. "We don't even know if Howard was murdered. He might have died of natural causes."

"I know this. If you find Trixie and Pippin, you'll have your killer."

"Holly, go home and let me do my job." Dave stepped inside and closed the door.

Without any discussion, Jim and I hopped on our golf cart. I started it and cruised along the street. At the corner closest to the green, I turned. We stopped briefly at each cross street, searching and listening for any indication of activity. It wasn't until we reached Sycamore Street that we heard an angry voice. I turned and sped to the source.

Old Mr. Finkelstein stood in the middle of the road. He was a small man with a balding head that was surprisingly round. His hands were balled into fists, which he shook in the air.

I stopped the golf cart and stepped out. "Mr. Finkelstein, are you okay?"

His face flushed red. "I hope you didn't hear any of the choice words I used, Holly. I apologize if you did. My dear departed wife would scold me for using language like that. But some idiot stole my golf cart! How am I supposed to get around? Why would someone steal an old man's transportation?"

Jim strode over to him and shook his hand. "Jim McGowen, sir. When did this happen exactly?"

"Well, it was still in the driveway when I had my coffee on the porch this morning. I remember that because I thought it needed washing. Then I drove over to"—he stopped abruptly and eyed me—"a friend's house for brunch. It was good, too! Country ham, corn bread, and green beans like my mother used to make. I came home, so I must have had the golf cart. I watched fishing on TV. I guess that meal was so good that I fell asleep. And then I thought I'd enjoy the night air a little bit and sit on the porch swing. That was my dear departed wife's idea. I never was much for swings, but it reminds me of her, so some evenings I sit in it for a while, mostly because she can't sit in it anymore. So I came out to the porch and sat down. And everything was all peaceful. I thought I saw some fireflies. And when I looked closer, I realized the golf cart was gone."

Jim grinned at me. "Is there any chance you forgot that you left it at your lady friend's house?"

"I don't recall saying anything about a *lady* friend, young buck."

Jim bent and peered at him.

"I'm not that forgetful either. I can't walk from her place to mine. Of course I drove home. How else would I get here?"

I pressed Dave's number on my phone. He wouldn't be happy to hear about a missing golf cart when he was dealing with a death, but if Howard had been murdered, chances were pretty good that the murderer could also be the thief.

"Did you hear any dogs barking?" Jim asked.

Finkelstein gave Jim an odd look. "Not while I was sleeping."

I stepped away to tell Dave what had happened. As I expected, he was less than thrilled to have to deal with a missing golf cart, but he promised to be there as soon as possible.

"Officer Dave is on his way over. Do you know the make and model of your golf cart?" I asked Mr. Finkelstein.

"Why are you asking such difficult questions?"

"What color is it?"

"Red with beige seats. Is that good enough for you?"

I smiled at him. I would let Dave ask him for more identifying information. The color was a good start. I phoned the parking lot where visitors parked their cars and told them to be on the lookout for Trixie, Pippin, and Mr. Finkelstein's red golf cart with beige seats.

Jim rubbed his eyes. "Really, Holly? You think a guy is going to murder someone, kidnap two dogs, steal a golf cart, and then leave through the main gateway in and out of town?"

"Murder?" asked Mr. Finkelstein. "You mean he would have killed me for my golf cart? I'm lucky to be alive!"

"Yes, you are," I assured him. To Jim, I said, "He stole a golf cart. Where else do you think he's going to go? He can drive somewhere, park the golf cart, and hike down the mountain. Or he can find a boat and row across the lake. If he wants to get out of here, which is what any smart criminal would do, his options are somewhat limited."

Mr. Finkelstein frowned at me. "That's just not true. He could thumb a ride. He could hide in the back of a delivery truck. He could pretend to be a guest and call a Wagtail taxi to pick him up."

I placed my fingers over my eyes. "I don't know where to look."

"Don't worry, Holly. Maybe the killer doesn't have the dogs." Jim patted my shoulder.

In my mind's eye, I could see Trixie cowering at Wade's feet. My poor baby. She must be so scared. He dumped her once. Why would he want her again? And then I remembered that someone seemed to know him. "Camille."

The men stared at me like I had lost my mind. "She knows something about that man. Let's go." I assured Mr. Finkelstein that Dave would arrive soon.

Jim jumped into the golf cart. "I'm glad these things don't go very fast. You have got to calm down."

I ignored him and steered the golf cart along the east side of the green. My phone rang while I was driving. I pulled over, hoping it was Oma with good news.

It was Zelda. "Holly, are you looking for Pippin and Trixie?"

"Yes! How did you know?"

"I'm having dinner at Hot Hog. Trixie and Pippin walked in by themselves, selected a table, and hopped up on a bench like they came to dine. Everyone is cracking up about it. The waiter brought them pulled chicken dinners. We're all wondering how they're going to pay!"

I started laughing, but tears came to my eyes and rolled

down my cheeks. "They're okay," I squeaked. I could barely
see anything through my tears. What a relief. I had never
been happier. My baby was safe. She wasn't in the clutches
of a horrible person. She would be fine and in my arms
again soon. I couldn't help myself. I laughed harder. I had
been scared to death, and now all that anxiety was released.
The tears kept flowing.

Jim peered at me. "If they're okay, then why are you
crying?"

"I'm just so relieved." I took a deep breath and wiped my
eyes. "We're on our way. Zelda, if you don't mind, could
you try to keep them there?"

"Sure thing."

"Where are they?" asked Jim.

"Apparently, they went out to dinner by themselves." I
gunned the golf cart toward Hot Hog.

When we arrived, Trixie and Pippin were still sitting at
their own table eating yogurt-frosted pupcakes for dessert.
They wagged their tails at the sight of Jim and me. After
hugging Trixie and making sure she was all right, I paid the
owner for their dinners and ordered enough takeout to feed
Oma and Pippin's crew back at the inn.

"Look at this," said Jim, showing me his telephone.
"Someone took a picture and it's going viral. They're calling it Pippin's date night out."

It was precious. I could only imagine that Trixie had
been to Hot Hog so many times that she knew the drill. The
scents that filled the air were certainly enticing. "I guess I
know now which restaurant is your favorite," I said to her.

Pippin and Trixie willingly followed us to the golf cart
and jumped into it. I had a feeling they were going to take
a long nap when we reached the inn.

We walked into the lobby to cheers and applause. Pippin
was used to that, but Trixie danced in circles as though she
understood that she had done something special.

Oma switched on the strings of pear-shaped lights that hung over the terrace. We carried the takeout dinners out to the terrace and shoved two tables together to accommodate everyone. I fetched two pitchers of iced tea and glasses of ice from the kitchen. Pippin and Trixie relaxed on the stone floor, but Gingersnap and Stella sniffed the air eagerly, hoping for their fair share of the takeout.

"So much for your theory that Wade murdered Howard," said Jim.

"Murdered Howard?" Camille screamed like an ingenue in a horror film.

# Twenty

Oma gasped. "The famous actor? Howard Hirschtritt?"

"Howard is dead? How did that happen?" asked Finch in his usual unflustered way.

Jim told them the sordid details. "Not the best dinner conversation. I'm sorry, guys. I wasn't fond of him, and I know you're not supposed to speak ill of the dead, but the guy may have had it coming."

Camille's mouth dropped open. "It sounds like he was murdered! You think he deserved that? How unbelievably cruel of you."

"He had a reputation. Of course, if any of that was true, you'd think he would have been axed in Hollywood years ago," said Finch. "Not here on vacation where no one has ever had to work with him."

"Finch is right, Camille." Jim bit into a rib that dripped with sauce.

"Oh, I just can't believe it." Camille sipped her iced tea

but didn't eat. "He invited Marlee and me to his place last night. When do you think it happened? What if we had been there?"

Marlee. In my fear that Trixie had been stolen by Wade, I had forgotten all about seeing Marlee at Howard's rental house the night before.

Jim shrugged.

I wasn't sure how much I should say about what I knew. "I saw him last night around eleven, so that narrows it down a little bit."

Finch's eyes met mine. "Was he with anyone?"

"He was all alone. He had come out of a bar, I think, and was stinking drunk."

"I hate to be so selfish at a time like this," said Camille, "but what about the show? Do you think it will be canceled?"

"He's a secondary character," muttered Jim.

"But he's so well-known." Camille still wasn't eating. "Roscoe said he didn't want anything to go wrong. Where's Rae Rae anyway? I'd say something has gone majorly wrong!"

I was thinking that Rae Rae couldn't prevent a murder but thought it wise not to say so. Especially since Rae Rae was probably going to be the prime suspect. Camille was upset. And rightly so. She had a lot riding on the success of Pippin's show. I gazed around the table. And where was Marlee?

Oma observed them quietly as she ate. I suspected she was thinking the same thing I was. We were sitting with the top suspects in Howard's murder.

"Pippin's the real star," Finch observed. "They can find someone else to play the role of a grouchy old man. All of us except for Pippin are expendable."

Camille's eyes opened wide. "You're missing the point, Finch. It's the publicity that will kill us." She waved her hands as though she wanted to erase her words. "I didn't mean to say that. Will kill the show. Are you sure he was murdered?" she asked. "He wasn't, like, staging his death and right now he's having a good laugh about it?"

"Not unless the cops were in on it," I pointed out. "But it's true that we don't know for sure that he was murdered. Dave made a big point of that."

Jim waved a rib when he said, "Dave was trying to stall rumors. We saw him. It was something I'll never forget. People who die of natural causes don't look like that. Listen up, now, everybody. They're going to try to pin this on us, but Howard had something else going on in Wagtail. Remember how weird he was when we checked in? Why would he rent a house unless he wanted to meet with someone without us knowing about it? Why wouldn't he stay at the inn or that other place in town?"

Oma nodded her head. "I think you may be on to something, Jim."

Finch leaned back in his chair. "Okay, let's work off that premise. But how would anyone be able to find out what Howard was up to? Unless someone was following him around, it would be impossible to figure out."

"Marlee," uttered Jim.

Finch shot him a look. "She and Rae Rae aren't here, so they're going to be our top suspects? If I weren't here right now, would you point your accusing finger at me?"

"Oh, come on!" Jim whined. "You really don't think those sunglasses and the wig are weird?"

"Wig?" asked Finch.

"Seriously, Finch. Don't you look at people?" Jim shook his head. "She's obviously not used to wearing it or wisps of brunette hair wouldn't show on the sides. And those sunglasses are a joke. She's like a private detective in a corny third-rate movie. What's that about?"

Finch raised his eyebrows. "Huh. Turns out Marlee might be much more interesting than I thought. I had her chalked up as another wannabe actor who wasn't having any luck breaking in. I meet way too many women like that. They want to be friends because I was a child star, but they're not really interested in getting to know me. They just want to meet any connections I might have. When they find out I don't have any, they leave so fast I can feel the icy air in their wake."

It was the first thing I'd heard him say along those lines. Maybe that was why he didn't show much emotion and had learned to be sarcastic to get by.

Camille pressed her lips together and looked worried.

"C'mon, Camille." Jim gave her a little nudge. "We'll get through this."

"My dear ones, Dave and Holly will uncover the monster who has perpetrated this sin on Howard. You mustn't worry. There is little you can do other than show your best faces in this terrible time." Oma rose and bid us all a good night. She whistled for Gingersnap and Stella, who followed her into the inn.

"She's right, you know," said Finch. "The media will come after us. It's best if we say how sorry we are and then change the subject to Pippin."

Camille nodded. "And what kind of face do we put on when the killer comes after one of us?"

Jim nearly spewed his iced tea. "What are you talking about?"

"You're assuming Howard was killed because of something he did. What if he was murdered because of the show?" Camille whisked her hair back off her face.

Jim and Finch stared at her like she was nuts.

"Why would anyone want to do that?" I dared ask.

Camille's expression changed to one of horror. She flapped her hands in the air rapidly. "It's Rae Rae. What do we know about her? We've been letting her tell us what to do. How do we know if she's really Roscoe's sister? How do we know if he actually sent her here? Maybe it's all a ruse and she's going to try to pin the murders on us. After all, she's the only one who really knew Howard. Right?"

I didn't say what I was thinking, because Camille was already agitated. No need to fuel that fire. But it had not escaped my attention that Rae Rae had known both of the victims. On top of that, they had both betrayed her. It had happened a long time ago, but sometimes people harbored resentment for decades. She had said it was a good thing she hadn't married Howard, but what if she really felt that they had stolen her life, her plans, her happiness? Was Diane the reason Howard had wanted his own place? Could he have murdered her? Did he need privacy where no one would keep tabs on his comings and goings?

"Holly!" Jim snapped his fingers at me. "We could all use a drink to help us relax. Want to come?"

What I needed was a hot mug of tea to settle my nerves. I declined their kind invitation. Besides, Oma had gone to her quarters. With a full house, I should stick around in case someone needed something.

"Before you go," I said, looking straight at Camille, "there is one thing I would like to ask. How do you know Wade Holt?"

Camille sucked her lips into her mouth and eyed us. "I heard that you thought he killed Howard, but I was hoping you'd forget about that. I am ashamed to admit that I was somewhat related to him."

"Somewhat?" laughed Jim. "Do you share DNA or not?"

"Not! My aunt married him, and now they're divorced. Wade is . . . a swindler. That's the kindest way I can say it. He's bad news. Frankly, I never thought I'd see him again. Last I heard, he was in prison in Ohio. When I spotted him here I was horrified. I honestly thought he might have escaped. But my aunt says he's been out for years. He's not even on probation anymore. Something I find very scary." Camille gazed around at us. "Please don't think poorly of me. A person can't help who her relatives marry."

Finch smiled at her. "If you dig deep enough, I bet most people have a relative they'd be happy to forget about."

"Sure," said Jim. "I have an uncle who gets staggeringly drunk at every family gathering. Not quite up there with being a con man but embarrassing nonetheless. Especially at elegant weddings."

I shooed them on their way and gathered up the takeout mess. Satisfied that the terrace was ready for use the next morning, I called Trixie and the two of us strolled down to the registration lobby to be sure the sliding glass doors had been locked for the evening. I left the lights on in case any guests happened down that way. We returned to the private kitchen to make the tea I craved.

I savored my tea quietly in the Dogwood Room, where I could see who came and went without seeming too nosy. Trixie hopped up on the sofa and rested her sweet head on my thigh.

I stroked her fur, relieved that she was okay and safely home with me. But I felt enormously guilty for imagining that Wade had murdered Howard and stolen Trixie and Pippin. Even if he was a swindler, I had jumped to conclusions in my panic and had been so wrong!

In fact, I felt a little bit better knowing that he was a lying cheat. For starters, it meant that maybe he was lying about Trixie having been his dog once. Maybe Dave had been right all along, and Wade had read about her in the magazine and gotten ideas. Additionally, I seriously doubted that Wade would pursue the matter in court, even if he *was* the person who dumped Trixie. My guess was that people who'd been imprisoned for conning others weren't keen on returning to a courtroom. And surely, the fact that he was a convicted liar and cheat would weigh in my favor if I ever wound up in court over Trixie.

Still, I felt a little bit guilty for jumping to the conclusion that he had murdered Howard.

The front door opened and Marlee burst inside. She closed the door and caught her breath as though she had been running from something, or someone. She didn't seem to notice me as she trudged to the grand staircase and up to her room. I heard her door close and wondered what that had been about.

I was itching to find a way to ask her about her wig and sunglasses, but nothing subtle had come to me yet.

Rae Rae entered the inn with her usual vigor. She spotted us right away and sank into an armchair opposite me. "Tell me, have you had a chance to chat with Marlee?"

"No."

"She just ran by me outside like she was afraid. Now, if she was scared, you'd think she might have grabbed on to me, wouldn't you? Either because there's safety in numbers or to tell me to run, too."

"Sounds logical," I said. "She came through here fast, too. Was she was crying? Or trying not to cry?"

"Do you think she's fallen for one of the guys?" asked Rae Rae. "Finch or Jim?"

"Funny you should ask that. Finch was just saying that he wrote her off as a social-climbing aspiring actress. He has a biting wit. Perhaps he offended her?"

Rae Rae gazed at the high ceiling and toyed with her earring. "I suppose that's possible. He's such a doll. I bet women chase him all the time."

"Jim, Camille, and Finch seem to be bonding and hanging out together. But I never see Marlee with them."

"Really?" Rae Rae's eyes narrowed. "That's most interesting. Then where has she been?" With a loud gasp, Rae Rae sat up straight. "Howard! She's fallen into Howard's clutches. I blame myself. I should have seen the signs. I'll have a talk with him in the morning."

I blinked at her. Either she didn't know or she was a better actress than I had suspected. "Rae Rae, I'm sorry to have to tell you this, but Howard has died."

Her face contorted from shock to doubt. "Are you pulling my leg? Is this some kind of trick where he'll walk in here and laugh at me?"

"I wish it were."

"You're serious? I was just speaking with him last night. No, it must be someone else."

"I saw him. It's definitely Howard."

"What happened? Heart attack?"

I wasn't sure how much I should tell her. On the other hand, she'd probably hear the grim truth sooner or later anyway. "Possibly, but we suspect he may have been murdered."

Rae Rae stared at me without moving. I wasn't sure she was even blinking. She finally tilted her head ever so slightly. "First Diane, and now Howard? What can that mean? What did they do?" She jumped to her feet and rubbed her forehead. "And I knew both of them. I might be the only person within a thousand miles who knew them both well. And we all know I had plenty of reason to be angry with them, even if it all happened a long time ago. I'm in a peck of trouble!"

# Twenty-one

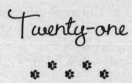

"Do you know any good lawyers?" Rae Rae paced back and forth in front of me.

My previous boyfriend happened to be a lawyer. He lived in Northern Virginia, but he was entirely too fond of using any excuse to make himself at home in my guest bedroom at the inn. I was certain she could find a lawyer in Snowball, if not Wagtail. But at the moment, my greater concern was that Rae Rae might actually have murdered them. "Should I call Dave?"

"Heavens, no! Why would you do that? But he'll come lookin' for me sooner or later. Maybe I should just get out of town. That might be easier. Then again, if I leave, they'll think that's a sign of guilt. What a mess! And this was such a fun vacation up to now." She gazed around blankly, as if she didn't quite know what to do. "Well, except for Diane's death. That wasn't any fun at all."

My phone rang, which was unusual at that hour. Dave asked if I had seen Rae Rae.

"She happens to be right here with me," I said, worried that he might be coming to place her under arrest.

"Great! Can you bring her over to Dr. Engelknecht's office? We need someone to confirm Howard's identity."

"They want you to identify Howard's body," I said to Rae Rae.

She drew in such a sharp breath that even Trixie looked up at her. "Yes, of course. I'm happy to cooperate with the authorities. That will look good for me."

I checked my watch. Casey would arrive for the night shift any minute. What I really wanted was to go to bed. But Rae Rae probably needed company, and she might have trouble finding the doctor's office.

As soon as Casey walked in the door, Rae Rae, Trixie, and I took a golf cart over to the three-story house where the doctor saw patients. I had never given much thought to the fact that someone had to have a place to store bodies in Wagtail until they were collected by a funeral home. The lights on the first floor were ablaze. An ambulance was parked on the street in front of the gate in the white picket fence.

I carried Trixie, whom I figured probably wasn't supposed to be in the doctor's office, but I wasn't taking any chances leaving her outside by herself.

Dr. Engelknecht greeted us, even Trixie, warmly.

Dave thanked Rae Rae for coming and led her to a back room. I waited at the doorway to the brightly lighted room.

Rae Rae gasped. She clamped a bejeweled hand over her mouth. She turned away from Howard with her eyes closed, and for a moment I feared she might faint, but she gathered herself and looked at him again.

"Howard, darlin', what happened to you?" She wiped tears off her cheeks. "Your tormented life is over. May you rest in peace. I guess we all knew you would end like this. It's probably a miracle that it didn't happen sooner."

Dave asked, "Can you confirm that this is Howard Hirschtritt?"

"Oh my, yes. It's definitely Howard."

"Thank you. I have a document for you to sign if you don't mind," said Dave.

"Of course." Rae Rae sighed loudly when she looked back at Howard. "It didn't have to be this way, Howie."

I blinked hard and watched Dave's expression. He didn't give away what he was thinking, but he sure was keeping his eyes on Rae Rae. Had she just implicated herself in Howard's death? Was it possible to murder someone yet be so calm and collected about it?

While Rae Rae signed the document, I asked Dr. Engelknecht what had caused Howard's death.

"I won't know until they do the autopsy. I didn't see any obvious wounds."

"What about his blue lips and fingernails?"

Dr. Engelknecht mashed his lips together. "Unfortunately, while there are a number of reasons for blue lips and fingernails, they are characteristic of death by fentanyl. Blue lips are seen in a lot of fentanyl overdose cases. If it hadn't been for Diane's death, I probably wouldn't suspect it in Howard's case, but I'll definitely be asking the medical examiner to check for a fentanyl overdose. That stuff is so dangerous. A pinch of it is enough to kill."

"That's just awful!" Rae Rae clasped her hand to her face.

"Doc and I are going to start carrying Narcan, a drug that temporarily reverses the effect. It's not perfect, but it can save lives." Dave looked worried. "We're hoping there won't be any more cases, but if we can get there fast enough, we might be able to help."

Minutes later, Rae Rae, Trixie, and I were on our way back to the inn. Rae Rae didn't say a word the entire drive.

But when we entered the lobby, she said, "I went for years without seeing Diane or Howard. I can't say I never thought of them. I've often wondered how differently my life might have turned out if it hadn't been for them. The two of them were the only two people who ever truly betrayed me. They spun my life in a completely different direction. But until my brother called and asked me to keep an eye on things this week, I didn't dwell on them. I assumed their lives were on track. I certainly never expected this."

She walked up the stairs silently and didn't look back.

In a way, I didn't think she had been talking to me so much as she had just been thinking aloud.

That night, I opened the French doors in my bedroom to let in the cool night air. On the third floor, I didn't have to worry about anyone walking in. A cat had managed to climb up the wall once, but I could handle that.

I snuggled in bed with Trixie and Twinkletoes. Poor Trixie probably wondered why I kept her so close by.

When I woke, I showered, pulled on khaki skorts and a melon-colored shirt, and took Trixie out to do her business. I stopped at the office for a trash bag and disposable gloves. Since I'd given Shadow the day off, I needed to tidy the doggy bathroom while we were out there. Most people cleaned up after their dogs, but there were always those who didn't bother.

I made of point of looking for Wade, but he wasn't on the bench where he'd sat before. I didn't see him anywhere.

I washed up and followed Trixie to the dining area. She raced ahead of me. There was no doubt she knew where her breakfast would be served.

Rae Rae had just joined Oma at an indoor table. Trixie ever so slowly approached the breakfast dishes that were meant for Gingersnap and Stella. Her head extended, she sniffed the air and drew ever closer.

"Trixie!" I scolded. I didn't know how Stella would feel

about another dog eating out of her bowl. Fortunately, Stella remained amazingly calm. Trixie knew she was being naughty and backed off.

I sat down with Oma and Rae Rae just in time to hear Oma say, "We have arranged for you and your group to go boating today. That way you and Pippin can relax a bit without crowds. And without the media looking for you."

"Oh, Liesel! That was so thoughtful of you. My brother phoned early this morning. Naturally, they're putting out a statement. He reminded me that people might be hounding us for quotes."

"They will pick you up at the inn's dock at eleven o'clock. You can swim, water-ski, and have lunch out on the lake away from prying eyes. They've promised me they'll have you back just in time for afternoon tea."

"That's marvelous. I'll try to round up the crew. Isn't it odd that the one who is always behind the camera seems to be the most elusive?"

"Marlee?" I asked.

"I can't imagine where she's spending her time, but it's not with us. She shows up for events and does her job, but before I know it, she's gone again."

When Shelley arrived to take our orders, Rae Rae said, "I can't help myself. I have to try the waffles with caramelized bananas. And a side of bacon."

Shelley grinned at me. "Shall I bring you the same?"

I usually tried to eat like a normal person would at home, but breakfasts at the inn were always so tempting. "Yes, please," I said meekly. "Is there a version for dogs?"

"I wouldn't forget our most famous resident. I have something special for her."

When Shelley returned with our waffles, she handed Trixie a bowl of sliced beef tips with gravy over rice and peas.

"Wow. That's quite a breakfast."

"Trixie deserves it." Shelley watched her eat for a moment before moving on.

Zelda sat down with us. "I've already had breakfast, and I promise I'll get right back to work, but I'm dying to know if the rumors are true."

Oma frowned at her. "What rumors?"

"That a woman was seen running away from Howard's house the night he was murdered."

Oma's eyes opened wide.

I looked over at Rae Rae, thinking she must be worried. But Rae Rae was stuffing her mouth with caramelized bananas and waffles as though she hadn't a care in the world.

"I'm sure this is nonsense. Nothing more than a silly rumor, Zelda." Oma buttered a piece of toast.

Rae Rae took a long swig of her coffee. "Are you the one who can read dogs' minds?"

"Yes!" Zelda said proudly.

"Can Trixie or Stella tell you who murdered Diane and Howard?"

"Oh, good question. Unfortunately, the answer is no. I've thought about this a lot. I think that Trixie knows who touched or was in the vicinity of a dead person. She can smell who was there. But even if she could say who it was, I don't think she could say which one killed the victim. I can pick up on a dog's emotions, but the dog can't point a paw at anyone. I have heard of cases where a dog was present when someone was violent with a person the dog loved. Later, when the dog saw the violent person again, he snarled or acted defensive."

"That makes sense," said Oma. "But a dog probably wouldn't realize that a person was being poisoned."

"Exactly. Like right now, Trixie is very happy with her breakfast. She's a funny girl. Her moods are easy to read. Some dogs are harder. Stella misses Diane. She's melancholy and confused. She doesn't know what will happen to her. But even though she might have seen the killer, she probably doesn't associate Diane's death with that person."

Rae Rae nodded. "Thank you for explaining that. It would be nice if the dogs could just lead us to the killer."

Zelda poured herself a cup of coffee and hurried back to her post at the registration desk.

Rae Rae waved her hands. "She's a sweet person, but honestly, I could have read their minds and figured that out."

"Rae Rae, you knew Howard well." Oma gazed at her. "Do you think he might have overdosed intentionally? Maybe he killed Diane and couldn't live with the regret?"

"Not a chance. Howard was too selfish. He didn't care about anyone but himself. It could have been accidental, of course, but Howard thought the world revolved around him. That's not the kind of thing he would do."

Oma excused herself just as Marlee walked through the door.

"Marlee!" Rae Rae beckoned to her. "Won't you join us?"

Marlee paused at our table, still wearing her sunglasses. "I've already eaten."

"Oh! Did you have these wonderful waffles?" Rae Rae asked.

Rae Rae's question startled me. I had assumed that Marlee hadn't eaten at the inn. But Rae Rae was being nosy and had deftly put her on the spot, while acting quite innocent.

"They look delicious!"

"What did you eat for breakfast?" Rae Rae prodded.

"Eggs."

I smiled. Marlee wasn't being sucked into confessing where she had been.

"Darlin', have a seat," said Rae Rae. "Would you care for some coffee?"

"I'm good, thanks. I'd just like to grab a shower."

"You're such a beautiful young woman. Why do you hide behind those sunglasses?"

# Twenty-two

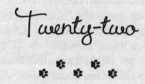

I nearly fell out of my chair. I choked on a bite of waffle I had just put into my mouth.

"Sensitive eyes." Marlee touched her sunglasses. "I've always been this way."

"I don't mean to be nosy, sugar, but I need to see what's under them." Rae Rae sounded sweet and sincere, but firm.

Marlee lowered her glasses. Her eyes were swollen and red as though she'd been crying.

"Oh, honey! Do you want to have a talk? Maybe Rae Rae can help."

"I'm so sad about Howard's death." Marlee sniffled. "I can't believe that he's gone."

As she spoke, it dawned on me that Marlee was the other likely woman who might have been seen running from the scene of the crime.

"Oh, sweetie. I suspected as much. He drew you into his web. Trust me when I tell you that you're better off without him."

Marlee slid her glasses back into place. "That's easy for you to say. Howard was my only hope. He could have helped me. He had connections."

"Here's the sad truth," Rae Rae said. "He had connections, but he never would have helped you. The only person Howard ever cared about was himself. You hung your hopes on the wrong star."

"But I heard he helped launch other actors' careers."

"He was good at taking credit for things he didn't do."

"He's the only real star I've ever had the opportunity to meet. I knew I shouldn't have come here." Marlee fled up the stairs.

"Do you suppose she thinks she looks sophisticated in those glasses? Like Jackie O?" asked Rae Rae.

"Something is up with her," I said. "And it's not sensitive eyes."

After breakfast, Trixie and I made our usual rounds through the inn. As was her habit, Twinkletoes spied on guests by entering their rooms when they were being cleaned. She was the nosiest cat I had ever met.

I noticed there was a *Do not disturb* sign hanging on the door handle of Marlee's room. The housekeeper gave me a thumbs-up.

Closer to her, I whispered, "Why the thumbs-up?"

"It's okay that I'm not cleaning in there. She hasn't slept in her bed since she checked in."

"What? How do you know that?" I asked.

The housekeeper smiled proudly. "I know how I make the beds. Even my own mother can't duplicate it perfectly. I don't know where she's been sleeping, or if she's been sleeping, for that matter, but I can tell you that she hasn't been in her bed."

Maybe Rae Rae was right. Had Marlee been sleeping in Howard's rental house? No wonder she was so upset. He probably promised her the moon, and now her dreams had turned to dust. Unless she had killed him, she would recover. Had she murdered him? Or had she been there when he was killed? Maybe that's why she was on the run when she returned to the inn last night. If she was a witness, she must be terrified.

Done with morning rounds, Trixie and I walked downstairs to the reception lobby. The door to the office was closed. I looked at Zelda.

"Big meeting between Dave and your grandmother. I have strict instructions not to interrupt unless someone else drops dead."

"Ouch. They must be talking about the murders."

Zelda leaned over the desk toward me. "I've heard that Howard used to date Diane. I think he came to Wagtail to get her back."

"Could be, I suppose."

"But that's not all. Diane was a beautiful, vibrant woman. I bet she was seeing someone on the sly and that's who murdered both of them."

"Also possible. Don't you think that driving Diane's body up the mountain and dumping it meant the killer was outrageously angry with her? Why not leave her where she died?"

"To buy time. The killer thought it would take weeks, maybe years or decades, to find her body in that ravine. Seriously, if Trixie hadn't found her, the vultures and possums would have. There wouldn't be much left by now. They work fast."

"That's a good point. Then why didn't the killer do the same thing with Howard's body?"

"Ah!" Zelda held up her forefinger. "He was interrupted."

I shouldn't have giggled given the seriousness of our discussion, but Zelda had an answer for everything. And she made sense! I wondered if Marlee had interrupted the murderer. "So how do we find the killer?"

"Well, I'm keeping my ear to the ground. Someone must

know who Diane was seeing, right? I mean, that's the kind of thing that's hard to keep quiet in a small town like Wagtail."

Hadn't Dave asked the same thing? But he had mentioned Augie, which was preposterous. How could Diane have managed to keep a romance under the radar when even visitors like Rae Rae had heard about Holmes and me?

At that moment, Pippin raced down the stairs and bowed to Trixie.

Trixie was game to play. I opened the sliding glass doors and accompanied them outside where they raced around on the grass.

A boat was arriving at the inn's dock. I walked down to give them a hand. To my surprise, the captain and crew for the day were Augie's son, Stan, and none other than Sugar McLaughlin, who had her eyes set on Holmes. I hadn't seen her since her cosmetic procedures, but she looked beautiful. It had been Augie who told me about her beauty treatments. I hoped Sugar had finally given up on Holmes and started dating Stan. At least they were about the same age. "Hi! It's a gorgeous day to play on the lake."

Sugar eyed me. "I guess I don't have to worry about Holmes arriving today while I'm out on the water."

"Oh?"

"You wouldn't have dressed like that if you thought he was coming today."

I probably should have been offended, but her games were too juvenile. I tried not to laugh but teased her a little bit. "Maybe I dressed like this to fool you."

Her smile faded.

Stan made a face. "She's messing with you, Sugar."

"I don't know . . ."

"You'll have a lot of fun with these folks," I said. "They're very nice."

Trixie and Pippin raced onto the dock followed by Jim,

Camille, Rae Rae, and Finch. Marlee walked down to the dock at a slower pace.

Pippin happily jumped on board the boat, quickly followed by his new best friend, Trixie. I coaxed her back to the dock with treats.

Stan helped the other passengers in. "Aren't we missing one?"

I turned, expecting to find Marlee inching her way toward us. Instead, she was fleeing up the hill in the direction of the inn.

"Well now, what's *that* about?" asked Rae Rae. "Honestly, I don't know what to make of that young woman. I suppose I should disembark and see what the problem is."

"You go and have a good time. I'll look after Marlee." I untied the lines and gave the boat a little shove as they cast off. I called Trixie, who reluctantly followed me back to the inn. There was no sign of Marlee.

Zelda gave me a strange look.

"Have you seen Marlee?" I asked.

Zelda flicked her eyes down.

"What does that mean?"

Trixie ran behind the reception counter and yipped playfully.

I looked over the counter and found Marlee crouched there.

"They're gone," I assured her. "How about I buy you lunch, and you tell me what's going on?"

Marlee emerged from her hiding place rather sheepishly. "Okay."

The door to Oma's office opened. Dave nodded at us and left.

"Zelda," said Oma, "this would be a good time for you to go to lunch. It will be very busy this afternoon, and I will need your help, ja?"

"Ja. Absolutely. Can I come with you guys?" asked Zelda.

I looked at Marlee. "It's up to you."

"Sure. The more the merrier. When they murder me, more people will know why."

"Oh, liebchen!" Oma placed a reassuring arm around Marlee. "We will not let anyone harm you. Do not be afraid. I'm sure these murders have nothing to do with a sweet young woman like you."

I wished I felt as sure as Oma that Marlee wasn't somehow involved.

Marlee, Zelda, Trixie, and I walked over to Café Chat. We settled at an outdoor table with a bright yellow umbrella that was imprinted with their logo of two back-to-back cat silhouettes and placed our orders for iced tea and their house specialty, grilled chicken and shrimp salads.

"Okay, so what's going on?" I asked.

Marlee paled. "I'm afraid of water."

I tilted my head. Surely, she wasn't going to try to dodge the question. I let a moment of silence convey my disbelief.

"I'm from Snowball." She removed her sunglasses. "I left here to go to Los Angeles and try to get an acting job. You see how well I did with that. I'm a social media guru for a dog!"

"And you were embarrassed about that?" asked Zelda. "I think it's such a cool job!"

"It's not my ideal job. I'd rather be an actor, but this pays the bills. Then they said Pippin was going on vacation. Woo-hoo! I would finally get to go somewhere interesting. And wouldn't you just know, they had to choose Wagtail, the one place I've been to a million times. I went full circle and came back to where I started."

"Do your parents still live in Snowball?" asked Zelda.

"Yes. I will admit that it has been nice seeing them."

"So that's where you've been spending your nights," I guessed.

"Yes. I felt safer there."

"Safer?" I sipped my iced tea. "Why don't you feel safe back home in the community you know so well?"

Marlee seemed uncomfortable and slid the sunglasses back on.

"Marlee, is there something we should know?" I wanted to add *about the murders*, but I thought she might tell us more if I didn't press that particular issue just yet.

The waitress brought our salads. Zelda and I dug in while waiting for Marlee to respond.

"I guess I should tell you that my real name is Mary Lee. I thought Marlee would be better for an actor. Mary Lee sounds so old-fashioned."

That wasn't the kind of information I had hoped for.

"I had these two friends, Sugar McLaughlin and Stan Hoover."

"And they were the crew on the boat today!" I said.

"Exactly. I've been trying to avoid them. It was so hard to stay away from Stan and his dad at Pippin's lunch on the mountain. I had to beg Finch to bring me food! I thought the boat outing would be safe enough. Everyone wears sunglasses on the water. But then there they were. The very people I wanted to avoid. Even with the wig and sunglasses, I knew they would recognize me. They know my voice. They know me far too well."

"Gosh, I'd think it would be fun for you to see your old friends," said Zelda.

"It wouldn't have been so great when they tried to drown me."

I stopped eating and watched her facial expression. She seemed serious and genuine. Would it be rude to ask her to remove her sunglasses? I wanted to see her eyes.

"We all went to the same college a few hours away from here. Everything started out okay. Sugar and I were roommates, and Stan hung out with us." Marlee munched on a grilled shrimp. "And then I started to notice things in Stan's dorm room."

"Things?" I asked.

"Yeah. Stuff that was weird for him to have. When I asked about it, he would tell me his mom had it sent to him."

"Maybe she did." Zelda speared a chunk of avocado with her fork. "Some moms are great that way. I can see Glenda sending care packages. She dotes on Stan."

"I know his parents are nice people, but would a mom really send her son an expensive vacuum cleaner or a Waterford Crystal bowl? He lived in a dorm room!"

Zelda winced. "Okay, so that's not typical care-package stuff."

"And then one day I found makeup in his room. One of those sets that has everything in it. You know, eye shadows, blush, lipsticks."

"I love those," Zelda exclaimed. "Was he majoring in theater?"

"It belonged to Sugar. My two best friends were having a romance behind my back. Sugar was still my roommate. And I noticed that she had a lot of new things, too. I didn't think much of it at first, but as time went on, she had a fancy new camera and a charger for power outages and"— Marlee took off the sunglasses and looked at the two of us— "this is what finally tipped me off—shoes!"

"Lots of women have a thing for shoes." Zelda sipped her tea. "I've been accused of that myself."

"You don't understand. They weren't her size. She even asked me if I wanted some of them because they were my size. Who has brand-new shoes, still in the boxes, but they're not the right size? I thought and thought about it. Even if you stole shoes from a store, you'd steal your size, right? So one day I followed them."

Zelda and I had stopped eating.

"They were porch pirates. They stole packages that had been delivered and left on people's doorsteps."

"That's really low," I said.

Marlee swallowed hard. "I reported them to the police."

That was the right thing to do, but I had a feeling it led to problems.

"Stan got three years in prison and a hefty fine. Of course, it totally messed up his college plans. When I was graduating, he was being released with ten years of probation. Sugar got one year in jail. I guess she's on probation, too. My mom said she heard that Sugar had finished school."

"And now you're afraid to see them," I stated.

"Not just them. Their families, too. Stan is his mom's pride and joy. She's furious with me. And Sugar's mom is just plain insane. She's a nut."

"But they were the ones that committed crimes," Zelda protested. "It's not your fault that you did the right thing."

"I don't trust them." Marlee took a deep breath. "And I don't want to take any risks."

# Twenty-three

❧ ❧ ❧

Zelda frowned. "I never heard anything about this. Did you, Holly?"

"Not even a peep or a hint."

"Their families kept it very quiet around here. Not that I can blame them. What they did was incredibly stupid. Someone told my mom that Stan had left college to assist a medical team in a remote area of Tanzania."

I snorted. "I suppose that would be difficult to confirm. But you're not really afraid they'll hurt you in some way, are you?"

"You bet I am! I know they're living here peacefully, and their crime, while horrible, wasn't violent. Stan is evidently working for his dad and taking on odd jobs. I have no idea what Sugar is up to these days. But Stan made it very clear to me that he will never forgive me for turning him in. He didn't come right out and threaten to kill me, but I'd rather not take that risk." Marlee toyed with her salad. "I couldn't refuse to come here with Pippin. Jim would have replaced me in a nanosecond. I may not have the job I want, but I need the money."

I wasn't sure what I would have done in her shoes. But I probably wouldn't have given up my job. "You had to hope all eyes would be on Pippin."

"Exactly. I could hide in my room or at my parents' house. Stan and Sugar didn't even have to know that I was in town."

I ate my salad, glad that Marlee's weird behavior had been partially explained and that it had nothing to do with Howard's murder. I debated asking her why she had been at Howard's house the night he was killed. Or was that line of questioning better left to Dave? Would she be more inclined to tell me?

I gazed at her while she ate and wondered if she was telling the truth. Was I getting jaded from hearing too many people lie? Dave could easily verify what she had said about Stan and Sugar. I might even be able to find news articles about it online.

"I think you're safest at the inn," said Zelda. "There are always a lot of people there, and we have a full house right now. If you so much as scream, a whole bunch of people will come running."

"I don't know what Sugar's momma is up to," I said, "but Stan's mother is busy looking for her stolen dog. I doubt that she's even thinking about you at the moment."

Zelda waved her fork. "Besides, they might yell at you, which would be embarrassing, but seriously, they're nice women who wouldn't hurt you. They're just very protective of their babies."

"You two have been so kind to me. You must have thought I was a complete nutcase."

I paid the tab for lunch and left a generous tip. "Sometimes it's better to tell people what's going on. Rae Rae, Jim, Camille, and Finch would stand up for you in a heartbeat. Maybe you should tell them," I suggested.

"Do you think Sugar and Stan will be invited to tea this afternoon?" asked Marlee.

"I don't know. I would suspect they'll need to return the boat and clean it up." We left Café Chat and strolled back to the inn. "After all they went through, I'm surprised that they're still friends. Are people on probation allowed to pal around together?" I mused.

"Ohhh! Don't start that. I've learned my lesson about turning people in," said Marlee.

Zelda hurried back to the reception lobby, and Marlee took the stairs up to her room.

I was on my way to see Oma when my phone rang.

"Holly, it's Donna, Diane's sister. Could you swing by for a minute? I'm a little worried about—"

"About what? Donna? Donna, are you there?" The line had gone dead.

# Twenty-four

I called Donna back immediately. Her phone rolled over to voice mail. Frustrated and worried, I called Dave and told him what had happened. "It might not be anything more than her phone going dead from not being charged. Or—"

"I'll meet you there. If you get there first, do not go inside. Did you hear me, Holly?"

"Yeah, yeah, yeah." I hung up and ran down the hallway to get a golf cart key. Trixie raced alongside me. She knew something was up.

I grabbed a key and told Zelda where I was going. I had some doubts about taking Trixie but paused long enough to grab a leash from the office.

When we drove up to Diane's house, I was relieved to see Donna standing on the sidewalk. I parked the golf cart and sprang out with Trixie securely on the leash. We dashed toward Donna. "Are you okay?"

Donna's cheeks were flushed. "I think my heart rate has

almost gone back to normal. Thank you so much for calling Dave. Someone was in the house!"

"Did you see him or her run out?"

"Not yet. Dave is in there now. I was scared out of my wits. The door to the closet in Diane's bedroom was cracked open just a couple of inches. I didn't think a thing about it. I called you because things weren't where I left them. Then I saw movement in the closet. I was so shocked that I dropped my phone! I ran out as fast as I could."

"I would have been terrified," I said. "But I don't understand why you called me. Did you think I had been in the house?"

"No. It seemed to me that someone was looking for something. Maybe that was why Diane was murdered? I called you to ask what that might have been. Were there any rumors about something special or valuable in her possession? Was she seeing anyone she might not have mentioned to me?" asked Donna.

Everyone seemed to be asking that. "Not that I know about. But I see what you're getting at. Maybe someone wanted something she had, and she caught him in her house."

"Exactly."

The front door opened, and Dave propelled a little boy forward, holding him by the collar of his shirt. "It appears that this young man was your intruder. I have called his mother."

"Jacob Minifree," I said, "what are you doing here?"

"Hi, Holly."

He didn't look the least bit flustered. I would have been crying if a cop hauled me out of someone else's home. "Jacob, what were you doing in Diane's house?"

He was completely serious when he said, "I came to see Pippin."

"Pippin?" asked Donna. "Why would you think Pippin was in the house?"

"Because I saw him." He blinked at us with innocent brown eyes. "He went into the house."

"When was that?" asked Dave.

"The day I saw him at the inn."

Dave's eyebrows jumped. "When was that?" he whispered to me.

"The day they arrived."

"Have you seen Pippin?" Jacob asked Donna.

Donna smiled at him. "I'm afraid not."

"Will Pippin come back to visit again?"

"Honey, I don't know. I don't think so." Donna gazed at me with a bewildered look.

Jacob faced Dave. "Am I under arrest?"

Dave's eyes met mine. I assumed he was wondering whether to scare the little guy.

"Yes," said Dave.

Jacob's mother rushed up at that moment.

"I'm under arrest," said Jacob proudly.

His mother took his hand. "How dare you frighten him? He's just a little boy. The mayor and the chief of police will hear about this."

Dave sighed. "Children are not allowed to hide in other people's houses. Jacob needs to learn that. It's called trespassing."

Jacob's mother turned her ire on Donna. "Everyone else loves it when my children visit them. What do you have against inquisitive little children? The nerve of you, calling the cops on a little boy." Still holding on to Jacob's hand, she walked away much too rapidly for his short legs.

"Donna says it looks like someone has been going through Diane's things," I said to Dave. "Could it be Jacob?"

"Possibly. You're locking the house when you're gone, right?" asked Dave.

"Absolutely. But from now on, the dogs will not be

sleeping out in their kennels. I will be surrounded by them when I'm in the house."

"Would you rather come stay at the inn?" I asked. "We're full up, but I have a guest room you could use."

"That's very kind of you. If anything else weird happens, I'll take you up on that. They tell me boxers are very protective, so I should be okay unless someone really does want something that's in the house. Though I can't imagine what it might be."

"Holly," said Dave, "have you talked to Pippin's owner about Diane?"

"He was with me when we found her—" I stopped short of saying the word *body* and was so glad I caught myself. Poor Donna was upset enough; I didn't need to be graphic. "So, yes, I guess I have."

"Before then. Did he ask for directions to her house or say that he knew her?"

"Not that I know of. He could have asked someone else. Want me to see what I can find out?"

"Don't say anything to him. I don't want him to be prepared when I question him."

"Can I get that screen replaced in the window yet?" asked Donna. "Or do you still need it to be the way it was the night Diane died?"

The three of us walked over to look at it from the outside. The window was located on the back side of the house, in Diane's family room.

Dave crossed his arms over his chest and studied it. "I always feel like this is important. If you don't mind, I'd like to take it as evidence. The person who went through it had to be slender. Initially, we suspected that Diane had the window open to enjoy the fresh air and that was how the killer gained access to the house. But once we found she had been poisoned by fentanyl, that didn't make any sense."

I understood what he meant. It wasn't as though someone would cut the screen, sneak into the house, and then present Diane with a fentanyl-laden brownie. No, it meant her killer was someone she knew and trusted. She had probably opened her door and welcomed that person into her home.

I stared at the screen. It was torn into an opening a little under two feet at the widest part. It was ragged, not neatly cut by a knife. Parts of it waved gently in the breeze.

I didn't know how much I could say in front of Donna without upsetting her or Dave. But I had to wonder if one of Jacob's older siblings had lifted him and pushed him through the screen to unlock the door. I couldn't imagine many people being able to get through that opening, especially since it was about four feet off the ground.

Dave was about to accompany Donna back into the house, but I grabbed him for a private word. "I keep meaning to tell you that I saw Marlee hanging around Howard's rental house the night he died. He had invited Marlee and Camille over, but I only saw Marlee there. Camille declined to go."

"Thanks, Holly. That's important to know." Dave headed for the house, and I left to return to the inn. On my way back, though, it occurred to me that the boxers hadn't been able to save Donna's sister. Had they been in their kennels?

Oma nabbed me the second I walked through the door. "Is Dave with you?"

"No."

"Ach. He should be here by now. Please place stanchions and ropes in the hallway to block people from the registration lobby." She handed me a sign that read, *Private Party*. "Then go to the kitchen and bring the pastries and teas. Ja? Zelda is calling Marlee to come down."

"Okay, Oma." I had no idea what was up, which was highly unusual. I hauled the stanchions and ropes up from the basement and used them to block the hallway. I hung the sign in the middle and headed for the commercial kitchen.

The cook pointed at a three-shelf food service cart. "The trolley is ready. Come back for the coffee and tea?"

I pushed it out of the kitchen. Trixie was waiting patiently by the door. It was loaded with goodies that made my mouth water. Glistening lemon squares that had been dusted with sugar, pink and white iced petits fours, tarts so tiny they only contained one blackberry and one raspberry, dainty watercress sandwiches cut into triangles, deviled eggs, miniature cupcakes with chocolate frosting, and one of my personal favorites, zucchini pineapple cake.

"Trixie, what do we have to do to be invited to this party?"

She wagged her tail, but her nose was focused on the lowest level, where iced dog cookies that looked like Pippin graced a plate. Miniature cupcakes with white icing were topped with tiny dog bones.

"I have a feeling you're invited."

We shoved it through the main lobby and along the hallway to the reception lobby, where I made a mental note that it served as a charming room for a small event. The vaulted ceiling rose two stories, and an elegant wrought iron balcony graced the second floor. In the middle, a giant antler chandelier added a lovely yet slightly rustic touch.

Gingersnap and Stella wore party hats decorated with paw prints and the word *Pawty*. They turned their twitching noses toward the cart. I had a feeling there might be peanut butter in the tiny pupcakes. Trixie examined the doggy table set up at a low eating height just for them.

Zelda slipped a pink party hat on Trixie that read, *Pawty Diva*. Marlee was already there taking photographs.

A second table had been set up for the people in Pippin's group.

Oma shooed me back to the kitchen for the coffee and

tea services. When I returned, I was dispatched to the lake to steer our guests to their special tea.

The first thing Jim said to me was, "Is Marlee okay?"

"She's great," I assured them.

I pointed everyone up the hill but stayed behind for just a moment to thank Stan and Sugar. I had to admit that I was seeing them through a new lens now that I knew about their crime spree.

Stan wore a baseball cap and swim trunks with a loud tropical pattern. Sugar didn't wear a hat at all. Her long hair had been windswept into a mess, but she was still beautiful.

"Thanks to both of you. Looks like they had a fun day."

Stan smiled at me. "I take people out all the time, and this bunch was way more fun than most. We're meeting them tonight for drinks."

Sugar turned her head coyly. "Have you heard from Holmes?"

Would I tell her if I had? It was so tempting to tease her again. But I needed to catch up to Pippin and his people. "Not a word."

She finally grinned. "Me, either."

I gave them a shove off and waved good-bye, then raced to catch up with the others. Dave arrived just as I walked through the door.

Our guests exclaimed over the trays of cakes and pastries. Only as I stood there watching them did I realize it was a brilliant method of detaining them while Dave interrogated each one in our office. I suspected Oma was the clever one who thought of it. My eyes met hers. She smiled, clearly pleased with herself.

Rae Rae beamed at Mr. Huckle as he poured her coffee. "This is simply delightful!"

What was Mr. Huckle doing there? It was his day off. Oma must have asked him to serve tea. It was just the sort of thing he loved to do.

"Pippin and I never expected anything like this." Jim watched as Pippin, Stella, Gingersnap, and Trixie contentedly gnawed on mock rawhide rolls.

A motion upstairs caused me to gaze upward. Sure enough, Twinkletoes was living up to her name. She spied on us from her perch on the railing one floor up. It always made me nervous when she did that.

Dave very politely asked if they would mind speaking to him about Howard. "After all," he pointed out, "you knew him, so maybe you can provide some insight into his untimely death."

Honestly, I didn't think they realized yet that they had been set up. They were as cheerful as most groups at tea. Even sarcastic Finch didn't have a sour word to say.

Rae Rae volunteered to go first. She smiled at Dave, and they disappeared into the office and closed the door.

"Who thinks Rae Rae murdered both of them?" Finch held up his hand, but none of the others did.

"That's not funny, Finch," scolded Camille.

"Finch is right." Marlee selected a cupcake from the tray. "None of the rest of us had a reason to kill Howard or Diane."

Jim was uncharacteristically quiet and appeared worried. "Has anyone noticed that when we go out at night, Rae Rae comes and goes?"

Camille gasped. "What are you saying?"

"He's right." Finch nodded. "She has had ample opportunity to run off and drug people before anyone misses her."

"Stop that!" Camille still hadn't eaten any of the goodies. "We can't let this turn us against one another."

The door to the office opened, and Rae Rae sashayed out as if she'd had a great time.

Surprisingly, Finch volunteered to go next.

I snatched a couple of sandwiches, deviled eggs, and slices of moist zucchini pineapple cake for Zelda and me. We noshed behind the reception counter.

Marlee glanced at Zelda and me. We both gave her a thumbs-up. Marlee squared her shoulders like she was bracing herself. "I want to apologize to all of you. I'm actually not who you think." With that, she launched into the story of her relationship with Stan and Sugar and their porch-pirating activities.

Her friends listened while they ate.

"I'm sorry I misled you. I hope you understand why I felt that was necessary."

Rae Rae was the first to speak. "Stan and Sugar couldn't have been nicer to us today. Especially that Sugar. Didn't everyone think she was darling? It just goes to show that you cannot judge a person by a brief meeting. Of course, I am all about second chances. I'd like to think those two learned their lessons and have changed their ways."

Jim looked repulsed. "I was flirting with Sugar. Ugh."

"They were both nice to me," said Camille. "But I can understand why you wouldn't have wanted to confront them, Marlee. I hope you'll hang out with us more now."

It wasn't long before Finch reappeared and Marlee took her turn with Dave.

"What did he want to know?" Camille asked Finch.

"Where we all were the night Howard was killed." Finch leaned back in his chair and bit into a chocolate éclair as though he had nothing to worry about.

"That's easy. We were all together," declared Camille.

"Well," Rae Rae spoke in a cautioning tone, "up until a point we were all together. But not all of us came back to the inn."

Finch sat up straight, suddenly looking amused. "We're supposed to bond over this. Don't you see? Howard's death is a fake. Look around. This was set up just for us. Isn't that a coincidence? Not!" He pointed at Camille. "We're supposed to give each other alibis. That's the point of this little exercise."

Camille turned a worried face to Rae Rae. "Were you sent to steer us in the right direction? Or to observe us? I'm sorry. You seem like a fun lady, but this is all kind of creepy."

Rae Rae patted her hand. "I'm afraid that's not the case. I saw Howard with my own eyes. When they needed someone to officially identify him, I felt obligated. Seeing as how I knew him well at one time, I felt I should go to him. It's so sad to die all alone in a strange place. Besides, I'm probably the only person around who knew him well enough to make an identification. It's not a prank. In no way was this part of the plan. I can promise you that. I know he's gone and not feeling earthly things anymore, but I suspect he had a lonely death."

Finch relaxed. "Does anyone else feel like we've landed in an Agatha Christie movie? You know, where each of us gets bumped off one by one . . ."

# Twenty-five

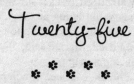

Camille froze with terror.

"Aww, knock it off, Finch." Jim tilted his head and smiled at Camille. "No one else is going to die. Howard's death was probably some kind of fluke."

"Yeah?" Finch grinned again. "Then why are you sitting here, waiting to be interrogated by a clueless small-town sheriff?"

I bristled at Finch's description of Dave and wanted to pipe up and defend him, but they *were* being interrogated. I didn't need to add to the drama.

Rae Rae broke the tension by laughing aloud. "You have watched way too many spooky movies, Finch. Next you'll be telling us that Howard's ghost is in the room and he will now tap on the shoulder of the one who murdered him."

Zelda was the one who stifled a laugh when every single one of them turned to look over their shoulders.

"Camille, you're not in a horror movie," I assured her.

"You haven't landed in a town where everyone is in on some sinister secret. You'll be fine."

At that moment, Marlee emerged from her interrogation, looking none the worse for it. "He'd like to see Camille next."

Poor Camille walked stiffly, as if she were headed to her doom. I could understand being anxious, but for the first time, I wondered if she had something to hide.

When the door closed, Marlee said, "Do you think Camille is always this high-strung?"

"Aw, give her a break, Marlee." Finch picked up a deviled egg. "She's a good egg."

The whole group groaned at his feeble joke.

Stella had finished her goodies. She raised her nose and sniffed. Walking slowly, she homed in on Jim's bag with all the pockets. She edged closer and surprised Jim by growling at it.

"What's up, Stella?" asked Jim. He touched the bag and Stella backed away, still growling. "Isn't that the weirdest thing?" he asked.

When the door opened, Camille emerged smiling. "Whew! It wasn't that bad after all. It's your turn, Jim!"

"Holly, will you keep an eye on Pippin?" Jim asked, picking up his bag.

Camille called, "Pippin! Pippin, come!" Pippin walked over to her, wagging his tail. Camille patted him and said, "I'll look after him. He's my buddy now."

Jim waved at us, squared his shoulders, and marched into the office.

Camille turned to Marlee. "What did he ask you?"

She rubbed her temples. "Mostly he wanted to know where we were night before last. It's funny, when we arrived, I thought it was cool that each of us had our own room. Now I wish we had shared a room. We could vouch for each other!"

Was Marlee still playing a role for her friends? Had she lied to us about spending nights with her parents?

"Now stop that," Rae Rae chided. "No one here has anything to worry about. Remember, Howard peeled off from this group on his own. There's no telling who he was with on the last night of his life. And I can tell you from experience that Howard was plenty good at getting himself into messes. The man was devoid of the sensibilities that most people have."

Finch frowned at her. "How long have you known him?"

"Oh, darlin'! How do I answer that without givin' away my age? Let's just say I was considerably younger than I am now." She winked at him. "Probably younger than you are now."

"You must have liked him to agree to come here," observed Camille.

"I thought I could tolerate Howard. It's been a long time since I saw him. As time goes on, one learns to cope with the slights and disappointments in life. Plus, I'm used to his self-importance. Other people get upset when he throws his little fits about inconsequential things, but I couldn't care less anymore, so they roll right off my back. I deluded myself into believing that he wasn't like that once upon a time. But age changes the way you see things. My daddy never did cotton to poor Howard. Now I understand why."

Camille sighed. "Howard's death will ruin the show. It will be canceled."

"Darlin'," said Rae Rae, "the show would get bad publicity if Pippin died. Maybe even if you or Finch passed. But for all of Howard's pomposity, few people outside Hollywood cared about him one way or the other. They might recognize him, but they won't actually miss him. Don't you worry, they'll find an even better actor to play his role."

Camille frowned. "I'd like to believe that, but Howard was legendary."

"Aww, sweetie, Howard would have loved workin' with you. Now don't you go believing that he had some kind of magic. The show will go on."

"How can you say that with such assurance?" asked Finch.

"I talked with my brother this morning. Honestly, I think a few people associated with your show are breathing sighs of relief. Howard was complicated, demanding, and narcissistic. I don't like speakin' ill of the dead, but quite frankly, it will be much more pleasant for everyone who works on your show. An actor once said to me that life was too short to be worth the trouble of working with Howard."

For the first time, Finch looked worried. "Good grief, Rae Rae, you make it sound like someone associated with the show knocked him off on purpose."

Rae Rae thought for a moment before saying, "Let's hope not. *That* could put a big crimp in things." She sank her teeth into a lemon square. "Mmm. Delicious!"

I wondered if Rae Rae was putting on a good face for the benefit of the others. As far as I knew, she was the only one who had been close to both Diane and Howard, which probably put her at the top of Dave's list of suspects. But Jacob's sighting of Pippin at Diane's house put a spin on that. If Pippin had visited Diane, so had Jim. He seemed like a nice guy, but why would he have paid Diane a visit? Better yet, why would he have visited her on the very day she died?

Camille stirred her tea. "I hope one of you had something helpful to tell Officer Dave, because I had nothing. I only saw Howard at night in bars, and I didn't know Diane at all."

Jim emerged from the office with blazing cheeks. I had a feeling it wasn't due to a sunburn. He walked over to the table, sat down, and asked Mr. Huckle for a glass of ice water. His hands shook.

Finch gazed at him in horror. "Are you okay?"

Camille placed her hand over his trembling one. "We'll stand behind you, Jim. No matter what happened. We're here for you."

Finch nodded. "We've got your back."

Dave appeared at the door and watched the group.

Rae Rae had stopped eating. "Is there something you'd like to tell us, Jim?"

He rubbed the icy glass across his forehead and took a long gulp of water. "Holly? Will you take care of Pippin?"

Camille's eyes grew large with fear. "Jim," she cried, "what's going on?"

"I didn't kill Howard. I swear I didn't." Jim looked over at Dave. "I don't know how long I'll be, Holly. He's a great dog. Please take good care of him." He stood up, gave Pippin a hug, and walked to the door with Dave.

Finch jumped up so fast that his chair turned over. "Wait! What's going on?"

Dave looked back at us. "Jim's coming in for questioning."

As Dave escorted Jim out the sliding glass doors, Dave was carrying the bag Jim always had with him. That couldn't be a good sign.

Pippin watched as if he knew he wasn't supposed to go with Jim. I walked over to him and tried to reassure him. I stroked his fluffy head and whispered, "It's okay. He'll be back."

Could Pippin tell I was lying? I wasn't at all sure that Jim would be back.

Jim's friends sat down at the table and gazed at one another.

Marlee finally spoke up. "I saw Jim at Howard's house the night before they found him dead. Howard had berated me. He was awful, telling me I would never be an actor. That I was just another pretty face. That he'd met hundreds of girls just like me and couldn't remember the name of a single one of them and that I would disappear into the mist of humanity just like the others."

Rae Rae tilted her head. "I'm sorry, Marlee. Don't believe a word he said. It's a tough business, but you keep tryin', sweetheart. Howard was an old fool."

"Did you see Jim go into Howard's house?" asked Camille.

"No. He stepped up out of the darkness like he'd been lingering outside, and he told Howard he was a vicious old has-been. Then he asked, 'Where's Lucy? What did you do with Lucy?'"

"Who's Lucy?" asked Finch.

Rae Rae stuffed a miniature cupcake into her mouth and diverted her gaze. Did she know something about Lucy?

"I have no idea. Howard was stoned or drunk or something. He wouldn't have known who his own mother was. Jim unlocked the door for him, and when Howard was inside, Jim and I walked over to Hair of the Dog. He was so nice to me. I was bawling. We had a drink and then came back to the inn."

Finch frowned. "I'm no lawyer, but that's hardly a reason to arrest him."

"Maybe he was checking up on Marlee," suggested Rae Rae.

"I don't think so," said Marlee. "I had been there awhile. It was the evening Howard invited Camille and me to come over to his house. When I got there, no one answered the door. I thought maybe he was on his way. Running late?"

Camille smiled at her sadly. "You are a true optimist."

"He invited us! I thought he'd be there," Marlee protested.

"Did you tell the cop all this?" asked Finch.

Marlee licked her lips nervously. "Yes, but there's more."

Finch rubbed his forehead.

"When I came back to the inn, you guys began playing

poker. I hung around my room for a couple of hours, but I was still so upset. I left my room, and when I started down the stairs, I saw Jim leave through the front door . . . without Pippin."

"That doesn't mean anything." Finch shrugged. "Each of us has gone out and about without the others. If he's been taken to the police station for questioning because of that, then they're just fishing and hoping he'll say something that incriminates him."

Camille spoke quietly. "You don't suppose he actually murdered Howard? It *is* somewhat suspicious that he emerged from the darkness like he was lurking around waiting for an opportunity to accost Howard. And do you remember them in the bar the first night we were here? Jim was really angry with Howard."

"That's right," mused Finch. "I forgot about that. Jim was insulted at the bar when Howard treated him like a lackey. What did Jim say? 'I am not your personal servant.' Something like that."

Pippin whined. Everyone turned to look at him.

"He knows Jim is in trouble," said Zelda.

I suspected it wouldn't be difficult for a dog to pick up on the tension in the room. They all probably realized that something was up.

"I suggest that we stick together," said Finch. "If we leave the inn with one another, we'll have witnesses who knew where we were and what we did."

"The buddy system!" Camille grinned. "I love that. Just like camp."

Rae Rae smiled wryly. "Finch, sugar, I fear the time for that kind of precaution has passed. Unless, of course, you expect someone else to turn up dead."

# Twenty-Six

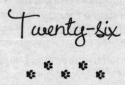

"That was just plain wicked," exclaimed Camille. Her eyes narrowed as she gazed at Rae Rae. "After
all, if I'm not mistaken, you're the only person in this entire
town who knew both of the victims."

Her sentence hung over us like a dark fog. It was true. As
much as I liked Rae Rae, I had to admit that if I were Dave,
I would be taking a hard look at her and her whereabouts
when the murders took place.

In spite of Camille's pointed accusation, Rae Rae re-
mained calm. "An astute and most likely accurate statement.
But I didn't murder anyone. What I'd still like to know is who
Lucy is. *That* might lead us somewhere."

At that moment, I truly missed Holmes. It would be nice
to have my old friend around to talk to. Holmes would undoubtedly tell me to concentrate on known facts.

Pippin's entourage broke up at that point and went their
separate ways.

Finch paused to ask, "Should I take Pippin?"

"Thanks. That's nice of you. But he's no trouble. He can hang with Trixie and me."

I did notice that Camille stayed back waiting for Finch. They walked away together.

Zelda cleared the dishes while Mr. Huckle and I put away the tables.

"Mr. Huckle, did you ever hear anything about Diane having an admirer?" I asked.

"She was a most attractive woman. I'm sure she must have had many admirers in her life."

"I meant here, in Wagtail."

His mouth twitched with a hint of a grin. "You know I don't gossip."

"Someone murdered her, Mr. Huckle. It isn't gossip anymore. Rumors could lead to her killer."

"Well, when you put it that way . . . I did hear someone speculating that she may have been a very close friend of Mr. LaRue."

I nearly dropped my end of the table. "Nooooo!"

"That was the scuttlebutt."

"But she was so refined and he's so"—I searched for a word that could describe him—"rustic."

"He's unusual but most intelligent. I must say that I quite enjoy his company. And he's an excellent cook."

"When are you in his company?"

"Not nearly so often as I should like. He's very well-read. And knowledgeable about the stars and ancient people. All around a fascinating fellow."

I still couldn't imagine Diane being interested in him. But sometimes people were attracted to each other for reasons that weren't immediately obvious. I wondered if Dave and Oma had known about Diane's relationship with LaRue. Perhaps that was the reason they had seemed reluctant to say much about him.

Mr. Huckle and Zelda went home, and Oma went out to

run a quick errand, leaving me to watch the inn. I felt a little like the Pied Piper with four dogs following me around. They ran ahead of me to the main lobby, and I thought it was lucky that Pippin and Stella had been spending so much time with Trixie and Gingersnap. The two of them probably felt much more secure with their new pack. If they had been alone, this would have been a more difficult time for them.

I found Rae Rae sitting on the terrace by herself watching a sailboat glide by on the lake. The dogs surrounded her and brought a smile to her face. She leaned forward in her chair and stroked each of them.

"Could you use some company, or would you like to be alone?" I asked.

"By all means, please, join me."

Rae Rae had changed for dinner. She wore a white dress adorned with chunky rhinestones along the neckline. "I was just sitting here thinking that Jim seems like such a fine young man. I never would have pegged him as a murderer. It's sort of mind-boggling. One minute I'm having a grand time with him out on the lake, laughing and water-skiing, and all the while he might have been planning another murder, for all we know." She looked over at me. "Do you know what they have on him? DNA evidence? Witnesses?"

"I don't have any idea. But it does appear that he may have known Diane. He paid her a visit the day you arrived."

Rae Rae stared at me. "I don't know what to think. Of course, that alone doesn't mean he killed her. How could he know her? Does this mean he killed both Diane and Howard?"

"Who knows? Dave must have something on him."

"I should be thankful it was Jim who was taken in for questioning and not me. I thought for sure I would be the prime suspect." Rae Rae studied her manicure. "You know, I'm going to miss having Jim around." She stood up. "If you'll excuse me, I'm off to meet Donna." She shook her head. "I'd have bet Marlee was the killer."

I enjoyed the cool evening air for a bit before going to the private kitchen to rustle up some dinner. To my surprise, Oma was there, looking happier than she had in days.

"Holly, could you take this up to Mr. Mason's cabin?" She pointed to a large insulated package.

"Sure. Is he ill?"

"Actually, I think he's quite well. But he doesn't cook much. And take all the dogs with you. I would like people to see that we are not afraid they will be stolen. Ja?"

"Who wants to go for a ride?" I asked enthusiastically.

All tails wagged and Gingersnap barked. I hoped no guests were around, because they romped through the hallway and out to the golf carts like they thought they were going to a dog park. I secured the package on a large golf cart, and they hopped in with panting smiley faces.

We drew a good bit of attention as I drove through the streets of Wagtail. Oma would be pleased about that. People waved at us, and a few dogs yipped greetings. We left Wagtail behind and began the slow ride up the mountain but away from the location of Pippin's Treasure Hunt. People and houses became scarce. Most of the cabins were on sizable lots for privacy and the enjoyment of nature.

When I pulled up to Mr. Mason's A-frame, flames blazed in a square outdoor firepit constructed of stone. Several rustic chairs surrounded it, but Mr. Mason wasn't outside.

The dogs hopped out, and all of them, except for Pippin, made a beeline to the cabin door as though they thought they would be rewarded with treats.

The door opened and they shot inside.

I hoped they hadn't knocked him over! Mr. Mason had to be in his eighties. I ran to the doorway and found Holmes on the floor with Gingersnap, Trixie, and Stella whining and vying for his attention. "Holmes? What are you doing here?"

He grinned as the dogs waggled and licked his face. "Hiding from Sugar McLaughlin."

"I brought food for Mr. Mason . . ." As I gazed around, I realized that Mr. Mason's furniture was gone.

Holmes scrambled to his feet and planted a big kiss on me. I tingled straight down to my toes. "I can't believe you're finally here!"

Still holding me in his arms, he said, "Mr. Mason moved into the town of Wagtail. He knew I was planning to come back here, so he wrote me and asked if I wanted to buy his cabin. What do you think?"

"I think it's great! But you could let a girl know you were coming."

He brushed back the sandy hair that waved in his face and chuckled.

Oh no. Oma and Holmes's grandmother were best friends, and they had been trying their best to throw us together. "Our grandmothers set us up again."

He laughed. "They set you up. I was expecting you."

"Apparently, I brought dinner for us."

"Is that Pippin?" he asked, releasing me to hold his hand out to Pippin.

"That's the real Pippin. Not a knockoff or a look-alike. I'm, uh, taking care of him for the moment."

Holmes carried the food outside to a table next to the firepit. He opened it and whistled. "There are even cocktails in here! And dinner for the dogs, in bowls and ready to be served."

Over watermelon coolers, shrimp crostini, London broil, herbed Dijon potato salad, and cheesecake squares, I told him everything about the stolen dogs, the murders, and the guy who tried to take Trixie. The only thing I didn't mention was Sugar McLaughlin's criminal history. In the first place, I wanted to confirm it with Dave before I mentioned it to anyone else. In the second place, I didn't want to be the woman who spread the details of Sugar's less-than-stellar past. Holmes would probably find out about it sooner or later. It had nothing to do with the murders or the missing dogs. Unless . . . Sugar and Stan were stealing dogs to sell them. Could *they* be the dognapping ring? Could Stan be so heartless that he would sell his own mother's beloved dog?

"Holly?"

"Hmm? Oh, sorry. I got distracted."

"Let me see if I have this straight. Rae Rae was the only person who admitted to knowing both of the murder victims. And she had a motive, although it's a very old grudge. Jim was seen arguing with Howard, was sneaking around outside his house the night Howard died, and paid Diane a visit on arriving in Wagtail, but you don't know any reason he would kill Diane."

"But Dave took him to Snowball for questioning. He must be on to something that I don't know about."

"And, of course," said Holmes, "the two murders don't have to be related. It could be that Jim killed Howard and someone local murdered Diane."

"Holmes, what do you know about LaRue?"

Holmes perked up. "He's the coolest guy ever. He never hangs around in town, but he's very interesting to talk to. There are all kinds of rumors about him, but I think most of them are the result of imaginations running wild."

"Like what?"

"That he's wanted for some heinous crime and is hiding out from the authorities here. Or that he's the leader of an online cult. There are people who think he's in the Federal Witness Protection Program because he testified against some Mafia types."

"What you're saying is that no one knows."

"Pretty much."

"I suspect Dave and Oma know. They're very close-mouthed about him. Any chance he was seeing Diane?"

Holmes nearly spilled his drink. "If there's one thing I have learned in this life, it's that the oddest people are often attracted to each other."

"I gather you never heard any rumors to that end?"

"Nope. Can't say I did. I'm guessing from these questions that you don't think this Jim murdered Diane?" Holmes asked.

"I don't know. Why did he go to see her? Why was Stella with Diane when we found her? Did the attacker mean to steal Stella but she got away?" I paused and reflected. "Jim is very good to Pippin."

Pippin raised his head and looked at me.

"You're being a very good boy, Pippin. It's not as though people who are kind to animals can't murder a person. But as you say, maybe someone else killed Diane, and Jim was somehow outraged by Howard and lost it. It's getting late. I'd better get back to the inn."

"Holly? Would you do me a favor and not tell anyone where I'm living?"

"Sure." That was odd. "Are *you* in the witness protection program?"

He laughed. "I need to be in the Sugar McLaughlin protection program. If she finds out this is where I'm living, she'll be hanging out at my doorstep day and night. While I was in Chicago, she drove my parents nuts by sticking around their house."

He was probably right. "If she sees you in town, she'll follow you out here."

Holmes chuckled. "Should we bet on how long it will be before she discovers where I live?"

I laughed aloud. "Okay. Loser buys dinner at the Blue Boar. And I bet she knows where you live in the next twenty-four hours."

"Oh, come on. I'm smarter than that. You don't think I can fool her for at least a week?"

"Why don't you just tell her you're not interested?" I asked.

"Hah! You think I haven't done that? Sugar does *not* listen."

"I heard she used to date Stan Hoover. Maybe we can get them back together again."

"Or maybe she'll be attracted to that new doctor, Engelknecht. A doctor is a million times better than an unemployed architect."

"I won't say a word about your new house, but I will enjoy that dinner at the Blue Boar." I gave him a big smooch that was long enough for the dogs to start pawing us to get our attention.

"Come on, you guys. Let's head back."

The four dogs hopped on the golf cart. I waved at Holmes as I drove away.

It was past midnight, and we had the tiny mountain road all to ourselves. I could hear a great horned owl calling, "Hoo hoo hooooo." It must have upset Stella, because she barked and leaped out of the moving golf cart!

I hit the brakes and yelled, "Stella!"

She stood at the side of the road, holding her head high, as if she were listening.

"Honey, it's just an owl."

But then I heard it, too. And it wasn't an owl.

# Twenty-seven

❧ ❧ ❧ ❧

Very faint high-pitched yapping came from somewhere. It didn't stop.

Stella ran along the road, turned to the right, and waited. After a moment, she trotted back to the golf cart and barked at us insistently. In a heartbeat, Gingersnap, Pippin, and Trixie flew off the golf cart. In the beam of the headlights, I saw Stella lead the way with the others chasing after her. They vanished from my line of sight.

I followed them in the golf cart. The headlights exposed an unpaved lane to the right. I turned and could make out the dogs running ahead in the distance. They disappeared when they rounded a bend, but when I caught up, I could see Trixie's white fur as she raced along a stretch through the woods. I was getting a little nervous about being in an isolated spot. But no matter how much I called them, the dogs were on a mission and refused to stop.

The lights on the golf cart finally fell on a small log cabin with a rustic porch and a stone chimney. I switched off the golf cart lights in case someone was home. But the truth was that the dog with the piercing bark had probably already awakened the residents. No one could sleep through that racket.

A bluish light flickered in one window. I suspected it was a TV set. Either someone was up or had fallen asleep watching TV.

I needed to get the dogs back on the golf cart and out of there before someone saw us!

Still, no lights turned on. And then, to my horror, I was close enough to see Stella slam her paw through a window screen and rip it open.

"Stella!" I hissed. "Come!"

But a tiny Yorkie came to me instead, followed by a Scottie. The Yorkie had stopped yapping and raced to me like I was her best friend. Both of the dogs hopped onto the golf cart as though they had been expecting me to pick them up. They had to be the missing Dolly and Tavish.

Panic set in. I held my breath, hoping the door of the cabin wouldn't open. All I could think of at that moment was getting out of there as fast as I could. Especially before the people in the cabin realized that the dogs were gone.

Happily, the other dogs followed Dolly and Tavish to the golf cart. It was crowded, but they all fit in. I turned it around in the dark and didn't flick on the lights until we hit the tiny road. I hauled down the mountain as fast as I could possibly go.

I sagged with relief when we drove into the town of Wagtail. As far as I knew, no one had seen me or was following us. But what to do with the dogs? Should I take them to their homes? Should I call Dave and wake him? Should I take them all back to the inn and deal with the logistics in the morning?

The latter would be the most sensible, but if it were Trixie who had been missing, I would have wanted her back in my arms immediately. And there was one other thing to consider. Dave might want the advantage of surprise if he was going to pay the house a visit. By morning, the dognappers would realize Dolly and Tavish were gone, and they might get out of town themselves. I phoned Dave.

His voice was groggy when he answered the phone. "Please tell me that Trixie didn't find another corpse."

"Nope. But Stella found the stolen dogs."

"What?" He no longer sounded groggy.

"Should I take them to their owners, or do you need to see them?"

"Wait a minute. Where were they?"

"In a cabin way off the road that goes up to Mr. Mason's cabin. I'll meet you at Clara's house."

"No. Take the dogs to the inn and secure them. I'll call for backup and meet you outside of Hair of the Dog."

"Okay." I hung up and steered toward the inn. When I parked, I expected them to run in every which direction. After all, Tavish and Dolly would be eager to go home. But either some kind of pack mentality set in or they were exhausted, because they all followed me up the stairs to the porch and inside the inn.

Twinkletoes leaped to the top of the desk at the sight of the dogs.

I ran my hand over her head.

Pippin raced to the Dogwood Room. I hurried over to see what was going on.

Jim sat up and rubbed his eyes. "Pippin!"

Pippin waggled like crazy and licked Jim's face.

Jim hugged Pippin. "Where have you been, Pippin? I was worried about you!"

"I'm glad to see you back. Did everything go okay?" I asked.

Jim sighed and ruffled the fur on Pippin's head. "As well

as it could, I guess. I hope they find the killer soon so I'll
be off the hook."

I had so many questions. But I needed to meet Dave and
didn't have time to chat. "Well, I know you'll sleep better
now that Pippin is home."

I started up the grand staircase, calling the dogs and
Twinkletoes. I feared tiny Dolly might have trouble with the
stairs, but she soared up them like the bigger dogs. Once
they were safely in my apartment, I took care to close the
dog door so no one would escape. I put down fresh water for
them. I had no idea when Dolly and Tavish had last eaten,
though now that I saw them up close they seemed to be in
pretty good shape. Still, I took a few minutes to feed them
all a midnight snack. They settled down, and I suspected
they would all be asleep shortly.

Twinkletoes didn't seem to mind that Stella, Dolly, Tavish, and Gingersnap were spending the night with us. When
the dogs were settled in our apartment, Twinkletoes roamed,
sniffing each dog discreetly. It was as though she tiptoed
among them. Either they didn't notice, or they were so
worn-out that they didn't care.

I quietly slipped away and locked the door.


Hair of the Dog, a popular bar and café, was
closing by the time I arrived. It stayed open later than any
other bar in town. Dave was waiting by the road along with
two police four-wheelers.

I stopped the golf cart, and he hopped in. "Let's go."

I headed up the mountain again. The four-wheelers followed us.

"What have you got on Jim?" I asked.

Dave was silent. For a moment I thought he wasn't going
to answer my question.

"There was a piece of paper on Howard's leg—"

"I saw it. On his thigh."

"Did you handle it?"

"No."

"It had Jim's name written on it. We have a handwriting expert checking it out, but that will take a while. Preliminary indications are that Howard wrote it."

I hadn't expected that and didn't know quite what to make of it. "So Howard wrote Jim's name on a slip of paper. That's not exactly a smoking gun. He arrived with Jim."

"True. I hoped Jim might be able to tell me what that slip of paper was about."

"And?" I asked.

"He seemed clueless. If he knew anything about it, he did a good job of pretending that he didn't."

"You're not thinking that Howard scribbled the name of his killer as he lay dying?"

"Stranger things have happened. It's something I have to consider."

I didn't like that at all. It was possible, I supposed. "Was the paper torn? It looked like a scrap to me."

"Yes."

"Don't you find that significant?"

"In what way?" asked Dave.

"I'm not sure. When do you write something on a piece of paper you've torn? When you don't have anything to write on. When someone needs the other portion of the paper."

"Hmm." Dave sounded unimpressed. "How did you find the dogs?"

"It's so quiet out here at night. I thought Stella was listening to the owls hoot. Suddenly, she jumped off the golf cart, and then I could hear Dolly. It was faint, so faint, I guess because the cabin is set so far back off the road. Even though I've been listening for dogs, I'm not sure I'd have thought anything of it. But Stella was determined. She even tore a window screen with her paw. And they came running out."

"Do you know whose cabin it was?"

"Not a clue. I didn't even know it was there."

"What were you doing up there this time of night anyway?" he asked.

"Visiting a friend."

"Does your friend have a name?"

"Why does that matter?"

"Why are you being evasive?"

"I just went to visit someone, Dave. It was no big deal. Okay, here's the drive that leads to the house."

"Pull over."

I steered the golf cart to the side of the road.

Dave looked at me. "I want you to go home. There's nothing you can do here. These guys might be armed, and I don't want you anywhere nearby. Not even here on the road, because someone could come tearing out or drive in. They could be on foot or in a vehicle. I honestly don't know what to expect, and I don't want to worry about you. Go home."

He hopped off the golf cart. "Thanks for showing us where it is. Now get going."

I was certain he thought I'd stick around, but the truth was that I didn't want to be there. I understood that I would be in the way and could even make their job harder. "Hey, Dave."

He turned to look at me.

"Stay safe."

He smiled, and I took off down the mountain, glad that I wasn't armed and walking into a house of dognappers.

I expected a chaotic greeting when I returned, but the dogs were so pooped, they barely stirred. Trixie yawned and followed me into the bedroom, where Twinkletoes was already curled up on the bed.

In the morning, after a shower, I stood in my walk-in closet and told myself that Holmes's return to town had nothing to do with the fact that I was eyeing a green-and-white-striped sundress instead of my usual jeans or skort. Taking a deep breath, I stepped into it, zipped it up, and slid my feet into white sandals. After all, I would be bringing Dolly and Tavish home this morning. I should be dressed appropriately.

I walked down the grand staircase with a pack of five dogs and one cat leading the way. Gingersnap showed the canine guests out to the doggy potty and back to the dining room, where they received a round of applause from Oma, Shelley, Zelda, and Mr. Huckle.

Shelley brought out a tray of dog breakfasts. It looked like barley, lentils, carrots, and cubed chicken breast topped with a fried egg.

"I hope you don't mind that we fed them first," Shelley said to me.

"I'm glad you did. They've been so good. I could use a mug of hot tea, please. And their fried eggs look delicious." I plopped down at the table where Oma and Zelda sat.

"You had quite a night." Oma smiled at me. "I can't believe that you found Dolly and Tavish!"

"Stella gets all the credit. You know, I think she recognized Dolly's bark. She was determined to get her out of there."

"She probably did recognize Dolly," said Zelda. "They were neighbors. I'm sure they knew each other. Stella must have heard Dolly bark every day."

"In fact," I said, "I think Dave should take another look at the torn screen in Diane's house. It seemed sort of odd, and

I think the assumption was that a person went through it, but it was child-sized. A guy like Jim, for instance, couldn't have entered that way. After Stella's performance last night, I suspect she has put her paw through a screen before. I wonder if she was locked inside the house and tore the screen to get out and follow Diane."

"She was dedicated to Diane. Poor baby," said Oma. "Dave called me early this morning. He wants to go with you when you take Dolly and Tavish home."

"I wanted to take them home last night. Did Dave say who they found in the house?"

"It was empty."

"You're kidding! I thought there was a TV on. Maybe the dognappers left when they saw that the dogs were gone?"

"He said it looks like a rental house. It was ready for use with the towels folded and the beds made. No one was there."

Shelley delivered my tea with a platter of fried eggs, home fries, bacon, toast, and a bowl of fresh fruit salad. "You deserve it. We're all so happy the pups have been found."

"I can't eat all this," I protested.

Zelda reached over and plucked a home fry off my plate. "I'll help you."

I sipped my tea. "Oma, that doesn't make any sense. If you were a dognapper, wouldn't you stay with the dogs? Why would you keep them in an unoccupied cabin?"

"To hide them," said Zelda. "The dognappers are probably staying in town where people would have heard the dogs barking."

"So they randomly found a cabin way back in the woods and kept them there while . . . what?" I asked. "While they looked for more dogs to steal?"

"Why are you surprised, Holly?" asked Oma.

"I guess I thought dognappers would put them in cages, or drug them so they wouldn't bark. Or at least stay with them."

"Perhaps Dave will have a fresh perspective. He must be exhausted," said Oma. "I can't believe how much happened while I slept. I'm so relieved. Finally, everyone is back home where they belong." Oma winked at me as she stood up. She gave me a hug. "Now, if you can solve the murders, Wagtail will be our lovely, peaceful little town again."

"Me?" I watched her walk away.

"What was that about?" asked Zelda.

I didn't want to say anything about Holmes being back, so I changed the subject in a hurry. "You should have seen Pippin last night when we came home. He was so happy to find Jim asleep in the Dogwood Room."

Zelda leaned closer, but I wasn't sure if it was to speak in a low voice or to help herself to more home fries. "Do you think Jim murdered them?"

I shrugged. "He seems like a nice guy. Dave must have had some reason to want to question him at police head-quarters. But he let him go. I guess that's good news."

After breakfast, I phoned Dave about returning Dolly and Tavish to their homes. He agreed to meet me at Clara's house.

Gingersnap stayed at the inn, but Stella and Trixie came along with me. It was probably silly of me, but I thought Stella should know where they went since she was the one who knew they were in the wrong place and rescued them.

# Twenty-eight

❁  ❁  ❁

I drove to Clara's cottage and parked in front of it.

Tavish knew he was home. He whined and hopped off the golf cart, ran to the gate, and pawed at it, eager to see Clara.

When I opened the gate for him, he zoomed to the front door and barked.

A bleary-eyed Clara, dressed in a blue flannel bathrobe, opened the door. "Tavish!"

There was no mistaking the joy in both their hearts at the reunion. Tears streamed down Clara's face. She sat down on her door stoop and cuddled Tavish. "I was afraid I would never see you again!"

The other dogs had followed Tavish and were investigating every inch of his yard.

Dave arrived on the run. He panted and rested at the gate for a moment, watching Clara and Tavish. He walked in slowly and whispered to me, "We'll talk. Don't tell Clara anything."

"Where did you find him?" Clara asked.

Oh swell. Why did I have to keep secrets? I dodged her question. "Stella found him."

"Stella? Come here, darlin'." Clara held her hand out to Stella, who readily went to her. "I'm going to buy you the biggest steak I can find!"

"You're certain this is Tavish?" asked Dave.

I gaped at him. Did he think I was cruising around picking up dogs at random?

"I just want to be sure," he muttered. "I don't need a phone call from someone missing a dog that looks like Tavish."

"He ran to his gate," I said. "He knew perfectly well that this is his home."

"There's no question in my mind, Officer Dave." Clara's smile said it all.

I called the dogs and made sure the gate was securely closed behind us.

"Want a ride over to the Hoovers' place?" I asked.

"There's not much room."

"There is if Trixie or Dolly sits in your lap."

He grumbled, but we all managed to squeeze onto the bench seats.

"Oma says no one was in the cabin."

"It's a rental and it was ready to go. The TV was on, and someone had left the windows open, probably so the dogs would get some air. The fridge was empty. There was no luggage or food, not even dog food. I don't know what to make of it."

"Had they broken in?"

"Not that we could see."

"Are you checking for fingerprints?" I asked.

He gave me an incredulous look. "Are you kidding? I know how to do my job. But it will take a while to get results."

I pulled up in front of the Hoovers' house and parked. Little Dolly announced her arrival at the top of her lungs, barking all the way from the street to her house. The front door of the brick rambler opened. Augie stepped outside and bent over to scoop up Dolly.

Glenda appeared right behind him. He turned and handed Dolly to her. Glenda's mouth dropped open. She clutched Dolly close to her and sank to the ground. "My baby! Where were you, sweetie pie?"

While they were fussing over her, I watched as Stella walked slowly toward Diane's house. She stood outside and looked at her home. If ever a dog wore a melancholy expression, it was Stella.

I could hear the other boxers barking inside. Dolly's exuberant yipping had probably set them off.

"I'd better go assure Donna that everything is okay," I said to Dave.

Stella walked to the front door with me. I rang the bell and shouted, "Donna, it's Holly. I brought Dolly home."

Donna opened the door. Mussed hair suggested she had been asleep. "What's going on?"

Stella walked right past her to join her old friends.

"We brought the missing Yorkie home to the Hoovers next door. I'm sorry she was so barky."

"You found her? That's wonderful! I don't mind being awakened for a happy occasion like that. I shouldn't have been asleep anyway. I was up late going through Diane's things. I found her will. She appointed me to find a person for Stella. And she named a couple of breeders who might be interested in taking some of the other dogs. So if you have any ideas about who might like Stella, please let me know. It might not be easy to find someone. Diane was very specific. Stella is to be an only dog. She must live indoors. No kennels. No crates. This isn't going to be easy!"

Stella returned to the doorway and politely looked up at Donna, who patted her. "Hi, Stella. We'll find you a good home. I promise."

And then Stella walked across the lawn and jumped into the golf cart. I wished Zelda were there to tell us what Stella was thinking.

"She knows Diane is gone," said Donna.

I had a feeling she was right. I said good-bye and walked across the driveways and grass to the Hoovers' house. A golf cart with a trailer behind it was parked in their driveway.

Stan had emerged from the front door in shorts and an old T-shirt. He rubbed his eyes as though he'd just rolled out of bed.

"About time you got up," muttered Augie.

"Dolly!" Stan ignored his father and reached for the dog. Glenda seemed reluctant to hand Dolly over to him.

Augie clapped me on my back. "We're so grateful to you."

I waved my hands in protest. "Stella gets all the credit. I'm just glad that Dolly is home and healthy."

When I returned to my golf cart, Dave was sitting in it, talking on his phone. Or, more correctly, listening to someone talk on the phone. Lack of sleep showed on Dave's face. He had taken the time to shave, but his eyelids hung heavy. No wonder he'd been testy with me.

He ended the conversation and hung up. "Mind giving me a ride to the inn? I need to talk with your grandmother."

"I'd be happy to give you a lift." I started the golf cart and steered toward the inn. "Any chance you can grab a nap?"

He nodded. "Looks like it. I still need to find the dog-napper, though. That's a funny word, isn't it? It sounds like someone who's napping like a dog."

At least he still had a sense of humor. When we arrived at the inn, he beckoned to me to join him in the office.

Oma looked up from her work.

"Zelda," called Dave. "You come in here, too."

I settled on the sofa, surrounded by dogs. Trixie must have been feeling neglected, because she jumped up into my lap.

"Our Dr. Engelknecht has been busy," said Dave. "The presence of fentanyl in Wagtail was of particular concern to him, because it takes such a tiny amount to kill someone. Other localities have had multiple deaths in a short period of time, and he wanted to prevent that. Apparently, it's showing up elsewhere mixed with other illicit drugs, so people don't realize they're taking it. They think they're taking heroin or cocaine, but it's mixed with fentanyl, and they die from an overdose."

Dave paused and appeared to collect his thoughts. "The fentanyl in Diane's system was compared with that in Howard's body, and they appear to have come from the same batch. That leaves us with a couple of possibilities. Obviously, Howard and Diane could have bought it from the same dealer and ingested it."

"But Diane was not a drug user," protested Oma.

"Exactly. I'm going to tell you this just the way the chief told me. There was no sign of forced entry into Diane's house or Howard's rental house. The chief's theory is that Howard visited Diane. She knew him and voluntarily invited him in. They reminisced or argued, maybe even partied together. She took the fentanyl on purpose to try it, or he surreptitiously added the fentanyl to her food. When she died, he panicked. He cleaned up the kitchen to hide evidence, loaded her onto a golf cart, drove her up the mountain, and dumped her body."

"Where did he get the golf cart?" asked Oma.

"One came with the house he's renting. The following day, Howard came here and made a scene about being the next to be murdered."

Zelda and I nodded our heads. We wouldn't soon forget that!

"He drank very heavily during the evening. Several people have confirmed this to me, including a bartender who was pouring him drinks. He went back to his rental house, partook of the fentanyl, and died. There were items among his belongings that have the slightest bit of fentanyl dust on them. It appears he brought it with him, hidden in his luggage as baby powder. But no appreciable amount seems to remain."

We sat silently, taking it all in.

"Hey, Zelda, I was up all night. I could really use a cup of coffee."

"Sure thing, Dave." She rose and left the room.

Dave closed the door.

Oma's eyebrows rose. "Do you believe this is what happened?"

Dave winced. "No. But it's what the chief believes, and it's the official story. I wanted Zelda to hear, because she'll spread it around. *If* there's any fentanyl still being sold, maybe that will scare people and stop them from buying drugs in Wagtail."

"So you think someone might still be selling this stuff here?" I asked.

"It's possible. But here's an interesting twist. Your guest, Jim McGowen, had a packet of the same batch of fentanyl in the tan bag he carries. And we know for a fact that he visited Diane and Howard shortly before they died."

Even though I knew Dave had information on Jim, I was shocked. I hadn't expected anything like this. I was fond of Jim, and it made me sad to think he could be the murderer.

Oma gasped. "Then he must be the dealer."

"Not necessarily," said Dave. "He claims he doesn't use drugs. He was willing to be tested, and everything has come back negative. On top of that, his fingerprints were not on the little bag containing the drug."

"Either he wore gloves, or someone else stuck it in there?" I guessed.

"Those are definitely possibilities. Unfortunately, he has been surrounded by people constantly. Anyone could have slid it into his bag. He also confessed a rather interesting story about Howard. See if he'll tell you. I've been in contact with the police in Los Angeles to follow up."

"Did it involve someone named Lucy?" I asked.

"You knew about it and didn't tell me?"

"No. Marlee said he was asking Howard about a Lucy."

Oma blinked and leaned forward toward Dave. "You have sent Zelda out of the room so she will not blab this, ja?"

"Ja."

"And what you are saying is that the case is closed. Officially, it is over. But *you* think there is still a killer among us."

# Twenty-nine

"That's exactly right, Liesel. The chief is a smart guy. His theory isn't implausible. We know that Howard visited Diane. We know that Howard had the drugs. We know that there was no physical violence. But it doesn't sit right with me."

"Me, either," I said. "I can believe that Howard was callous enough to drug Diane. But he'd been in Wagtail less than twelve hours at that point. I guess I can imagine him partying with an old friend, and I can understand the panic. If he was partaking of the drug, maybe he wasn't able to help her or call for help."

"All possible," Dave agreed.

"I didn't know Howard well, but I sure have heard a lot about him. And what I don't think he would have done is drag Diane out to a golf cart, drive her up the mountain, and dump her body. If he sobered up and found that she was dead, he might have cleaned up in a panic. He might have wiped his fingerprints, but I think he would have left her in her house. He strikes me as a hands-off kind of guy. He pays people to do things for him. He doesn't do things himself."

Oma tapped her fingers on her desk. "Two accidental deaths from the same drug. If Howard was the one who brought fentanyl to Wagtail, why would Howard place it in Jim's bag? Did he harbor some kind of anger toward Jim?" asked Oma. "Something is not right with this story."

"What about Mr. Finkelstein's golf cart?" I asked. "If Howard took an overdose accidentally or intentionally, then who stole Mr. Finkelstein's golf cart?"

"One of many questions that remain unanswered." Dave took a deep breath. "It's possible that it wasn't related to Howard's death at all."

"Has it been found yet?" I asked.

"It was abandoned down by the lake. The theory is that some kids were probably joyriding. But back to Liesel's point, if Jim's story about Lucy is true, Howard might have wanted to get rid of him. Ladies, I would appreciate it if you kept a lid on this. Obviously, I can't go around openly investigating a closed case. And I certainly don't want to upset my boss or get in trouble because of this."

"But you're going to investigate anyway?" I asked.

"I did not say that." He cast a glance at me. "The case is closed."

Zelda opened the door and brought coffee for all of us, along with a tray full of savory sandwiches and sweet pastries.

"Wow. I didn't expect this." Dave guzzled the coffee. "Thanks, Zelda."

"This leaves us then with the matter of the dognapper." Oma picked up a chicken salad sandwich.

"I'm still working on that. In fact, I'm in the process of something that might help us develop leads."

# Thirty

Zelda stopped nibbling on an egg salad sandwich. "What is it?"

Dave grinned. "Can't say just yet." He promptly chowed down on a sandwich.

I had a few ideas of my own that I wanted to follow up on. I'd had an enormous breakfast, so when I finished my coffee, I excused myself.

As soon as I stood up, Trixie jumped to her feet and watched me expectantly. Stella, however, seemed content to stay with Oma and Gingersnap. Trixie accompanied me on my rounds through the inn.

I discovered Finch on the window seat in the tiny inn library. "Are you hiding out?"

"No. I'm waiting for Camille and Pippin." He winced. "Do you think Jim murdered Howard?"

I sat down on the window seat. "What do you think?"

"He's a nice guy. I can see hanging out with him when

we go home." Finch's eyes narrowed. "Has he told you that he thinks someone is following him?"

"That's news to me. How can he tell? When Pippin is with him there's always a crowd around him."

Finch rubbed his beard. "I've been watching him at bars when we go out at night. He was always hounding Howard."

"What do you mean?"

"Howard would change seats to get away from Jim, and Jim would move so he was in Howard's line of sight. It was a little creepy."

"But you still want to be friends with him."

"He only acted that way around Howard. The rest of the time he's a lot of fun. You . . . you don't think he'd kill one of us?"

I smiled at him. "I'm not certain that he murdered anyone."

I left Finch to his thoughts in the library and hustled out the front door before anyone else could waylay me.

My first stop wasn't official inn business. I popped into Pierce Real Estate. They carried the largest selection of rental homes in and around Wagtail. I thought it likely that they managed the house where Dolly and Tavish had been kept. Some residents had rental homes that they handled themselves, but many of the owners resided elsewhere and used Pierce to take care of their properties.

Nancy Friedman's corgi greeted us at the door. "Hi, Clover." I would have patted him, but he was far more interested in Trixie.

Nancy, a tall blonde, laughed at our dogs. "Have you noticed that the dogs who live in Wagtail have their own little social group? I'm not sure they care about us at all!"

I didn't plan to fudge or skirt the law, even though I suspected that Nancy couldn't answer everything I wanted to ask. I got right to the point. "Can you tell me who owns the cabin where Dolly and Tavish were found?"

"Wasn't that the strangest thing?" Nancy's eyes opened wide. "I'm so glad they're home. I've been watching Clover very carefully. And yes, I can tell you. It's public record anyway. It's owned by George and Frieda Popolov. They live somewhere in New Jersey, and as far as I can tell from our records, they haven't been here since last fall. Owners have to tell us when they're coming so we won't rent out the cabins during that time. Their cabin has been rented several times since then but not recently. It's a cute place. I always recommend it when people are looking for a lot of privacy."

I tried to sound casual. "Glenda was telling me about the problems you have with people who don't return the keys to the rental properties. We go through the same thing at the inn."

"We've been trying to figure out a better way to handle the issue of the keys. We can't go through the cost of replacing the locks each time guests leave. We're considering instituting a fine equal to the cost of replacing the lock. Maybe that will get their attention!" She lowered her voice to a whisper even though no one else seemed to be there. "Dave was over here first thing this morning asking the same questions. He wanted to know who had rented the cabin and whether the keys were all accounted for. Fortunately, they are. I can't imagine how the dognappers got into the house."

I probably shouldn't tell her that I had no trouble using a credit card to enter the house Howard rented. If the locks on the cabin were anything like those locks, even I could get in. "How about the house Howard rented?" I asked. "Did you get the keys back from the police?"

"Not yet. You won't believe this, but a few people have called about renting it! That grosses me out. It's owned by LaRue. Do you know him? The weird guy who lives in the woods? He decided he's not going to rent it for a while. He's repulsed by the idea that people want it because Howard Hirschtritt died there."

"Ugh. That's sort of sick. Good for LaRue. Instead of making money off Howard's death, he's doing the right thing." I switched her back to the subject of the keys. "So I guess it was other homes that Glenda was making keys for?"

"Probably. She's been checking a lot of the rentals to be sure nothing happened over the winter that we don't know about. Now that we're headed into the summer season, we need to be prepared. Everyone gets a set of two keys. Can I tell you how often someone calls in the middle of the night because they've misplaced *both* of them and they can't get into the house? My husband complains every time it's my turn to answer the calls at night. Invariably, I have to get up and schlep over here for an extra key to let them in."

"What about the keys to the golf carts?" I asked.

"Those are on the same ring as the house keys." She pointed to a pegboard located behind a counter. "Like those."

I didn't get any helpful information from her. But I knew one thing. Either the dognapper was a local who knew about the cabin, or someone from out of town had scoped out Wagtail thoroughly. "Did Dave ask you for a list of the people who rented the private cabin in the last few years?"

Nancy grinned. "Holly, you're beginning to think just like him! I gave him that list this morning."

It was a long shot. But people who had stayed there would have known how isolated it was.

And so would Stan Hoover.

I thanked Nancy and left the building with Trixie. I stood outside, watching people for a minute. Stan came across as a likable fellow, but he clearly had a darker side. His mom had access to tons of rental cabins. Could he have swiped keys from her? Maybe he went to the office with her sometimes and helped himself to keys. I couldn't get around him stealing Dolly, though. Was he angry with his parents? Did he mean to hurt them by taking their little Yorkie? Or was that to throw people off? Did he plan to sell Tavish and miraculously rescue Dolly?

It seemed absurd. I was getting way too far off track.

But as I stood there watching people, I wondered where the gray-eyed man was staying. Was he still in town? The fact that he wanted Trixie didn't mean he was the dognapper, but I had such a bad feeling about him.

I stepped back inside. "Nancy, there's a guy named Wade Holt who claims Trixie is his dog. Is he renting a house from you guys?"

Nancy gasped. "What are you going to do?"

"I've been avoiding him. I haven't seen him recently. I'm hoping he gave up and left town."

Computer keys clicked as she typed. "Wade Holt. Nope, he's not on *our* roster."

"Thanks."

Dave had said that everyone leaves something behind at a murder scene. As far as I knew, they hadn't found anything incriminating. Trixie and I strolled over to Diane's house. I knocked on the front door.

Donna opened it surrounded by boxers. "Holly! I didn't expect to see you again so soon."

"Would you mind if I looked around a little bit? I'm trying to figure out what happened here the night of Diane's death."

"I'm so glad to hear you say that. Come on in." She closed the door behind Trixie, who romped with the boxers. "The chief of police called this morning to inform me that Howard was responsible for Diane's death and probably killed himself, too. It's been a very long time since she was pregnant with his child, so I have some trouble imagining that their feelings about everything that happened would still be so raw that anything as drastic as murder would be necessary. Besides that, one tiny thing keeps coming back to me. It's probably meaningless, but it doesn't quite make sense." She led me into Diane's family room.

A rustic stone fireplace dominated the room. The ceiling was vaulted with exposed mahogany beams. The oversize sofa was a plush brown and looked as though it had gotten a lot of use. A prim Louis XV chair had been upholstered with a soft floral fabric. The room appeared to be a comfortable mishmash of things Diane had loved. A sliding glass door led to the backyard, and a sturdy blue armchair stood below the window with the torn screen.

"What did you find peculiar?" I asked.

"I'm no expert on any of this, of course. But it's my understanding that fentanyl works very fast. So if someone, presumably Howard, poisoned food that she ate, where is the plate?"

"Have you moved anything around?"

"Not a thing. I just have trouble imagining someone taking the time to wash the plate and put it away. Maybe they both had plates, and forks, and glasses or mugs. Would Howard take a serving plate or a box from a bakery with him? It wasn't in her trash."

"Maybe the police collected them?"

"Not according to Dave. They emptied the refrigerator to test the food, but they didn't find anything with brownie residue. No dirty dishes, boxes, or cutlery!"

"That's interesting. I'm not sure what that means. I did think that Howard might have cleaned up in a panic. But maybe it tells us that the killer was someone tidy?"

"And heartless!"

That went without saying. I strode over to the torn window screen. It would have been easy for Stella to jump on the chair, paw the screen, and leap through it. If I was right about that, it meant Stella saw the killer remove Diane's body, but the killer had locked Stella in the house.

"What are you thinking?" asked Donna.

"About Stella. If Diane died in this room, then the easiest way to remove her body would have been through the sliding glass door. But how did the killer manage to do that while keeping Stella inside?"

"But I thought Stella was outside with Diane."

"She was with Diane when we found her. But after seeing Stella tear a screen with her paw to rescue Dolly and Tavish, that's what I suspect happened here."

"Stella is very well-behaved."

"Even so. If someone was dragging Diane outside, I suspect she might have gotten agitated. If I opened the sliding glass door right now, all the dogs would run outside." I pointed to an interior door. "Where does that door go?"

"Into the kitchen."

I opened it. "The killer probably coaxed Stella into the kitchen, closed the door, and dragged Diane's body outside. Then he had to come back inside anyway to lock the sliding glass door. He let Stella back into the family room and left through the front door, which he locked behind him."

"And it was Stella who pawed through the screen and jumped out to be with Diane," said Donna. "I wish I could take Stella. I love that dog."

"Why don't you?"

"I have six cats and a dachshund. It wouldn't be fair to Stella or to them. Besides, Diane requested that Stella be an only dog."

"Too bad. But I can understand that. Would you mind if I stepped outside?"

"Not at all. I'll call the dogs into the kitchen."

It was a perfect example of what the killer had probably done. When the kitchen door closed, Trixie and I stepped outside onto a concrete patio.

Diane must have spent a lot of time in her backyard. Plants were beginning to flourish in pots and flower beds.

A fence enclosed the patio and part of the yard, no doubt so dogs could run and play. I tried to imagine what had happened that night. The killer must have dragged Diane along the concrete toward the gate that opened to her driveway. It was wide enough to have easily pulled Diane through it. If the murderer had parked there, it would have been possible to drag her onto a golf cart. I gazed around. Diane had had plenty of neighbors, including the Hoovers next door, but if it happened around two or three in the morning, it was unlikely that anyone would have noticed.

The Hoovers' driveway ran next to Diane's with a generous twenty-foot swath of grass between them. Their garage probably helped buffer any sounds coming from Diane's house. One of them had already taken their garbage to the street to be picked up the next day. The house seemed peaceful and quiet. I presumed they had all gone to work.

We returned to the family room. I closed the sliding glass door behind us, and Donna let the dogs out of the kitchen.

"Well?" she asked.

"I'm afraid it would have been fairly easy. Zelda, who works at the inn, thinks the murderer was banking on the passage of time. He took Diane up on the mountain to dispose of her body, where he thought it wouldn't be discovered for a long time, if ever. He washed the dishes or took the box that the brownie was in with him and locked the doors. He thought no one would miss her for days. And honestly, if Trixie hadn't found her body, we wouldn't know about the fentanyl, or the brownie, or the dish being cleaned up."

Donna frowned at me. "But the dish is just conjecture, right?"

"He had to bring the brownies in something. It must have been someone she knew. Someone who brought her deadly brownies. Someone Diane invited into her home. She probably offered him a cup of tea."

Donna had turned ashen, and I realized I had been too graphic. "I'm so sorry. I didn't mean to distress you even more."

"It's all right. I think you're correct."

"Dave says a killer always leaves something behind at a crime scene. But I don't see anything. Have you found something that seems out of place?"

Donna smiled sadly. "I wish I had."

Trixie and I took our leave with Donna promising to be on the alert for anything unusual.

At the end of the driveway, a piece of paper flapped on a trash bag full of shredded paper that the Hoovers had set out. I peered at their house, hoping no one was home to accuse me of going through their trash. As fast as I could, I walked by their garbage and bent to yank that slip of paper off the garbage bag. It was adhered so tightly that it tore a small hole in the plastic. Yikes! I tried to act casual but walked away as fast as I could.

# Thirty-one

The paper stuck to my hand, too. As we walked, I glanced at it and then heard my name being called.

I looked up to see Glenda running toward me. I'd been caught. Like a guilty child, I folded what looked like a mailing label from a package and slid it into my pocket.

"Hi, Glenda."

"Holly, I don't think I ever thanked you properly for bringing Dolly home this morning. It was such a shock. I had almost reached the point of giving up on her and then, ba-boom, there you were with her."

"No thanks necessary, Glenda. I was thrilled that Tavish and Dolly were alive and well."

Glenda cocked her head. "What were you doing up on the mountain in the middle of the night?"

For absolutely no good reason, I was alarmed by her question. Since her son, Stan, hung out with Sugar, I wasn't about to tell her the truth. I fudged. "I was delivering inn leftovers. There are quite a few folks around here who can't get out."

Her smile faded. "Well, you're just the little angel, aren't you?"

She knew I had snatched something from her garbage. I could see it in her expression. Thanking me had been nothing more than an excuse to run after me. I forced a smile. "How's Dolly doing? She must be so glad to be home."

"She has barely left my side."

"I'd better get going then. Oma sent me out with a whole list of things to do."

"Did she? Take care, Holly."

I tried not to walk away too fast. And I resisted the urge to look at the mailing label until I reached town. I stepped into the drugstore and walked to the very back where I would notice if Glenda were following me.

I pulled the label out of my pocket.

Initially, I found it boring. Just a mailing label torn off a shipping box. But then I realized that it was addressed to Diane.

If I hadn't heard Marlee's story about Stan Hoover's porch-pirating activities, I would have assumed that it blew across the lawn and just happened to be stuck to the Hoovers' trash. But it was more likely that Stan had snatched something off Diane's doorstep. After all, she was dead. No one would know. Unless . . .

I checked the shipping date. It had been shipped before Diane's death, but there was no telling when it had been delivered or what was in the package.

There was no sign of Glenda, so I dialed Dave's number as I left the store. When Dave answered his phone, I whispered, "Do you know anything about Stan Hoover and Sugar McLaughlin being on probation?"

For a long moment, Dave didn't say anything. "Theft is a long way from murder."

"I'm not accusing them of anything . . . yet. So it's true? They went to prison for being porch pirates?"

"Yes."

"But you never told Oma or me?"

"Holly, there are a lot of people in Wagtail and everywhere else who have a past. I don't tell you about them, either. Is there a problem?"

"I don't know. I found a shipping label addressed to Diane stuck to one of the Hoovers' garbage bags. It looks like they were shredding things and maybe this one got stuck on the outside of the bag and no one noticed."

"You know, when you tamper with evidence, it's inadmissible in court."

"I didn't know it would be evidence. It was on their trash bag, for Pete's sake."

"Okay. Don't say anything to anyone. I'll keep an eye on him."

I hung up. What if Diane caught Stan stealing a package from her front door? Would he have murdered her for that? Would he have been afraid she would turn him in and he would have to go back to prison?"

My head was swirling at the thought when Trixie suddenly raced toward her buddy Pippin, who led his entourage along the sidewalk.

"Holly!" called Rae Rae. "We're on our way to lunch at Tequila Mockingbird. Would you like to join us?"

How convenient. As a matter of fact, I would. This would be a great time to find out about the mysterious Lucy. "Sure!" I felt just a touch guilty about joining them to weasel information out of them, but not sufficiently guilty to turn them down.

As its name implied, Tequila Mockingbird was a popular nighttime spot, but it also had great food. And if you were lucky enough to get one of the outdoor tables that felt like they were hanging over the edge of the lake, you had one of the best seats in town. It was a gorgeous day to watch sailboats and fishermen. The sun glittered like diamonds on the lake as the water moved.

Pippin's star power earned us an outdoor table.

I ordered three baskets of their thick-cut onion rings for the table, iced tea with a chicken strawberry salad on greens for me, and their Tempting Chicken Tenders for Trixie. After everyone had ordered, the group launched into a lively discussion about a possible replacement for Howard on the show. Although I found little to like about Howard, especially if he had murdered Diane, I felt a twinge of sadness for him. He had only been dead a couple of days, and he was already being replaced as though he never existed.

The waitress delivered our drinks.

"Holly, you'll have to come out to LA and watch us shoot the show one day," said Camille.

"I would love that. It's all so exotic to me."

Finch, in his usual I'm-only-vaguely-interested way, asked, "Is it true that Howard murdered Diane?"

Oof. Why was everyone asking me things I had to skirt around? "That's the official verdict. I was over at Diane's house just a little while ago. Donna said she had received a call to that effect."

Marlee, still wearing the wig and sunglasses, raised her tea glass in a toast. "Looks like you're off the hook, Jim! What did the cops want with you?"

Jim's relief was visible. His entire body relaxed. "I went to see Diane the day we arrived. Someone must have seen me going into her house and reported it to the cops."

Rae Rae sat back in her chair and eyed him. "Did you know Diane?"

"I didn't. I had never met her before. But I had heard of her, just like I had heard of you. I went to talk to her about Howard."

The waitress brought the onion rings to the table.

"Howard?" Rae Rae plucked a hot onion ring out of the basket. "Darlin', why?"

"He murdered my babysitter." Jim spoke as though it was a matter of fact.

"In front of you?" Camille gasped.

"No. She lived next door. The sweetest girl you can imagine. She walked me in my stroller when I was a baby and was like a big sister to me. When I was five years old, she disappeared." He paused to bite into an onion ring. "They never found her remains. But I knew who did it."

"Because you saw him?" asked Rae Rae.

He looked ahead as he spoke, not meeting anyone's gaze. It was as if he was seeing it all again through the eyes of his five-year-old self. "It must have been after six o'clock in the evening, but it was still broad daylight. My mom had just come home from work, and Lucy left. I was standing inside the screen door of our house, watching her walk home, when he pulled up in a blue car. He didn't get out. She ran over to his car window and spoke with him. She liked him. She laughed and was happy to see him. Then she willingly walked to the passenger side and stepped into the car. I saw his face, clear as could be. I'll never forget it. He looked straight at me. Besides Howard, I was the last person to see her. The trouble is that when you're five, no one listens to you."

He stopped talking when our lunches were served.

"That's horrible. Did the police question you?" asked Marlee.

"Never. I was five! After a couple of days, when she didn't come home, her dad asked my mom if she had seen anything. I told him then that a man picked her up in a blue car. But I don't think he took me very seriously."

"And you think that man was Howard?" Finch looked doubtful.

"Definitely. There's not a doubt in my mind. He had more hair back then, but I'd have recognized him anywhere.

I was always on the lookout for him. And then one day, I happened to catch him on TV being interviewed about a hit show that he starred in. I knew it was him. I knew instantly. He has a fairly distinctive face."

"Did you go to the police then?" asked Rae Rae.

He looked at her. "Even I realized that they wouldn't take the word of a witness who was five years old at the time. Howard wasn't easy to approach, either. He wasn't the kind of guy you run into at the gas station or walking his dog in the park. And I wasn't in the entertainment business. But once I knew who he was, I researched everything I could find on him. You can learn a lot if you locate the right people. There were rumors of him having strangled a girl overseas, but everything was hushed up. That's how things were back in the day. If you were a moneymaker, if you drew an audience, then people made your troubles go away. You'd be surprised how many women claimed he attacked them. A lot of them didn't want to talk about it publicly."

"So that's how you found out about Diane?" I asked.

"I knew her name but couldn't locate her until her dogs started winning championships. I went to see her as soon as we arrived in Wagtail. I was so sorry that she died. She was really nice to me. She remembered Lucy being on the news but never made the connection with Howard."

Finch was mesmerized by Jim's tale. "You must have flipped out when you got the call for Pippin to be on the same show as Howard."

"You bet! I think all of you wanted the show because of famous Howard Hirschtritt. I was excited to get a call asking if Pippin would be interested in a TV show. The fact that Howard was part of it was icing on the cake. I knew that job was meant to be. Actually, I may have been the reason he declined to stay with us. Camille and Finch probably remember the meeting we had in LA a couple of weeks ago. He was sitting there, ignoring everyone, so I sat down beside him like he was just anybody. He was checking e-mail on his phone. And as calmly as I could, I said, 'I knew Lucy Zankowski.' His fingers stopped moving, like he was in shock."

Rae Rae held her hand over her mouth. "I can't believe you did that!"

"We were surrounded by people. What was he going to do?"

"I don't know if I would have had the courage," I said. "But you were right—he recognized her name."

"He whispered, 'I haven't heard that name in a long time. How's she doing?' I said I was pretty sure he knew how she was. He took a long look at me and asked what I wanted. I told him I wanted to know where she was. He looked me straight in the eyes and laughed when he said, 'No one will ever find her.'"

# Thirty-two

"And then he said, 'You must have been the little kid who was watching at the door.'"

Even Finch gasped. "That's like a confession!"

"It gets better. He pulled a line that sounds like it was out of an old movie script, 'If you know what's good for you, you'll never mention this again.'"

"They ought to take a cadaver dog into his yard and have her sniff around," said Finch.

Rae Rae frowned. "Did you think Diane was involved in Lucy's disappearance?"

"I had no reason to think that. But both of you knew Howard around that time. I thought she might have heard him mention Lucy. Maybe she saw something that didn't make sense, or he canceled a date." Jim finally bit into his burger.

"What did she say?" asked Rae Rae.

"She heard a rumor way back when, but the only Lucys she ever knew were a basset hound and a black cat. She was very friendly and nice about it. She told me she knew he had a reputation for being a bad boy. He was good-looking, unbelievably vain, recklessly fun, and very charming. Women chased him all the time. She'd never heard of him being rough or physically abusive with anyone, but there was no telling what he might have done to preserve his reputation."

Rae Rae looked at her plate, but I didn't think she was seeing it. She shook her head. "Diane was right. She might not have realized anything was awry. Howard was notoriously late and erratic in the way he conducted his life. If he hadn't been such a good actor, people might not have tolerated that kind of behavior." She gazed at Jim. "I remember when the cops were looking for Lucy. I never knew her, but I saw her picture in the newspaper when she disappeared. I'm so sorry."

Jim nodded. "I wondered if you knew her. He never sold the house where he lived then. Even when he was rich and famous. He moved out, but he rented it. I think he was afraid someone would dig if he sold it. Now that he's dead, I think I'll make a stink and see if we can get into his yard before the house is in someone else's hands."

I looked from Jim to Rae Rae. They were both somber. Their lives had been impacted by Howard. Both of them had motives to murder him. Could one of them have poisoned Howard? Or Diane? What if Jim was sugarcoating his encounters with the two of them? What if his visit with Diane hadn't gone exactly as he was telling us?

If Howard actually murdered Lucy all those years ago, he might have murdered Jim too, just to keep him quiet about it. But it worked out in reverse. Someone had killed Howard. And Jim had the murder weapon of fentanyl in his bag . . .

I picked at my lunch. Trixie, not as distressed over the murders, had finished her lunch and was sitting on the deck next to me, gazing at me hopefully. I relented and sneaked a slice of chicken breast to her.

Rae Rae very kindly picked up the tab for everyone. With a wink, she said, "Lunch is on my brother." When we were leaving, one of the bartenders nabbed my elbow. I hung back as the others walked out the door.

When it swung shut, he said, "Tell Dave that redheaded guy, the one who was a child star, was in here Friday night. He was having a humdinger of an argument with Howard. He kept walking away from him, but the redheaded guy followed him and started it up again every time."

Finch? Up to now, Finch hadn't really been among my suspects. "Any idea what it was about?"

He heaved a sigh. "I couldn't swear to it, but it sounded to me like it was about a woman."

"Thanks. I'll let Dave know."

"Rumor is that Howard killed Diane and himself. But as a bartender, and that means a pseudo-shrink, it wasn't Howard. The man expects to be waited on by everyone. He was always bossing people around. 'Get me another drink, get me some pretzels, get me something to eat.' If Howard killed Diane, I bet he paid someone to do it for him. Now that Howard's dead, I thought I'd better pass along the info on the redheaded guy before he leaves town and gets away with it."

I thanked him again and left the restaurant thinking about how many people probably do get away with murder, like Howard did. Everyone seemed to think he expected other people to do everything for him. But could he have developed a nasty habit of drugging women who then died of an overdose? Did he see that as a hands-off way of ridding himself of someone?

I had barely taken two steps with Pippin's crew when Sugar and her momma, Idella, marched toward us like they were out to kill.

"Mary Lee Seidel!" cried Idella. "You stop right there. I want to have a word with you."

"I'll back you up," said Jim. "What did you do to them?"

Idella said, "Laugh, Sugar. We want to look as though we like her."

The two of them put on a show smiling and chuckling. They were a pair of nuts!

Idella gazed at Pippin and his entourage. In a highly annoyed tone, she muttered, "Would you mind? This is a private matter between Mary Lee and my daughter."

I turned to Marlee and her friends. "It's okay. Go on back to the inn." Facing Sugar and Idella, I asked, "What can I do for you?"

Idella leveled a hateful gaze at me. "Mary Lee! You come here right this minute."

Marlee, known locally as Mary Lee, whipped off her wig. Shiny brunette hair tumbled around her head. I could see her hand shaking, but she stood up to Idella.

"Mom, I told you she was Mary Lee," hissed Sugar.

Marlee stared at Sugar. "I'm tired of hiding."

Idella's eyes blazed. "How dare you come back here and make a ruckus? I thought we were through with you."

Marlee spoke calmly. "Get over yourself, Idella. You have no business telling me what I can do or where I can go. In fact, if you weren't standing here making a fuss in front of everyone, they wouldn't know a thing was wrong." She shifted her gaze to Sugar. "I'm sorry about the way things turned out. Now if you'll excuse me, I'm here on a job."

Marlee joined Pippin's group, and they walked away, high-fiving her.

I was proud of Marlee. She hadn't lost her temper, and she had made perfect sense.

Idella fumed and turned her ire on me. In a bitter and angry tone, she said, "You better keep your mouth shut about Sugar and Stan. And I don't want to see you digging through my trash, you hear?"

Now *that* was interesting. Considering that I hadn't dug in anyone's trash and that the only trash I had been near belonged to Glenda Hoover, it was clear to me that Glenda had immediately phoned Idella. I could certainly understand why they didn't want Stan's and Sugar's criminal behavior to become public knowledge in Wagtail. But it was intriguing to me that Glenda and Idella were worried. Maybe I was on to something. Could Diane have caught Stan and Sugar stealing a package? They had only been on the periphery of my radar, but Idella's words had moved them up.

"You're just doing this to make me look bad to Holmes," sniffled Sugar. "Have you heard from him?"

Oy. I was doing way too much lying for my comfort. This time I told the truth. "Not today."

I had nothing more to say to them. Without the courtesy of a good-bye, I turned on my heel and walked away. I could hear Idella say, "Well I never! She's going to ruin everything for you, Sugar."

The funny thing was that I had no desire to ruin anything for Sugar. I didn't plan to say a word about her porch-pirating days unless packages went missing in Wagtail. The truth was that I felt sorry for Sugar. She had made a terrible mistake, and it was just a matter of time before someone in Wagtail learned about it and blabbed it all over town. It had to be awful living with that fear hanging over her head.

I put them out of my mind and followed Trixie, whose nose was to the ground. We were at the far end of Wagtail, where the Wagtail Springs Hotel was located. When Trixie walked up the steps to the entrance, I followed her and opened the door.

Jimmy Bocuse was working at the front desk. A friendly guy in his twenties, we sometimes shared stories about quirky guests. "Hey, Holly!" He came around the desk into the lobby and handed Trixie a little treat. "That was a great article about you."

Trixie wagged her tail.

"So how is it with Pippin in residence?" he asked. "Are people breaking in to see him?"

"Not yet. He's been pretty accessible to the public."

Jimmy grinned. "He's keeping us busy. One fellow checked out this morning, and we sold his room within the hour."

"We're full up, too."

"We were sorry to see Wade go. He was a very generous tipper."

"Wade? Not Wade Holt?" I asked, feeling a little queasy.

"Yeah! Do you know him? Great guy!"

Great guy? How could that be? I treaded cautiously. "I've met him."

"I've worked at the hotel since it reopened, but he was the first person who ever paid for his room in cash."

I thought about it for a moment. I couldn't recall anyone paying cash for their stay at the inn. But if he was an unemployed con man, maybe he couldn't get a credit card. Cash might be his only option. I hoped he wasn't pulling cons around town. "He seemed to have a lot of cash?"

"Why are you surprised? He writes Internet games about superheroes. I'm telling you, he was really cool."

Wade was a good liar. I hadn't expected that from the man I met in the woods. "But he checked out?"

"We almost cried when he left!"

I honestly felt a weight lift off me. I reached for Trixie and stroked her. That was one worry gone. I hoped he would stay away for good. "Did he say where he was going?"

"Las Vegas, I think."

I breathed a sigh of relief even though I realized it was probably just another lie. As long as he wasn't in Wagtail, I would be thrilled.

"I heard that Pippin's owner, Jim, is the one who murdered Howard Hirschtritt. I don't know if I'd like having a suspected murderer staying here."

"Really? Who told you that?"

"Wade. But everyone is talking about it. I wonder what would happen to Pippin if Jim went to the slammer for murder?"

Wade? I wanted to think there was something sinister about Wade discussing the murders. But the truth was that everyone in town had probably heard about them, even the visitors. And if rumors were circulating that Pippin's owner had committed the murders, then that was even more interesting for the visitors.

Trixie received one more tiny treat from Jimmy before we departed. I left feeling much less tense. There were still plenty of problems in Wagtail, but the big one that had been hanging over *my* head had left. I was practically giddy when we walked back to the inn through the green.

Marlee and Rae Rae sat on the porch drinking iced tea. Marlee had ditched the wig and glasses. Gingersnap and Stella lounged at their feet, and Twinkletoes sat on the porch railing. It was a charming scene.

"Did everything go okay with that lady?" asked Rae Rae. "She seemed very angry."

"They're afraid I know about the porch pirating." I flipped my hand through the air casually. "No big deal. You two look like you're enjoying the afternoon."

"It's so peaceful," said Rae Rae. "And guess what. Stella knows some words!"

Marlee snickered. "They all know a few commands."

"That's not what I mean. She knows perfectly well what"—Rae Rae spelled out the words—"i-c-e c-r-e-a-m means. She gets all excited if you say it."

"That's so cute," said Marlee. "Maybe that's her favorite treat."

"It probably is," I said. "Dogs understand around five hundred words. I bet she's had enough i-c-e c-r-e-a-m to know it's delicious!"

Trixie and I went inside and headed to the office. It was

so quiet in the inn that I wondered where everyone had gone.

Zelda latched on to me when I walked by her. "It's so boring around here today."

"Zelda, this is a good thing," said Oma. "We have a full house, and all our guests are happy and content."

I sat down opposite Oma. "I'm feeling very happy right now, too. Apparently, the man who claimed Trixie belonged to him checked out of the Wagtail Springs Hotel." Trixie jumped up into my lap and kissed my nose. "We don't have to worry about *him* anymore."

Oma frowned at me. "There are still the two deaths."

Zelda chirped up, "I thought they were solved and the cases were closed."

Oma turned as red as a beet. "Um, yes. They are still very troubling."

Oy! I needed to change the subject and fast. "Hey, Zelda, did you mention something about Stan and Sugar's porch pirating to anyone?"

"Of course not. Marlee asked us to keep it quiet. Why? Is someone on to them?"

I pulled the label out of my pocket. "I found this sticking to the Hoovers' garbage bag."

"Holly!" Oma said my name in a scolding way, but she leaned forward. "What does it say?"

"Nothing important. It's a shipping label that must have been on a package destined for Diane's house. It was stuck on the outside of a garbage bag, kind of hanging there flapping in the breeze."

"Why would it be on the Hoovers' trash?" mused Zelda.

"Precisely. Idella and Sugar tracked me down, and Idella had a little hissy fit and threatened me if I said anything about 'what I knew.' It was very strange."

"She admitted what Sugar did?" asked Oma.

"Idella never mentioned it. She was never specific."

"Ohhhh," Oma moaned. "I do not like this. Why would she threaten you? Even if you did snatch something off the Hoovers' trash."

"It was out on the street. It's not like I broke into their garage."

"Holly! It's still not right. But perhaps it is good that we know this. Zelda," said Oma, "we must be very subtle, ja?"

"You can count on me."

She had barely finished speaking when we heard angry voices.

# Thirty-three

Jim burst into the office. "Have you seen Pippin?"

He was so agitated that he woke Gingersnap and Stella.

Jim gazed around the office and ran to the sliding glass door. He looked out at the lake. "One minute he was with me and the next he was gone. A crowd of people gathered around us, and he somehow disappeared. Pippin!" he shouted. "I don't know what to do. I've looked everywhere."

I stood up. "Oma, you stay here and coordinate. Call Dave and let him know. Zelda, find little Jacob Minifree. He has a Pippin obsession." I pulled out my phone and sent a lost dog alert to the Wagtail community.

"Let's walk over to Hot Hog. He and Trixie had a good time there. Maybe he went back. I'm sure he's fine, Jim. He's just kicking up his heels while he's on vacation." I hoped I sounded assuring, because I didn't feel confident at all. We still hadn't found the dognapper. The deaths had overshadowed the problem of the missing dogs, especially once they were found. I took Trixie with us so she wouldn't disappear.

Jim was distraught. I assured him that Trixie would probably notice if Pippin were roaming the green. But he was inconsolable.

Our hopes were dashed when Pippin wasn't at Hot Hog. They promised to keep him at the restaurant if he showed up. From there, we walked over to the house Howard had rented. Jim and I called Pippin's name over and over, but there was simply no sign of him. The house lay silent, with crime scene tape still draped across the doors.

The day flew by as word spread and helpful people called in sightings. A fisherman was sure he'd seen a guy washing Pippin in the lake. Jim and Finch spent a couple of hours cruising the lake with Stan, while I stayed at the inn to take calls. Two hikers thought they'd seen Pippin at the top of the mountain chasing squirrels. And three people reported him playing with other dogs in the dog park on the green.

None of the leads panned out.

Jim was beside himself. "I should have used the GPS collar you offered. After he and Trixie went out to dinner, I should have realized the importance of those collars."

"Don't be hard on yourself," I said. "Pippin usually sticks close to you."

"I swear he was there one minute and gone the next. I don't understand. How could I have let this happen?"

"Don't give up yet. I'll take the dogs and drive up to the cabin where we found Tavish and Dolly. It's a long shot, but maybe it's worth a try."

"I'd go with you," said Jim, "but I'm afraid there might be a sighting of Pippin."

I nodded. "It's better if you stay here and pursue any leads." I called Gingersnap, Stella, and Trixie, grabbed a golf cart key, and drove to Pierce Real Estate. Nancy Friedman was at the desk.

"Has the Popolov house been rented?" I asked.

She checked her computer. "No. What's going on?"

I explained the situation.

Nancy handed me the keys. "Normally, I'd go with you, but Al's back went out on him, so I have to cover the desk."

"No problem. I'll have them back to you soon."

I hopped in the golf cart, and the three dogs joined me. We drove up the mountain. I watched Stella for a reaction. The scents probably reminded her of the night she found her friend Dolly. I turned off the main road, drove up the long driveway, and parked in front of the house. If Pippin was there, he wasn't barking. Before I stepped out, I watched the dogs to see their reactions. Unfortunately, Stella didn't bark, and Trixie didn't jump out to track anything.

Feeling discouraged, I stepped out and unlocked the front door of the house. The kitchen, dining area, and living room were all one uninterrupted room, anchored by a river rock fireplace at the end. Large beams held up a wood ceiling, and green French doors overlooked woods in the back.

The dogs ran around sniffing the floors, undoubtedly smelling Dolly and Tavish. I wished they could tell me if Pippin had been there.

I wandered into the kitchen. It looked like a rental. Neat and orderly, but sparsely equipped except for an air fryer. Maybe the Popolovs were big fans of fried foods.

A door led to a single bedroom with a bath. It was a very small place but cozy and warm. I could imagine snuggling up by the fireplace on cold nights. The bedroom was ready for the next guests. Towels were stacked on the bed and tied with a ribbon to show they had been laundered. I checked the hardwood floor. There was no sign of dog fur.

"Well, guys," I said to the dogs, "I'm sorry I dragged you out here." I stood near the fireplace and turned around, taking in everything. The police had probably checked it out thoroughly. But I felt like this particular cabin had to be key. There were plenty of cabins out in the woods around Wagtail. But the dognapper chose this one. The roster of suspects would include everyone who worked at Pierce Real Estate and all the people who had ever rented the place. It didn't end there, but it was a good start.

There was one other odd connection, though. Glenda Hoover worked for Pierce Real Estate, and her dog, Dolly, was the first to be kidnapped. Did someone at the real estate company have a bone to pick with Glenda? Why did Stan Hoover keep coming to mind? Because he had a record of theft? Would he steal his own mother's dog? I felt a little bit guilty for jumping to Stan as a suspect. Just because he had been convicted of a crime once didn't mean he was continuing down that path.

And why leave the dogs here? If I were stealing dogs, I would have gotten them out of town right away. Of course, Dave had been kind enough to point out what a lousy criminal I would make. Had the dogs been hidden here with the intention of sneaking them out of town in a month or two when the hubbub had died down and people weren't looking for them anymore? That was dangerous. What if someone rented the cabin?

I let the dogs out and watched to see if their noses led them in a particular direction. Birds chirped in the trees, but there weren't any other sounds. If Pippin was barking somewhere, I couldn't hear him.

The three dogs sniffed in different directions.

I sighed. What was I overlooking? I returned to the kitchen and poked around. The air fryer was so new that the instructions were still inside it. I opened kitchen cabinets. They were largely unimpressive. Just like an ordinary kitchen, there were dishes, plain glasses, and mugs decorated with cats and dogs. But way in the back, something glistened. I pulled a chair over and stepped on the seat to see it better.

After moving everything aside gingerly, I withdrew a heavy crystal decanter. I'd heard of these but hadn't seen one. Roughly eight inches high and six inches across, the decanter was carved so the base looked something like a dog's paw. The crystal stopper was the shape of a hound's head, probably a beagle. I turned it over to see the hallmark—Waterford. I didn't know exactly what they cost, but I knew they weren't the sort of thing usually found in a rental house.

Stan. Could he be using this house to stash things he found in packages he stole? I replaced the decanter carefully and snooped some more. A brand-new, ultramodern heating and cooling fan with no blades was stashed in a closet. I had seen one in a store and knew it was pricey. It was impossible to know what belonged to the owners and what might have been hidden there by Stan.

In any event, I had dawdled long enough. I needed to get back to the hunt for Pippin. I stepped outside and locked the door. When I turned around, Gingersnap and Stella were growling. Wade stood not fifteen feet away from me.

# Thirty-four

I stopped breathing. I'd thought he was gone! A bedraggled dog with a kennel leash looped tightly around his neck stood next to Wade. Its black and yellow fur appeared wet and matted. It looked like it had mange. A rope harness kept the dog's mouth shut so it couldn't bark.

But it whined.

Gingersnap and Stella showed their teeth, and their hackles were up. They were positioned in front of Trixie as though they were protecting her from Wade. Trixie seemed scared and immobile.

"We meet again, Holly Miller," he said.

Thoughts swirled through my head fast. Was he the dog-napper after all? Had he been using this cabin? I tried to stay calm and pretend to be civil. "Hello, Wade."

"You know my name. I'm flattered."

My heart beat like crazy. I was still close to the door. Could I unlock it and get everyone inside before he attacked me? I didn't know that he even wanted to attack me. I assumed he still wanted Trixie.

He called her name. "Here, Dummy. C'mon."

Trixie pinned her ears back and lowered herself to the ground. Slowly and grudgingly, she moved forward.

There was an old saying, *Emotions run up and down the leash*, meaning a dog could feel what his person was feeling. Right now, I was panicked. I stepped forward and crouched fast to pick up Trixie when something flew over my head, barely missing me. It was so close I felt the air moving my hair.

I jerked upright with Trixie in my arms. In front of me, Wade fell to the ground with a bloodcurdling scream of pain. An arrow jutted from his thigh.

"LaRue?" I yelled. "LaRue? Is that you?"

I heard someone running through the woods. There was no time for anything but getting out of there.

Gingersnap leaped forward and grabbed the leash of Wade's dog. As I ran for the golf cart with Trixie in my arms, Stella, Gingersnap, and the other dog raced toward it.

I jammed the key in the ignition, turned it on, and drove down the road as fast as I could, leaving Wade alone and injured. For all I knew, the archer in the woods might have another arrow. I wasn't going to stick around.

When we reached Wagtail, I breathed with relief. I didn't stop until I pulled up at the reception entrance of the inn. I didn't even bother to park the golf cart properly. Trixie was the first to jump off and open the automatic sliding doors. The other dogs and I followed.

It was ridiculous of me, but I ran behind the reception desk and hit the button to lock the doors. Had Wade been on foot? Maybe he had stolen a golf cart and left it hidden up on the mountain somewhere. I wasn't taking any chances. With that arrow in his leg, I didn't think he would be moving very fast, but he might be the kind of guy who muscled through the pain.

No one was in the office. There was no sign of Zelda. I picked up the phone and called Dave. While it was ringing, I grabbed some dog treats and handed them out. "You guys were so brave. You saved Trixie!" I gently removed the rope halter and leash from the mangy dog. As I looked at his face more carefully, I recognized his eyes. "That idiot dyed your fur!" I shouted. Pippin smiled and crunched his treat.

When Dave answered his phone, I told him what had happened. "Wade is probably out there somewhere with that arrow in his leg."

"You didn't see who shot it?"

"No. I can only imagine that it was LaRue. You know how he appears and then is gone in an instant. I did hear the sound of leaves crunching as someone ran through the woods."

"And you have Pippin?"

"Yes. And, Dave, there's one other thing. I'll tell you about it after you deal with Wade."

I hung up. I was still shaking. I needed a cup of strong tea. "What's the doggy equivalent of tea?" I asked.

If Zelda had been there, she could have interpreted their response, but I had a strong feeling it might be a good hard cookie to chew on.

I walked toward the main lobby. Pippin raced toward Jim and jumped up in his arms.

Stella watched sadly. She seemed resigned to being alone. I hugged her and told her again what a great dog she had been to defend Trixie.

Her tail wagged, but I knew it wasn't the same as if Diane had been there for her.

The lobby appeared to have become the heart of the search for Pippin. Oma, Zelda, and Pippin's entourage cheered. Everyone wanted to pet him.

"What is this stuff on your fur?" asked Jim. "What did they do to you? You're a mess!" In spite of his complaints, he hugged Pippin fiercely.

The dining area had long since closed. I hurried into the private kitchen for dog cookies and a mug of tea for me.

When I returned to the lobby and sat down, all four dogs came to me for a cookie. While they contently ate their treats, the humans in the room demanded explanations.

I didn't tell them my theory about Stan, but I gave them the whole story about how the dogs protected Trixie from Wade.

"Why would he ruin Pippin's fur?" asked Jim. "Gosh, I hope this stuff comes off."

"I guess he thought no one would recognize Pippin with dark, mangy fur," I suggested. "How else would Wade be able to get Pippin out of town?"

Oma placed her hand on my arm. "Thank goodness someone shot this Wade and defended you."

I gave her a sideways look. "I wouldn't go thanking anybody just yet. That arrow passed very close to my head. I'm not sure it was meant for Wade. If I hadn't bent to pick up Trixie at that precise moment, I might have been hit."

Oma's hands flew to her red cheeks. "Are you saying *you* were the target?"

"I don't know. I guess it could have been an inept archer. I thought maybe it was LaRue."

"You better stick around the inn," said Zelda. "But who would want to shoot you?"

"You mean other than Idella and Sugar?" I asked.

"Ach, you joke," Oma grumbled. "They might make a big fuss, but they would not harm you."

"To be honest, I'm perfectly happy to hang around here until we figure out what happened." I tried to seem nonchalant, but the more I thought about it, the more I realized the arrow had been meant for me.

I relaxed when Pippin became the center of attention.

"He's damp," said Jim. "Maybe this stuff will wash out."

Oma examined Pippin's fur. "We have several excellent groomers in Wagtail. Perhaps one of them could strip this black dye."

Camille began to laugh. "They're going to have to rewrite the script for the first show. I have a feeling Pippin will be getting into paint in the first episode."

"Not funny, Camille." Jim sighed. "Liesel, can you hook me up with one of these expert groomers?"

"It would be my pleasure." She motioned to Jim to follow her.

I could see that Rae Rae and Marlee felt obligated to stay with me. "You guys go on and have fun. I'll be fine. In fact," I lied, "I believe I might take a nap. I'm a little worn-out." I stood up and disappeared into the private kitchen. Trixie, Gingersnap, and Stella accompanied me. I settled in an armchair in front of the fireplace and put my feet up. Twinkletoes appeared out of nowhere to purr on my lap.

It wasn't long before the hubbub in the main lobby died down. I wondered if Dave had found Wade yet. He would have to take him to Dr. Engelknecht or to the hospital in Snowball. That wound had looked awful to me.

At least Dave could charge him with stealing Pippin. It probably wouldn't keep Wade off the streets for long, but it was a start.

I closed my eyes and heard someone at the kitchen door that led outside to Oma's herb garden. Trixie, Gingersnap, and Stella raised their heads and perked their ears.

When someone knocked on the door, all three of them barked. I turned around, afraid it might be Wade or some deranged archer.

But the dogs had run to the door and were wagging their tails.

Clutching my phone in case I needed to call for help, I edged closer.

In the fading light of day, I made out Holmes through the window in the door. Feeling foolish, I flung it open.

"Hi! Could you use some company?" His grin chased all my fears away.

"Did Oma call you?" I locked the door while he petted the dogs.

"You bet. Her favorite granddaughter was nearly murdered up on the mountain."

I flopped into my chair. "That may not even be an exaggeration."

Holmes sat down on the fireplace hearth facing me. "She said something about an arrow."

I told him about Wade and the arrow nearly hitting me. "I've come to the conclusion that I may be too close to uncovering something. But I'm not sure what."

Holmes rose and walked behind me. I could hear him running water in the kettle. "Have you eaten dinner?"

"No."

"Let's see what's in the magic refrigerator. Ohh, nice! Chicken salad. Mac and cheese! Looks like doggy meat loaf for Trixie and lake trout for Twinkletoes."

The next thing I knew, he placed a tray of goodies on a table between the two armchairs. He brought over two mugs of steaming tea, two forks, two knives, and two napkins. No plates. We ate right out of the containers. He'd even taken a minute to heat the mac and cheese in the microwave. It was positively sinful.

"Okay, so let's look at the facts."

I cracked up laughing. He was so predictable. But he was right. "It all began when Glenda's dog, Dolly, was stolen. Clara's dog, Tavish, was reported missing the next day. By Saturday morning, Diane was missing. We know the dogs were being kept at the rental cabin on the mountain. And

Glenda works for the real estate company that handles that cabin. Diane had been driven up the mountain where her killer dumped her body in a ravine."

"You left out Wade. He claimed Trixie belonged to him. Right?" asked Holmes.

"Correct. Holmes, I didn't want to tell you this, but Dave has confirmed that a few years ago Stan and Sugar were convicted of being porch pirates."

"Sugar McLaughlin?"

"I'm afraid so. Their families have tried very hard to keep it a secret."

"Wow. Sugar's a pest, but I never imagined she would do anything like that. They're so young. Why would they be so stupid?"

"I'm afraid the lid is going to blow. I found a few things in the cabin where the dogs were held that seemed out of place. There's an expensive crystal decanter, an air fryer, and a pricey vacuum."

"You think the two of them are at it again and hiding their treasures in the cabin?"

"I think Stan is. I have no reason to think that Sugar is involved this time. But if I'm right and he's stashing things in the cabin, it leads me to believe that Stan might also be the dognapper."

Holmes scooped up a bite of chicken salad. "I'm trying to think of a reasonable alternative explanation, but the only one I can imagine is that the owners of the cabin placed those items there."

I told him about the shipping label I found on the Hoovers' trash.

"Have you told Dave?" I could hear the doubt in his tone.

Eyeing the mac and cheese, I said, "He's busy looking for a guy with an arrow in his leg."

"That would take priority. At least Stan didn't murder anyone."

"I wouldn't be so sure about that." I ate a giant mouthful of mac and cheese. "Mmm. I love it when it's creamy like this. I'm very much afraid that Diane might have caught Stan stealing a package from her front door."

"Aww, come on. He wouldn't kill her because of that. And I thought you said the fentanyl is believed to have been on a brownie."

"What? Stan can't buy a brownie? Maybe he brought her one from a bakery and tampered with it or poured the stuff into a drink."

"But to murder someone over a package?" Holmes shook his head. "That's hard to believe."

"What if he murdered her so he wouldn't end up back in prison?"

"Seems like a stretch, Holly. Maybe the owners of the cabin just have nice stuff. And maybe the label on Diane's package blew over to the Hoovers' house. If Diane lived across town from Stan that might be different. Besides, I heard the case was solved and that Howard killed Diane. What happened to that?"

I swallowed another forkful of the heavenly mac and cheese. "I think it's wrong. It's all so nicely probable, but it's also terribly unlikely."

"What about that guy Jim?" Holmes asked.

"He and Rae Rae had motives and opportunity to kill Howard. They were both out and about in the wee hours. I don't know of any reason Jim would want to murder Diane, though. It could be that Stan murdered Diane and Jim killed Howard. Apparently, Jim was hounding Howard. And someone saw him leave the inn late the night Howard died."

Holmes held a piece of chocolate cake in front of me. "The facts just don't add up, Holly. This might make you feel better."

"What about the fact that someone just shot an arrow at me?"

# Thirty-five

"Do you think that was related to the murders?" Holmes handed me a dessert fork for the cake.

"I've been pondering it. The way I see it, there are three possibilities. The first would be the best scenario—someone was aiming for Wade and I happened to get in the way. But I'm not hopeful that was the case, because the archer ran away. If he had meant to injure Wade and help me, why wouldn't he have stuck around to help me?"

Holmes licked chocolate icing off his finger. "Good point. Could have been a clumsy hunter, but it's not hunting season."

"Or, I know something that someone doesn't want me to blab."

Holmes looked over at me. "That's pretty serious. You think the archer meant to kill you?"

"I don't know. I don't want to think that's the case, because it scares me. The third possibility is that someone wants me to stay away from that cabin."

"Ahh, he meant to frighten you, but his near miss was too close. That makes more sense. But what's in the house that he wouldn't want you to see? Seems pretty dire to protect crystal and a vacuum."

I gave Holmes a look just as Dave swung the door open. "Liesel said I'd find you here. Hi, Holmes. Glad to see you back in town."

"Want some dinner?" Holmes held out the mac and cheese for Dave to see.

"Sounds great. I've been chasing Wade with no time to eat." He pulled up a chair.

"Uh, Dave? We've been eating out of the containers." It was only fair to warn him.

He plunged a fork into the mac and cheese. "I'll consider you poison testers. You both seem to be alive and well."

"So far," Holmes quipped, handing him a mug of tea. "Have you got Wade in custody?"

"Not yet. I have to give it to him—he's a hardy guy. I figured I'd drive up there and call an ambulance to come get him. But he was gone. I found blood on the grass. He left a trail of it to the house and broke in. Near as I can tell from the lack of blood leaving the house, he must have bound it somehow with a towel or a sheet that he tore up. He left the medicine cabinet open. I assume he stole some aspirin."

He paused to finish the container of mac and cheese. "I'm starved. I may get calls while I'm here. Headquarters sent a couple of Snowball officers over to track him. It's getting dark, though. I don't know if they'll be able to do much at night unless he happens to approach the wrong cabin and someone reports him. I've put out an announcement to be on the lookout for him."

"If he's smart, he'll leave the area," observed Holmes.

"I don't know how far he'll get without someone noticing the arrow sticking out of his leg. Aside from the pain, it has to make it hard for him to walk." I ate the last bite of my slice of chocolate cake. Holmes was right. I did feel better!

"Liesel and I agreed that I should stay here tonight. The inn will be a central point of contact for me. I hope that's okay."

I grinned, because Dave clearly wasn't asking. It was a done deal. "Sure. Is there anything I can do to help you?"

"Not yet."

Holmes was staring at Dave in a way that I didn't like. He looked worried. "Sure. Holly and I will stay with you. Whatever you need. You just say the word."

"Thanks. I appreciate that. Hate to eat and run, but I'd like to keep an eye out for Jim and Pippin. They're out to dinner somewhere. We've locked up the reception entrance, so I'll see them when they come in."

"Why don't you go with Dave?" I said to Holmes. "I'll clean up in here and put on a pot of coffee."

Dave and Holmes left the kitchen. The first thing I did was make sure the back door was locked. I started coffee brewing, washed and dried our utensils and food containers, and tidied up.

As awful as he was, I felt sorry for Wade. It was hard to imagine being alone in the dark woods with an arrow in my thigh. Maybe the cops would locate him soon.

I loaded a tray with mugs, sugar, milk, and coffee and carried it out to the Dogwood Room. As I approached, I heard Holmes ask Dave, "You don't think this Wade guy is coming here to harm Holly, do you? Is that why you're staying here tonight?"

"Partly. We know he wants Pippin and Trixie. And both of them will be here. Like Holly pointed out, he's not in very good shape. I didn't find the arrow, so it's probably still in his leg. If it were me, I'd be more interested in leaving town. But this guy has a long rap sheet. He doesn't think the way we do. There's no telling what he might do."

"Any violence on that rap sheet?" I asked as I set the tray on a table.

"Surprisingly little, actually." Dave poured himself a mug of coffee. "Mostly con jobs. Stealing dogs and selling them is right up his alley."

"I don't get it." I sat down with them. "Pippin is so famous. He would be recognized right away if someone bought him."

"You'd be surprised how many people would pay to own the real Pippin, even if they had to keep him hidden."

"You were right all along, Dave. He probably came here to steal Pippin and happened to read about Trixie. I don't understand why he would want Trixie. I love her to bits, but if she was his dog, he threw her out. Why does he want her back now?" I gazed at her, and she hopped in my lap. Wrapping my arms around her, I whispered, "You're staying right here with me."

"Are you kidding?" asked Dave. "It's all about money, Holly. He probably thinks he can get a good price for her now that she's been featured in a national magazine."

As Pippin's entourage filtered in, they joined us in the Dogwood Room. Wade Holt and the arrow in his leg were the main topic of conversation.

I made more coffee and raided the freezer for high tea leftovers. Before long, it looked like a party with chips and dip, fruit tarts, cookies, and a raspberry swirl cheesecake.

Oma joined us and brought Gingersnap and Stella along. She hit the stash of liqueurs and offered everyone after-dinner drinks.

The only ones missing were Jim, Pippin, and Marlee. Their absence was notable.

"They were with us at dinner," said Camille.

Dave strode to the front door and stepped out on the porch. He returned quickly. "No sign of them yet." His phone buzzed, and he took a quick call. When he hung up, he said, "Jack Klausner says his German shepherds are, and I quote, 'barking their fool heads off.' He has pretty good lighting around his place, but he doesn't see anyone."

"Where's that?" asked Rae Rae.

"Just outside of Wagtail. If it's Wade and not a deer, then he's made good progress for someone with that kind of injury."

"I'm getting worried about Jim," said Camille. She hastened to add, "And Marlee and Pippin! They should have been here by now."

Finch, in his usual deadpan way, said, "They probably went to a bar. I wouldn't worry about them yet."

Oma shook her forefinger. "It is not safe for Pippin to be out tonight. Jim should bring him home."

Another half hour passed before Jim, Marlee, and Pippin arrived to our cheers.

Casey followed them in to take the night shift.

Trixie, Gingersnap, and Stella rushed at Pippin as if they had been concerned, too.

Oma breathed a sigh of relief. She walked over to me and whispered, "I am going up to bed now. I will take Gingersnap and Stella with me. Good night, liebchen! Please call me if anything happens." She walked down the hallway and disappeared into the elevator with the two dogs.

For a while, the party atmosphere continued. But one by one, Pippin's entourage bid us good night and went upstairs to bed.

By three in the morning, I had come to the conclusion that I would have made a lousy cop, because I didn't have the patience to sit around and wait. I curled up on a sofa in the Dogwood Room listening to Holmes, Casey, and Dave talk about Wade.

The next thing I knew, Mr. Huckle was saying, "Time to rise, Miss Holly."

I opened my eyes. He smiled at me and waited for me to

sit up before handing me a steaming mug of tea. "Where is everyone?"

"Holmes and Casey went home. Officer Dave is having breakfast with Liesel."

"Did they catch Wade?" I asked.

"Alas, he is still at large."

Since I was already downstairs, I took Trixie out to the doggy bathroom. It was another gorgeous day. The sun shone high in an azure blue sky. Wagtail and the lake were calm. A lone red canoe was tied to our dock. No one would ever have guessed a dog thief and possibly a murderer was on the loose. I sipped my tea and waited for Trixie.

The door behind me opened, and Pippin ran out to join Trixie. Jim followed him, carrying a mug of coffee.

"That was quite a night." Jim yawned. "I don't imagine it will go on like this much longer. That wound has got to be unbearably painful, and it's probably getting infected by now."

"If it had been me, I would have begged for an ambulance," I said. I knew it was nosy of me, but I asked anyway. "Where did you and Marlee go last night after dinner?"

Jim chuckled. "She bought me a drink to thank me for being nice when Howard said such cruel things to her. That's all. It was no big deal. We didn't realize everyone was looking for us."

I dared to ask, "You went back to Howard's house later, didn't you? The night he died?"

He seemed surprised. "After I brought Marlee back to the inn, I played poker for a while. Then I left Pippin in our room to get some sleep, and I went to Hair of the Dog. I never saw Howard again until we walked into his house together."

That would be easy enough to confirm. I happened to know the owner of Hair of the Dog pretty well. Of course, unless he was flirting with her, she probably wouldn't have noticed if Jim slipped away for half an hour to murder Howard.

"Listen," he said. "Some part of me might have wanted to throttle Howard for what he did to Lucy. But my goal was to find her remains. His death pretty much ends any hope that she will be found. Nope. I wanted that jerk to be alive and tell us what he did with her."

I watched Trixie chase Pippin down to the lake. They ran along the shoreline then raced to the dock, where Trixie froze.

# Thirty-six

"Trixie?" I called. I dropped my tea mug and ran toward her as fast as I could.

"What's wrong?" cried Jim behind me.

"I don't know." By the time I ran onto the dock, Trixie had shaken her fear and was barking loud and nonstop.

Pippin lifted his nose and sniffed the air. He barked at the edge of the dock like he was agitated.

A rough green tarp in the canoe moved. Trixie and Pippin launched themselves at it.

A hideous scream filled the air as the tarp thrashed and the canoe turned over.

"Pippin!" howled Jim.

Where was Trixie? She knew how to swim, but she hated the water. I jumped into the chilly lake. Trixie's head bobbed up a couple of feet away. In two strokes I had her in my arms. Pippin swam steadily beside me.

But when we reached the shore, I realized that someone was thrashing in the water. Jim wasn't on the dock anymore.

"Jim!" I yelled. He turned to look at me. "What are you doing in the lake?"

And then Wade's head emerged from under the water. He reached out for Jim's neck. The two of them wrestled, trying to shove each other under the water.

I ran back to the dock. The tarp had sunk when the canoe flipped, but a wooden canoe paddle floated by the dock. I picked it up, took a running start, and leaped into the water while cracking it over Wade's head with all the strength I had.

The churning in the water stopped.

Out of the corner of my eye, I saw Dave running down to the lake from the inn.

Jim and I turned around in panic. There was no sign of Wade.

Dave ran across the dock and dove into the water. I grabbed hold of the ladder on the dock and hauled myself out. I'd barely stepped on the dock when Dave's head came up. He had Wade under his arm and swam toward me.

Jim clambered up the ladder. Our eyes met for a brief instant. Did we really want to save this guy? We knelt on the side of the dock and heaved his lifeless body out of the water.

"I killed him," I whispered. "Oh no! I killed him!"

Jim nodded. "Looks like it."

I rolled him on his side and watched as water dribbled out of his mouth.

"Shove over, Holly." Dave knelt next to me, rolled Wade on his back, and started chest compressions.

Wade sputtered and spewed water. He coughed several times. His steely eyes landed on Jim. "I should have killed you when he told me to. Never was any good at following instructions."

It wasn't until I stood up that I realized the arrow was still in Wade's thigh. He had cut off his trouser leg. The wound looked pretty bad. Jim was right. It had become infected.

The rays of the sun gleamed off Wade's watch. It was a fancy silver model with a brown band. I had seen it before.

The chaos continued as two of Wagtail's volunteer firemen showed up and moved Wade to a gurney. They carried him up the hill to wait for the ambulance.

"Did he say what I thought he did?" asked Jim, whose face had turned ashen.

Dave nodded. "I think so."

"Who?" Jim started to run uphill after the gurney. "Who? Who told you to kill me?"

By that time, it felt like everyone in town had shown up. Oma hurried toward me. "Are you all right?" She picked up my hand. "You're cold as ice!"

We walked up the hill with Dave and watched as they loaded Wade into an ambulance that had arrived.

Jim was still shouting, "Who?"

And suddenly I thought I knew who.

Dave placed a hand on Jim's arm and spoke calmly. "I'll find out." To the rescue squad, he said, "I'll swing home for a change of clothes and meet you at the hospital."

I took Dave aside and whispered, "Was Howard wearing a watch when he died?"

Dave looked at me like I had lost my mind. "I don't know. We'll talk later, okay?"

"Dave! Check Wade's watch. I think it belonged to Howard."

Dave took off, and the ambulance departed only minutes later.

I was drenched and shivering. It was too early in the summer for the lake water to have warmed up enough for a morning swim. "C'mon, Trixie."

After I took a shower and Trixie had a bath, I dressed in jeans and a thick fuzzy top that was better suited to winter weather. I wasn't sure I would ever be warm enough again. I rubbed Trixie's fur with towels until she'd had enough, and we went down to breakfast.

Jim was already there, sitting at a table with Oma and Rae Rae. "Tell them!" he said to me.

Pippin and Trixie didn't romp around like they usually did. I suspected they were exhausted.

I sat down at the table wondering if I should tell him my suspicion. "What I heard him say, and he was looking straight at Jim, was 'I should have killed you when he told me to.'"

Rae Rae and Oma were horrified.

Shelley arrived at the table to take our orders. "You two are town heroes. Everyone saw what happened. People who were dining out on the terrace started screaming. The cook and I ran outside to see what was going on."

"Jim wrestled with him in the water!" said Rae Rae. "It was amazing."

"Did you call the ambulance?" I asked Shelley.

"That was me." Oma placed her hand gently on my arm. "I was afraid someone would drown."

"What would you like for breakfast?" asked Shelley.

"How about a nice hot ham-and-cheese omelet. The dog version for Trixie, please."

Jim piped up. "I'll have the ham steak with eggs and hash browns, please. Pippin would probably like what Trixie is having."

While he ordered, I could hear the buzz about our morning swim at the other tables. Frankly, now that it was over, I was enormously grateful that I hadn't killed Wade. How could murderers live with themselves and go about their lives knowing what they had done?

While we were eating, Dave called Oma from the hospital in Snowball. Jim would have to wait a little longer to find out who wanted him dead. They had taken Wade straight into the operating room to remove the arrow from his leg.

Rae Rae grimaced. "How do they do that? Ugh."

"I'm going to be there in his room when he wakes up," grumbled Jim. "The first thing he sees when he opens his eyes will be me looking down at him. And I will stay there until he tells me the truth."

I understood Jim's frustration, but I had a feeling that I knew who had asked Wade to kill him. "Jim, do you remember the fancy watch that Howard wore?"

"The one he pointed out to everyone? We have laughed so many times about that crazy watch. It was good-looking. I'll give him that. But who flashes a watch around bragging about it?"

"I think Wade was wearing it."

The look on Jim's face was priceless. He sank back into his chair. "Do you think Wade murdered Howard? He would never have given up that watch willingly."

"I've asked Dave to look into it. I imagine they did an inventory of his belongings. Especially anything he was wearing at the time of his death."

Rae Rae's mouth actually hung open. She snapped it shut. "Jim, you and Marlee were the last to see him. Do you recall if he was wearing it?"

"It was dark and I was angry. I wasn't paying attention to his watch. It's quite distinctive, though. I'd like to see the one Wade had on. One thing's for sure, if it was really the same expensive brand, then I bet Wade stole it from someone."

We ate in silence for a moment. And then Jim asked, "Does that mean it was Howard who told Wade to kill me?"

# Thirty-seven

"Has Pippin had his massage yet?" I asked.

"Are you serious? Someone wants to kill me and you're talking about dog massages?" No sooner were the words out of his mouth than he apologized. "I'm sorry. This has got me on edge. Will someone rush at me with a knife? Will my food be poisoned? It's pure agony."

"All the more reason for both of you to relax with a massage," said Oma. "I will book them for you." She bustled away to the phone.

"Do you suppose that's why Wade came here?" Rae Rae held her coffee mug in both hands. "Howard hired him to murder you?"

Jim mashed his eyes shut for a moment. "It's a funny thing. I would have sworn that I was being followed when we got to Wagtail. You know how you just have that feeling? But there were so many people around Pippin all the time that I couldn't pick anyone out. I thought I was imagining things. Now I know I wasn't."

"Sort of ironic, actually," I said. "While Dave was thinking you might have committed murder, someone was planning to murder you!"

Jim started to choke. He waved us away and caught his breath. "I've been running around trying to get in Howard's face and annoy him. It never even occurred to me that he might try to get rid of me. It could be me in the morgue right now instead of Howard."

Rae Rae blinked. "It will be interesting to find out why Wade spared you and killed Howard instead."

Jim's face flushed. "He spared me, and I was trying my best to drown him today. Everything is turned around."

I tried to act like it was just a regular day. Around eleven in the morning, I finally felt warm enough to change into a coral sleeveless blouse and a white skort. While Pippin was off being pampered, Trixie and Twinkletoes helped me do my rounds at the inn.

Holmes found us on the second floor. He rushed at me and picked me up in a bear hug. He set me down, his eyes wide. "Are you all right? I leave the inn for a few hours and you incapacitate the man everyone was looking for?"

"You're making too much of it. But it appears that he might have had a hand in Howard's murder." I told him my theory about the watch.

"Holly Miller, you never cease to amaze me." He grinned and planted a big smooch on my lips.

"I believe I'm going to enjoy having you back in town."

Trixie placed her paws on my thighs, demanding her fair share of attention.

"Did Dave figure out who shot the arrow?" asked Holmes.

My elation subsided. In the frenzy of capturing Wade, I had completely forgotten that someone had taken a shot at me. Trying to act nonchalant, I said, "Well, I'm alive and kicking. There have been no attempts on my life this morning." But I wondered where Stan was.

Holmes frowned at me. "My mom says that Sugar won some archery competitions in high school. I didn't live here then. I'm not sure I ever knew that."

I teased him a little bit. "Get over yourself, Holmes. Even Sugar wouldn't kill for your love."

He didn't smile. "Idella might."

"Stop that. Have you seen Sugar yet?" I asked.

"I guess I should go over and say hi. That would be the right thing to do. And maybe the subject of archery will arise. I won't tell them where I'm staying. They'll probably assume that I'm at my parents' house."

"Holmes Richardson! You've been back less than two days and my bad snooping habits are rubbing off on you."

We walked down the stairs, and he slipped his hand around mine. "There have been two deaths in Wagtail. I don't want you to be the third."

I appreciated his concern, but when he put it like that, it scared the pants off me.

Holmes left reluctantly. I assured him I had work to do and he would feel better if he did the right thing and went to see Sugar. After he left, Trixie and I headed for the inn office.

Oma sat in a wing-back armchair looking at the lake. The French doors were open, and a gentle breeze blew in through the screens. "Holly!" She reached up for my hand. "You scared me this morning."

I sat down on the sofa, and Trixie jumped up next to me.

"I know you could not help what happened. Evil lives in that man, Wade."

"Is he out of surgery?"

"Yes. They don't know how much use he will have of that leg, though. On a happier note, Augie phoned to invite Pippin and crew, and us, to dinner at Chowhound. I think he wants the publicity." She laughed. "He wasn't happy that Pippin and Trixie chose Hot Hog all by themselves for their dinner date. Apparently, there's now a line every evening to dine there!"

"Sounds good to me. It's nice of Augie to include us."

Oma gazed at me. "You must be worn-out."

"A little bit. I'm just enormously relieved that I don't have to worry about Wade snatching Trixie anymore. And if we're right about him murdering Howard, he'll be in prison for a good long time."

Late that afternoon, I donned a simple sleeveless black dress for our dinner at Chowhound. A gold herringbone necklace and hoop earrings dressed it up just a bit. I pulled my hair up into a loose twist. Trixie watched carefully as I dressed. I pulled out her special collar with a vibrant yellow flower on it. She looked adorable, and I could tell she felt special wearing it.

We met in the main lobby. Casey had agreed to come in early so both Oma and I could attend the dinner. We walked over to the restaurant as a group. I was happy to see that Marlee was no longer hiding behind the sunglasses and wig. She smiled broadly and finally seemed to be enjoying herself.

During the walk to the restaurant, I found myself with Finch. "I heard you had quite an argument with Howard before he died."

Finch's eyebrows rose. "How could you possibly know about that?"

"I never divulge my sources," I teased.

"For a long time, no one cast me because I was little Tiger, except I wasn't little or cute anymore. There's been a long drought for me. This show is the first decent chance I've had to revive my acting career. I'm being very careful, because I don't want to mess this up. Poor Marlee was dying for Howard to pay attention to her. Meanwhile, Howard

could not stop flirting with Camille, who wasn't interested.
She did her level best to be polite, but Howard just kept coming on way too strong. I was determined that Howard would
not ruin this opportunity for us. I've been around the business long enough. I knew why Roscoe sent Rae Rae here.
Howard was notorious for misbehaving toward women. That
big argument we had was me telling him to knock it off and
him calling me a childish has-been."

"Ouch!"

"That wasn't news to me. It's not easy to be finished with
your career before you're out of puberty. I hope this show
is everything we expect."

"I hope so, too."

At Chowhound, Augie had arranged tables so our whole
group could sit together. He had selected the entire menu
himself and beamed when his waiters served an appetizer
of deviled eggs, shrimp, and colorful crudités with a zesty
aioli sauce. There were so many of us that the waiters
brought three giant platters for us to share.

As we ate, Rae Rae dinged her glass with a fork. "I have
an announcement." Everyone quieted down. "I've been quite
sad to know our week in Wagtail will soon be coming to an
end. I have loved getting to know you all. As you are aware,
Howard's death left an opening in the show. I heard from my
brother today that they have filled the role of the cranky father. It's me!" She raised her hands in the air in celebration.
"But I won't be the cranky father. I'll be the nosy mom!"

The air filled with applause. I glanced around. All the
actors were pleased. They had been through a lot with Rae
Rae. I was certain she would fit in well. And the role suited
her perfectly.

The second course was crab cakes with blanched sugar
snap peas. Marlee was busy taking pictures and posting
them on social media. Just when we thought Augie couldn't
top himself, a parade of waiters brought us beef tenderloin

with a mustard and sage crust, served with mashed potatoes and roasted carrots. It was a meal that we would remember. Trixie, Pippin, Stella, and Gingersnap were served a doggy version of our delicious feast.

An exhausted Dave arrived just in time for the main course. We scooted over to make room for him. Naturally, everyone quieted down to hear what he had to say.

Dave guzzled ice water before he began. "For starters, the operation was deemed a success. For your information, should you ever be hit by an arrow, do not remove it yourself. There's a huge chance that you could bleed out very fast. Wade didn't know what to do, but as it turned out, he did the right thing and most likely saved his own life by leaving the arrow where it landed."

Dave took a bite of mashed potatoes and swallowed. "I'm starved. The hospital cafeteria left a lot to be desired."

"Did he murder Howard?" asked Jim. "What about the watch?"

"There was no watch on Howard's person when his body was found. We have photos of him, and there's no question about that. His belongings were packed up, inventoried, and tested for fentanyl. There are no watches on the inventory."

Everyone except Finch stopped eating and listened.

"The watch Wade was wearing at the time of his capture was a Hermès brand watch."

"Howard wore it everywhere," said Camille. "I bet the bars have cameras that might have caught it."

Dave smiled. "That won't be necessary. Wade admitted that he took it off Howard's arm. In fact, he said rather gleefully that he removed the watch while Howard still understood what was happening."

Rae Rae gasped. "That's cruel! It was Wade who gave Howard the drugs then?"

Dave looked at Jim. "Maybe we should discuss this after dinner."

Jim groaned. "Nooo! We can take it. I've been waiting all day for this."

Dave nodded. "Howard contacted Wade from LA. One of Wade's friends is a thug in Hollywood. For a fee, he put Howard in touch with Wade. Howard offered to pay Wade if he would come to Wagtail this week to eliminate Jim."

Oma gasped. "This is horrible!"

"Howard brought the fentanyl with him. Apparently, Wade is not lying, because he knew that Howard hid it in a small baby powder container, which is exactly what we found in his luggage. Howard gave him some fentanyl to use to kill Jim but refused to give him the advance payment he had promised. That riled Wade, who sold part of the fentanyl on the street in Wagtail. Wade saw the *Dog Life* article about Trixie posted everywhere and recognized the dog he had abandoned. He had no desire to have Trixie back. He was desperate for money and planned to sell her and Pippin."

# Thirty-eight

My heart sank. I had hoped Wade hadn't been her owner once. But I reminded myself that he would be in prison, so I no longer had to worry about Wade claiming Trixie. I looked down at her sitting so politely with her buddy Pippin and handed each of them a tiny bite of tenderloin.

Dave continued to talk. "Wade says Howard treated him like slime and refused to give him any money. He spent the first couple of nights sleeping in unoccupied cabins. Seems he's adept at picking locks, too."

Jim shot me a look. I knew he was thinking about the way I broke into Howard's rental house.

"Since Howard was reneging on the deal he had offered," Dave continued, "Wade decided he would come out ahead if he stole Pippin and Trixie and sold them.

"The night Howard died," said Dave, "he was intoxicated. We know that from the autopsy and countless witnesses. Wade waited until he saw Jim leave the property with Marlee. Howard let him in and told Wade to make him a drink. Wade poured fentanyl into the beverage, handed it to Howard, and started looking for Howard's money. He didn't take the credit cards, because he knew they would be tracked. He collected the cash that Howard had promised him, leaving a couple hundred dollars so it wouldn't appear that Howard had been robbed. He says Howard was beginning to feel the effects of the fentanyl when Wade helped himself to the fancy watch."

"Why?" asked Jim. "Why would Howard want me dead?"

Finch spoke up. "Because you were hounding him about Lucy. If the truth about Lucy had made the news, he would have been finished. He was trying to silence you."

"What about Diane?" asked Rae Rae. "Did Wade murder her, too?"

Dave's eyes met mine. "Wade insists that he didn't know Diane. He heard rumors about her around town but asserts that he had nothing to do with her death."

"Howard murdered her." Rae Rae appeared distressed. "After all these years, he came to town and killed her. Why couldn't he have let her live her life in peace?"

I looked at Dave. I had to talk to him about Stan.

Now that Wade had confessed to murdering Howard, everyone was more relaxed. Dessert arrived with great fanfare as Augie lit the cherries jubilee. Gingersnap barked at the flame and backed away from it.

Stuffed to the gills, we thanked Augie for the delicious meal. When we left Chowhound, Marlee's posts were already having an impact on Augie's business. A line of people waited outside for the opportunity to eat there.

Pippin and his entourage headed for a bar to celebrate Rae Rae's new role in their show.

Dave offered to walk Oma and me back to the inn. Finally, I had an opportunity to tell him my theory about Stan.

While we walked, I told him about the items I found in

the cabin. "And the shipping label on the Hoovers' trash backs up my theory that Stan is stealing again."

In a distressed tone, Oma asked, "Could it have been Stan who shot the arrow at Holly?"

"Holmes says Sugar is pretty good with a bow and arrow," I pointed out. "I wonder if she was defending Stan."

"Or if they're both involved again," said Oma.

Dave hadn't said anything. He walked us up the stairs to the front door of the inn. "You two keep this under your hats. If that's what happened, I don't want them getting wind that we're on to them."

"If one of them shot that arrow at me, then I think they already know."

"Still, I want to keep this quiet so I can watch them. And I'll have another look at that cabin. For now, I want both of you to tell everyone that it was Howard who killed Diane. Got it?"

Oma grasped my hand. "Perhaps Holly should stick around the inn, ja?"

"An excellent idea, Liesel. Don't hesitate to call me if anything happens that worries you. And close off the reception lobby entrance early tonight. It's easier to watch one door."

Dave took off in a hurry. He had to be worn-out after no sleep and working all day. I was slightly nervous, though. The person with the bow and arrow was still out there.

When we were safely inside, Oma suggested, "Perhaps you would be safer staying with Aunt Birdie until they catch this person. No one would know you were there."

"I think death by arrow might be preferable."

Oma smirked. "Then I will leave Gingersnap and Stella with you tonight, ja? The dogs will let you know if anyone is lurking around." She hurried off to close the reception lobby doors.

I thought about sitting on the terrace for a while, but that might make me an easy target. Instead, the dogs and I settled in the Dogwood Room with Casey. We could easily see who came and went.

Casey wrapped his arms around Stella. "Word around town is that LaRue shot that arrow. It was meant for Wade."

Uh-oh. People didn't think Howard had killed Diane. I guessed that I shouldn't have been surprised. After all, it was Augie who had pointed out in the beginning that he thought it was someone local. I bet he didn't think it was his own son when he said that. But Wade wasn't local. I tried to steer Casey the way Dave had requested. "That doesn't make any sense at all. Why would he do that when it was Howard who murdered Diane?"

"The way I heard it was Wade sold Diane the fentanyl, which made him the drug dealer. When she died, he took her up the mountain to dispose of her body. LaRue wanted revenge, but you nearly got whammed instead."

Part of me wanted to believe that. It would mean the arrow wasn't intended for me. But logic dictated that wasn't the case. Wade murdered Howard, but he didn't drag his body up the mountain or try to dispose of him in any way. In fact, if he had just left town instead of trying to steal the dogs, he might have even gotten away with Howard's murder.

The phone rang, and Casey left the Dogwood Room to answer it. A guest probably needed another blanket or more towels.

Quiet as a mouse, Glenda walked into the inn. "Holly! Just who I wanted to see." She held out a luscious lemon tart and said, "This is to thank you for bringing our darling Dolly back home. And to make you feel better after that arrow nearly hit you!"

Stella stood up and walked over beside me. Her nose twitched, and she raised her muzzle.

When Glenda held the lemon tart out to me to take, I saw the powdered sugar on top and my blood ran cold. Was this how she had murdered Diane? Had Glenda presented her with a brownie covered with powdered sugar and fentanyl?

In that instant, Stella jumped up, hitting the bottom of the tart with the top of her head.

It arced straight up and smashed in Glenda's face.

"Leave it! Casey! Casey! Grab the dogs!" I shouted. "Don't let them lick anything." I shooed Trixie and Ginger-snap away.

"Holly!" Casey came running. "What are you doing?"

Glenda looked at me with panic in her eyes. Her face was covered with the sugar and lemon. In desperation, she tried to wipe it out of her mouth with her fingers. She rubbed her nose, but I had a bad feeling that it was too late. She had probably inhaled and swallowed some fentanyl, and it was all over her face.

"Water," she gasped. "Where do you have water?"

Casey was doing a great job with the dogs. I could hear him saying, "Leave it."

Glenda's legs grew unsteady, and she sank into a chair. Weakness overcame her much faster than I could have imagined.

I pulled out my phone and called Dave, then Dr. Engel-knecht. Hopefully one of them would arrive soon with the medicine to counteract the fentanyl.

Behind me, Casey said, "I've called 911. What happened?"

"Glenda killed Diane."

She could still hear. I knew because her eyes turned to me.

"Why, Glenda?"

"To save my baby."

"You mean Dolly?"

"Stan," she breathed. "Diane was going to turn him in. He would have gone back to prison."

"So you baked brownies to kill her? And now you've baked a lemon tart to murder me?"

Glenda reached a hand out to me. "Please, Holly. You have to help me. I don't want to die!"

I stared at the sweet-looking, plump woman. "You baked everything, but Stan helped you get rid of Diane's body."

"No! I swear! He knew nothing about it."

"How did you take her up the mountain?" I asked.

"Oh no! I'm going to die just like she did!"

"Glenda! How did you move Diane's body?"

"In Augie's truck. He has an open utility trailer hooked on the back. I drove her up there, brought her to an isolated spot, then threw her over into the ravine. No one would have ever found her there if it wasn't for your crazy dog."

I was afraid to touch her. There was probably fentanyl all over. On my shoes and clothes. On the hardwood floor. It probably wafted through the air.

"Glenda, Doc and Dave have something that can reverse the effects. I've already called them." At that moment, I felt very sorry for Glenda. She must have been terrified. But there was some weird justice in Glenda suffering and knowing what Diane had gone through. Glenda was reaping what she had sown.

Dave and Dr. Engelknecht rushed into the inn together. I stepped aside to make room for them. Dr. Engelknecht pulled out a syringe and plunged it into Glenda's arm.

We watched her silently. It took effect, and she was able to sit up.

"It's hard to tell how much fentanyl you have in your system," said Dr. Engelknecht. "Chances are good that you will need more of the Narcan. I'll stay with you until you're in the hospital, okay? But I need to know where you got the fentanyl."

Glenda already looked considerably better, but she was obviously scared. "From a guy in town. I was planning to go over to Snowball to buy it, but then I heard some guy was selling it in Wagtail."

"What was his name?" asked Dave.

"I only know him as Wade."

"Incredible," I said. "So I guess we know who bought at least some of the fentanyl Howard gave him."

Dave took a deep breath. "Wade obviously needed cash, and it took him no time at all to find eager buyers. I wonder how many other people bought fentanyl from him."

Dr. Engelknecht gazed at me. "Are you feeling any effects?"

"No. I'm fine. I've been watching Glenda. She seems to be okay, too."

I told them exactly what had happened.

"Interesting," said the doctor. "They're training dogs to pick up the scent of fentanyl. It's very effective, because the officers don't have to open bags to see what's inside. Stella probably remembered the smell from the night Diane died."

"Glenda?" Dave shook his head. "What were you thinking?"

"Diane caught Stan stealing a package from her front door. She gave him a warning. But he did it again. That time she came over to talk to Augie and me. She didn't want to get Stan into trouble. I don't think she knew about his past. She said we had to get control of him. And that if it happened again, she would report him to Dave. I couldn't let him go back to prison. He's my little boy. Do you know what it's like there?"

I had a feeling that she would be experiencing prison firsthand very soon. "Are you the one who shot the arrow?"

Glenda winced. "It was so easy to get rid of Diane. If only you hadn't ducked, we wouldn't be going through this right now. That arrow had your name on it."

After the ambulance whisked her away, Dave took control of the cleanup. I was sent to shower. All three dogs were bathed, and the Dogwood Room was off-limits to everyone while it was cleaned from top to bottom.

# Thirty-nine

Glenda Hoover was released from the hospital the next morning and was taken into custody, but she was the talk of Wagtail. Parents wondered how far they would have gone to protect their own children. But everyone agreed that Glenda had lost her mind. Poor Diane thought she was being considerate toward her neighbors by not reporting Stan's thefts. And in the end, she died because of her kindness.

At breakfast, Marlee crowed that she had been wise to wear a disguise. "I did the right thing and turned them in, but you can see that they're nuts and would have come after me. I'm lucky to be alive."

After doing our rounds in the inn, Trixie and I hopped into a golf cart and were on our way to pick up some items the cook needed when Mr. Finkelstein waved me down. "Can I have a ride? Somebody took my golf cart again!"

I wondered if his brain was beginning to fail. Maybe he shouldn't be driving. But I was more than happy to help him out. He stepped into the golf cart.

"Where to?" I asked.

"The other side of town, please."

He gave me directions as I drove.

I knew the street we were on very well. My ornery aunt Birdie lived there. She had been oddly silent in recent days, which caused me to wonder what she was cooking up.

"Right here!" said Mr. Finkelstein. He stepped out of the golf cart. "You don't mind keeping my little secret, do you?"

"Secret?"

"Now you know where my lady friend lives."

Aunt Birdie's front door opened, and she looked out at us. She was, as always, impeccably dressed in a chic dress that showed off her slim waistline. "Holly?" Aunt Birdie strode toward the sidewalk.

"Birdie," said Mr. Finkelstein, "someone stole my golf cart again. I don't know what's going on in this town anymore with murders and golf cart thefts.

"Thank you for the lift, Holly," he said, as a golf cart just like Mr. Finkelstein's parked directly in front of me.

Cute old Mr. Ledbetter from the bakery shouted at Mr. Finkelstein, "What do I have to do to keep you away from Birdie?"

"Did you steal my golf cart, you old curmudgeon?"

"So what if I did? You have no business here with Birdie."

I could hardly believe my eyes. Two adorable old men arguing about my cranky aunt Birdie?

"Now, boys," she said, "I think you're both wonderful." She tilted her head coyly.

Was she flirting with them?

"Why don't you both come in? I made plenty of food."

The two old fellows followed her up the walk to her front door. I could still hear them muttering at each other.

Trying not to laugh out loud, I drove away fast, fearing one of them might decide to rope me in as a mediator. At least we knew now who the golf cart thief was.

Trixie and I hustled to pick up the items the cook had requested. I loaded them onto the golf cart and drove back thinking how wonderful it was not to be afraid of an arrow zinging through the air at me anymore.

I delivered everything to him and headed for the office to see what else needed to be done.

Rae Rae was talking with Oma and Zelda. She held a leash with tiny glittering rhinestones on it. The moment she saw me, she fairly sang out, "I'm adopting Stella!"

Zelda said, "Stella is so excited. She loves Rae Rae and her sparkles. It's a wonderful match."

"Are you flying her home?" asked Oma.

Rae Rae appeared appalled. "I'm not going to make this sweet girl fly in a crate! I've rented a car and bought a guide to all the best dog parks and dog-friendly hotels." She fastened a collar covered in giant rhinestones onto Stella's neck and slid a pair of blinged-out goggles over Stella's eyes. "Road trip, Stella! In a convertible!" Rae Rae bent over and held up her palm. "High five!"

To my complete astonishment, Stella raised her paw and touched Rae Rae's hand. "Did she already know how to do that?" I asked.

Rae Rae smiled. "Jim taught her. Isn't she darling? We're going to have so much fun. And we'll both remember Diane fondly. I like to think that Diane's spirit will be with us."

Although the Sugar Maple Inn never served dinner, on that night, Oma asked the cook to prepare a special meal for Pippin and his entourage, as well as members of the Wagtail community.

At six o'clock in the evening, Trixie, Twinkletoes, and I were out on the terrace that overlooked the lake. Mr. Huckle and I had set up a buffet. The cook and Shelley were busy bringing out corn bread, beans, Southern fried chicken, barbecued short ribs, and an array of salads and vegetables. Two buffet warmers were labeled *For canine guests*. It looked like they were having a choice of chicken breasts with yellow squash and rice or beef tips, barley, and broccoli in a sauce.

"Thanks for helping me."

I whipped around. Dave wore a red golf shirt and shorts. "No uniform?"

"I'm pretending to take a day off. But I mean it, Holly. If you hadn't whacked Wade over the head, there's no telling what could have happened. I appreciate it."

"I'm glad I didn't kill him. What does *pretending* to take a day off mean?"

"I did a lot of paperwork today. I'm still trying to wrap some things up."

Oma and Gingersnap bustled out onto the terrace. "Ohh, it smells so good out here. It must be the short ribs. I don't see drinks in your hands."

"I just arrived, Liesel." Dave hugged Oma as if she were his own grandmother.

Holmes bounded up the stairs that led to the lake. At the same time, Pippin and his crew emerged from the inn. The party was on!

Poor Dave was bombarded with questions. We gathered around him with icy drinks and listened.

Marlee grimaced when she asked, "What will happen to Stan?"

"He has violated his parole by stealing again, so he's headed back to prison. Interestingly, his mom, Glenda, was so intent on protecting him that she hid the items he stole in the rental cabin where Stella and Holly discovered the missing dogs. I don't think we'll have any trouble providing ample evidence of his crimes."

"Then Glenda knew all along where the missing dogs, Tavish and Dolly, were?" I asked.

Dave groaned. "I'm afraid she staged the theft of her own dog. She took Tavish because she knew Clara didn't keep a close eye on him. She thought it would be easy to snatch him."

"But why?" asked Rae Rae. "Why would she do that?"

"Because she planned to kill Diane. She thought if dogs went missing, it would point a finger at a nonexistent dog thief. It almost worked. A lot of people thought Diane might have been murdered by someone who wanted her dogs."

"Stan had nothing to do with it?" asked Marlee. "What about Sugar?"

"So far we haven't found any connection to Sugar at all. And while Stan did steal packages, it appears that only Glenda was involved in Diane's murder."

We settled at tables and ate the feast our cook had prepared. The setting sun glowed red as it sank behind the mountain, and lights twinkled in cabins across the lake from the inn.

After dessert, when most people had gone home or out to a bar, I sat down on the top step and looked out at the lake.

I had been too busy to realize that a full moon was in the making. It reflected on the water in a wide, golden swath. Trixie nudged her nose under my arm and nestled next to me. Twinkletoes leaned against my legs. And just when I thought life couldn't get any better, Holmes came up from behind and joined us on the stone stairs.

He grinned at me. "It's good to be home."

# Recipes

One of my dogs suffered from severe food allergies that did not allow him to eat commercial dog food. Consequently, I learned to cook for my dogs and have done so for many years. Consult your veterinarian if you want to switch your dog to home-cooked food. It's not as difficult as one might think. Keep in mind that, like children, dogs need a balanced diet, not just a hamburger. Any changes to your dog's diet should be made gradually so your dog's stomach can adjust.

Chocolate, alcohol, caffeine, fatty foods, grapes, raisins, macadamia nuts, onion and garlic, salt, xylitol, and unbaked dough can be toxic (and even deadly) to dogs. For more information about foods your dog should not eat, consult the Pet Poison Helpline at petpoisonhelpline.com /pet-owners.

# Zucchini Pineapple Cake

Not for dogs.

Krista's note: This is an incredibly moist cake. While you do not have to wring liquid out of the zucchini and pineapple, you also do not want to use any excess juices that might collect. Drain them before adding to the batter.

¾ cup milk (2% or higher)
1 teaspoon white vinegar
3 cups shredded zucchini
1 8-ounce can pineapple chunks (drained)
2 cups flour
2 teaspoons ground cinnamon
2 teaspoons baking powder
2 teaspoons baking soda
½ teaspoon salt
3 eggs
2 cups sugar (if you plan to use frosting then
    only 1½ cups sugar unless you like it very
    sweet)
¾ cup vegetable oil
2 teaspoons vanilla

Grease and flour a 13-by-9-inch baking dish. Preheat oven to 350°F.

Measure the milk, and add the vinegar to it. Set aside. In a food processor, shred the zucchini and the drained pineapple. Set aside. Combine the flour, cinnamon, baking powder, baking soda, and salt in a bowl and stir well with a fork to combine. Beat the eggs lightly, add the sugar, and beat until thick. Slowly beat in the oil, milk, and vanilla, then the flour mixture.

When well combined, drain any juices from the shredded zucchini and pineapple and stir the zucchini and pineapple into the batter. Bake 45–50 minutes.

Serve with lightly sweetened whipped cream.

# Oma's German Pancakes with Strawberries and Whipped Cream

A non-oily bite of a pancake may be shared with dogs, but *not* the strawberries or the whipped cream.

German pancakes are thicker than crepes but thinner than American pancakes. They're easy to make, and once you know how, you won't even need to measure the basic ingredients of flour, milk, and eggs. You can just gauge whether the batter is the correct density. The trick is to use a nonstick or well-seasoned pan. If you don't have one, you can still make them, but you'll likely need more oil.

This recipe makes approximately 3–4 pancakes. Double the recipe for 7-8 pancakes.

## Strawberries

*16 ounces strawberries*
*¼ cup sugar*

Wash, hull, and slice the strawberries. Sprinkle with ¼ cup of sugar, turn a few times to spread the sugar, and let sit while you make the pancakes.

## Sweetened Whipped Cream

    1 cup heavy whipping
       cream
    ⅓ cup powdered sugar
    1 teaspoon vanilla

Beat the cream until it begins to take shape. Add the powdered sugar and vanilla and beat until the cream makes a firm peak.

## Oma's German Pancakes (Pfannkuchen)

    1–2 tablespoons or more oil (mild-flavored olive
       or canola)
    2 large eggs
    Pinch of salt
    ½ cup milk
    ½ cup flour

Crack the eggs into a medium bowl and whisk lightly. Add the salt and the milk and whisk. Add the flour and whisk until smooth.

Use a nonstick or well-seasoned pan to cook the pancakes. Heat the pan over medium heat and add the oil. As the oil warms, lift the pan and rotate to spread the oil around the pan. When the oil is hot, pour batter in the pan about five inches in diameter. Lift the pan, slant it, and rotate so that the batter runs around the edge of the pan's base. Set the pan back on the burner. Lift the entire pancake with a thin spatula (Oma likes to use a super-thin cookie spatula) and flip. When the underside is done, remove from the pan and serve.

Note that there is no sugar in these pancakes, so they work well with sweet or savory fillings. No strawberries or whipped cream on hand? Use the trick of German Omas and spread with your favorite jam. They're delicious with maple syrup, too.

### Assembly

Place the pancake on a plate. Spoon the fruit in a line near one side. Roll the pancake up so the fruit is in the middle. Garnish with additional fruit and a dollop of whipped cream.

Alternatively, spread a thin layer of your favorite jam or preserves on the pancake and roll it up. Sprinkle the top with a pinch of sugar.

# Herbed Dijon Potato Salad

Not for dogs.

3 pounds red potatoes
   (roughly 6 medium red potatoes)
2 teaspoons salt, divided, plus extra to taste
3 hard-boiled eggs
¼ cup mayonnaise
1 tablespoon apple cider vinegar
2 teaspoons Dijon mustard
2 teaspoons tarragon
2 teaspoons minced shallots

Cut the potatoes into ¼-inch cubes. Add water and 1 teaspoon salt to a large pot. The water should be sufficient to cover the potatoes by about an inch. Cook the potatoes in boiling water with the peel on until they can be pierced easily with a fork. Chop the eggs and add to the potatoes. Mix together the mayonnaise, vinegar, Dijon mustard, tarragon, 1 teaspoon salt, and shallots. Pour over potatoes and turn to coat. Salt to taste.

Serve warm or cold. Note that you will want to make more dressing if you eat it warm. Warm potatoes will absorb the dressing. If you allow it to cool first, you can use less of the dressing to suit your taste.

# Waffles with Caramelized Bananas

Makes 12 waffles.

*2 cups flour*
*2 tablespoons sugar*
*2 teaspoons baking powder*
*1 teaspoon baking soda*
*¾ teaspoon salt*
*2 eggs*
*1½ cups buttermilk*
*3 tablespoons vegetable (high heat) oil*
*1 teaspoon vanilla*

In a large bowl, mix together the flour, sugar, baking powder, baking soda, and salt. Lightly whisk the eggs.

Mix with the buttermilk, oil, and vanilla. Pour over the dry ingredients and gently whisk to combine. Do not overmix.

Place a baking rack in the middle of the oven and preheat to 250°F.

Use nonstick spray or brush the waffle maker with oil and preheat. Follow the instructions for your waffle maker or add the batter and close. You may wish to spread the batter toward the edges. If you find the batter is too thick, you may thin it with a couple of tablespoons of milk. Cook for 3 minutes or until the waffle maker indicates they are ready. Serve immediately or place on the rack in the oven to keep warm. Freeze any extra waffles!

## Caramelized Bananas

For people only, not for dogs.

Note: This makes enough for 3–4 servings. If planning to serve all the waffles, double or triple the amounts for the bananas.

*2 fresh bananas*
*4 tablespoons butter*
*4 tablespoons dark brown sugar*

Slice the bananas about ½-inch thick. Melt the butter in a pan. Add the brown sugar and let it melt. Add the bananas and cook about 4 minutes on each side. Note: You can also keep the caramelized bananas warm in the oven with the waffles.

## Sweetened Whipped Cream (optional)

   1 cup heavy whipping cream
   ⅓ cup powdered sugar
   1 teaspoon vanilla

Beat the cream until it begins to thicken. Add the powdered sugar and vanilla and beat until it holds a peak.

## Assembly

Make the waffles. Ladle fresh caramelized bananas and sauce over the waffles. Top with sweetened whipped cream (optional).

# Lemon Tart

Not for dogs.

## Crust

   1¾ cups flour
   ¼ teaspoon salt
   ½ cup granulated sugar
   1 stick butter, frozen

Preheat oven to 375°F. Mix the flour, salt, and sugar and place in a food processor. Using the shredding disk, shred the butter. Swap the shredding disk for a blending blade. Pulse until it forms a loose ball or small balls that can be packed together. Remove from food processor and roll out. Place in tart pan. Fill with dried beans in aluminum foil or pie weights. Bake 17–20 minutes until baked through. Cool on a rack.

## Lemon Filling

> Please be sure to use a sieve. This is super easy to make, but it's prettiest if it's smooth.

*4 eggs*
*2 egg yolks*
*¾ cup sugar*
*1 cup fresh lemon juice*
*Pinch of salt*
*12 tablespoons unsalted butter*

Place the eggs and egg yolks in a heavy-bottomed pot and whisk together. Add the sugar, lemon juice, and salt, and whisk. Add the butter and bring to a simmer over medium high. Cook until it thickens, stirring the whole time, about three minutes. Pour through a sieve into the prebaked tart shell. Refrigerate until set.

## Chocolate Cupcakes

**NOT** FOR DOGS.

### Cupcakes

*2 tablespoons unsalted butter*
*⅓ cup vegetable oil*

1 cup flour
½ cup cocoa powder
(not Dutch process)
1 teaspoon baking powder
¼ teaspoon salt
¼ teaspoon baking soda
1 teaspoon instant coffee
1 tablespoon warm water
1 cup sugar
2 large eggs
1 tablespoon vanilla extract
½ cup buttermilk

Preheat oven to 350°F. Prepare a cupcake pan with cupcake papers.

Melt the butter with the oil and set aside to cool. In a bowl, mix together the flour, cocoa powder, baking powder, salt, and baking soda. Dissolve the coffee in the water. Beat the butter mixture with the sugar in a separate bowl. Beat in the eggs one at a time. Add the vanilla and the coffee. Alternate adding the flour mixture and the buttermilk. Fill the cupcake wells slightly over ½ full. Bake 16 minutes or until a cake tester comes out clean.

You can also bake mini cupcakes. Bake them for 9 minutes or until a cake tester comes out clean.

## Chocolate Frosting

**NOT** FOR DOGS.

¼ cup butter
½ cup unsweetened cocoa powder
Pinch of salt

1 teaspoon vanilla
2 cups powdered sugar
4 tablespoons 2% milk

Melt the butter and mix in the powdered cocoa until smooth. Allow to cool. Mix in the salt and the vanilla. Beat powdered sugar into the butter mixture ½ cup at a time. Add the milk as needed to achieve desired consistency. Beat for 4–5 minutes.

# Peanut Butter Pupcakes

For dogs as a treat.

Makes 12 regular pupcakes or about 36 mini cupcakes. Please note that there is no baking powder or baking soda in this recipe. The cupcakes will rise, but you have to beat the eggs white separately and fold them into the peanut butter batter.

2 eggs, room temperature
½ cup peanut butter
½ cup honey
¾ cup flour
1 banana, cut into slices

Preheat the oven to 350°F. Line a cupcake pan with cupcake liners. Separate the eggs. Beat the egg whites on slow for about one minute. Raise the speed and beat them on medium for at least one more minute, until they hold a shape. Beat the egg yolks, peanut butter, and honey together and gradually add the flour and the banana. Beat well to combine. Fold the egg whites into the peanut butter batter. Distribute among the cupcake papers. Bake 16 minutes or until a cake tester comes out clean. **Remove the cupcake paper before serving to your dog.** If your dog gulps food instead of chewing it, please cut the pupcakes into small pieces before serving.

# Greek Yogurt Peanut Butter Frosting

For dogs as a treat.

   1 cup unflavored and unsweetened Greek
      yogurt
   ½ cup peanut butter

Swirl together. Frost cooled cupcakes.
   Decorate with mini dog bone–shaped cookies.

# Gobble Gobble Goodness

For dogs.

   2 tablespoons olive oil
   ½ pound 93% lean ground turkey
   ½ 10-ounce package frozen carrots and peas

2 *cups cooked barley or rice*
1 *tablespoon cooked cranberries (optional)*

Heat the olive oil in a frying pan. Add the ground turkey. Break it up and cook until no pink shows in the meat. Meanwhile, cook the carrots and peas. Add the cooked barley, carrots and peas, and cooked cranberries (optional) to the meat. Stir to mix.

## Chicken Salad for Dogs

½ *tablespoon olive oil*
2 *chicken breasts*
1 *teaspoon sliced celery, without strings!*
6 *thin slices of cucumber, quartered*
½ *apple*
2 *cups cooked barley*

Preheat oven to 400°F. Pour olive oil in a baking dish. Dredge the chicken breast through the olive oil and flip to coat both sides. Roast in the oven for 25 minutes. Remove when they reach 165°F and no pink shows inside the chicken breasts. Set aside for 5 minutes.

Meanwhile, slice the celery and the cucumber. Peel and core the apple, cut into thin slices, and cut each slice into four pieces.

Cut the chicken breasts into cubes approximately ¼-inch-by-¼ inch. Combine the chicken breast cubes with the celery, cucumber, apple, and barley. Pour the juices from the chicken pan over the mixture and stir.

Ready to find
your next great read?

Let us help.

**Visit prh.com/nextread**